P9-DWH-303

SPRING OF HOPE

SPRING OF HOPE

Cora Harrison

SEVERN
HOUSE

First world edition published in Great Britain in 2021 and the USA in 2022
by Severn House, an imprint of Canongate Books Ltd,
14 High Street, Edinburgh EH1 1TE.

Trade paperback edition first published in Great Britain and the USA in 2023
by Severn House, an imprint of Canongate Books Ltd.

severnhouse.com

British Library Cataloguing-in-Publication Data
A CIP catalogue record for this title is available from the British Library.

ISBN-13: 978-0-7278-5051-5 (cased)
ISBN-13: 978-1-4483-0717-3 (trade paper)
ISBN-13: 978-1-4483-0716-6 (e-book)

All Severn House titles are printed on acid-free paper.

33614082790261

Typeset by Palimpsest Book Production Ltd.,
Falkirk, Stirlingshire, Scotland.
Printed and bound in Great Britain by
TJ Books, Padstow, Cornwall.

ACKNOWLEDGEMENTS

This book is dedicated to my son, William Harrison, M. Eng., without whose enthusiasm and help it could not have been written.

Very sincere thanks to my agent, Peter Buckman, who never fails to produce incisive and helpful advice promptly and well-seasoned with humour. I am also very grateful to Publisher, Kate Lyall Grant, who takes time from a busy schedule to read my books and offer praise as well as insight. Editors Anna Telfer and Sara Porter remain good-humoured while running a fine comb through my many errors and muddles. Their job is unenviable and I thank them for their tact as well as their hard work.

PROLOGUE

Letter to Nina

Wilkie Collins
Wimpole Street
London

September 14, 1889

Mrs Frederick Lehmann,
Highgate,
London

My dearest Nina,

You, Frederick, and I have been friends for so many years and now that our time together is coming to an end, I want to make one last demand upon your never-failing kindness and generosity.

Nina, for many years I have had a story written, carefully stored in that brimming-over box which all novelists have: a box filled with ideas, sketches, stories which have been lovingly worked upon; stories which are almost ready for the sharp eye of a publisher, but still need thinking about, reworking, and worst of all, pruning down. But this story is special because I wrote it as if I were telling you, my dear friend, about something that happened to me – happened to me thirty years ago from this night.

I've just found, at the back of the drawer, the account published on that spring day thirty years ago. Here it is, Nina:

Terrible Accident in London Warehouse
Our readers will be shocked to read of a terrible

accident which occurred within the precincts of a London warehouse late yesterday evening. No names have yet been released, but our reporter believes that in the course of a demonstration of mechanical engines to an audience of some attendant engineers, an unfortunate man became entangled in some apparatus of machinery and a piece of metal pierced his throat, severing, according to the medical report, a large artery and the unfortunate man bled to death. We understand that the terrible death was witnessed, not only by the engineers present at the demonstration, but also by an audience which comprised, not just members of the laity but gentlemen of all professions, including a very well-known novelist, but also some members of the weaker sex and even some children were present to witness the terrible sight.

The proprietors and employees of this newspaper send our condolences to all who were afflicted by this most terrible event, especially, of course, the relatives of the unfortunate victim. Further details will be published as soon as released by the police.

I remember it well, Nina. That terrible night. The *Courier* had its boys on the streets by eleven o'clock that night selling their paper with this column inserted into the early evening edition. The streets rang with their cries of 'Terrible accident! Read all about it! Read all about it!' as I made my way home. After I parted with Dickens, I joined a queue of late-night theatregoers, and purchased one for myself. Standing there at the street corner, I read it through before folding it and hiding it in my pocket. Once home and alone in my room, I got a pair of scissors, cut out the above paragraph. I would keep the cutting, I thought. It would be a unique memory for me to mark my place in the history of our great capital city.

I had wanted this story to be published after my death, some names changed, of course. I had thought that I would leave it in as perfect a state, ready for an editor's eye, as is possible. But the day of my death seemed a long way ahead back in that time in the twentieth year of the reign of our dear Queen, that time when that terrible 'Summer of the Great Stink' in 1858 had been followed by the 'Spring of Hope' in 1859. I knew that the story would have to be changed in places. Certain things would have to be obliterated; others subtly altered.

But time has moved on – moved on by a good thirty years. Dickens, of course, is dead – dead for many a long year – and so is his brother-in-law, Henry Austin. And others from that cluster of talented engineers and ambitious politicians now lie in their graves. Disraeli is gone, that restless seeker after fame now lies quietly in his grave in a country village in Buckinghamshire. John Phillips is dead, of course, and David Napier, also, poor fellow. And Andy Wainwright. He died of malaria out in India. And others too, their faces that seem so clear to me when I read through this book, they, too, are now in their grave – some that I have lost touch with, others whose careers I have followed with interest. Nevertheless, some names will need to be changed and it may be best to change all names. And you, Nina, you and Frederick will know what else to change and how to deal with its ending. The curious can try to work out matters for themselves, but the feelings of those who remain will have to be safeguarded. I, the world's worst procrastinator, have left it too long. But the story, as a story, is finished, and I know that you will do what is needful.

So farewell, my dear friend! I am dying, Nina. My doctor has been very gentle, but I read the sentence of death upon his face and he did not deny it. Just quietly asked me whether I had made my last will and testament and was at peace with God and man. He will stay by my side. He has promised me that. And he has promised that I will have all the laudanum, my old friend, that I need to keep mind and body relaxed and at peace.

Caroline has written today to most, telling them the news, but there are some special friends for whom I wanted to make the effort for myself. So this, Nina, is a goodbye and a last request.

I'm alone now, Nina, alone except for the night nurse. Dear Caroline, worn out by weeping, has gone to bed and Carrie, my faithful amanuensis, having placed my box of writings on the bed beside me, has eventually gone home to her husband and to her children. It's thirty years now since we all met, but now I must leave them.

So, I'm alone, Nina, and I can talk to you without interruption. When I finish this letter, I shall enclose my story of that time, over thirty years ago, now. And then I shall ask my doctor to seal and stamp it, put it in the post, and then it is yours. I can trust you, I know, to do what is needed. You and Frederick have been my dearest friends for many a long year.

Don't weep for me, dear friend. I am perfectly happy. I have had a good life, have known good friends, had some splendid meals and swallowed some excellent wine, have lived, despite all my ill-health, for sixty-five years. I have been a happy man during those years of my life, have written some books that may give pleasure after my death, and now my dear physician, my old friend, Frank Beard, has come to my aid and given me the laudanum that my heart, my spirit, my mind and my body had craved – well, now I shall die peacefully and happily. God bless him for his compassion and his understanding to a man who has been weak all through his life.

And so here is that story that I promised to tell you, promised long ago. It is still so clear in my memory. That night in the warehouse, that explosion, that ominous sound, that scream of a dying spirit, the body falling upon the floor, the blood! Blood everywhere, splashed on the wall, staining the floor, soaking into the man's clothing. Blood smells, you know, Nina, a terrible sweet smell. And that scream! It still rings in my ears. I never knew that a man could scream like that, a high-pitched sound like a pig in a slaughterhouse.

So, Nina, my dear friend, soon after it happened, when I knew truly what had happened and why it had happened, thirty years ago when I was strong and well, I wrote this account, locked it in my box, and it explains everything about me, me and my new little family, and how I got involved in the Great Stink of London and the secret of what really happened on that day in what would eventually prove to be the Spring of Hope.

Goodbye, dear friend. Plant a rose in my memory and don't forget to allow the ivy, my favourite plant, to clothe the wall behind it. Light and shade. Our lives are made up of the two elements.

Your friend and admirer,
Wilkie Collins.

ONE

London, 1859

Tonight, I have decided to begin to write down what I remember from this spring of 1859. The events of these last months fester in my memory and disturb my sleep. I shall write it like a novel, evening after evening, week after week and month after month, just as event followed event, and then lock the sheets of paper away in a box. Like that the burden may be lifted from my mind. Someday, when I know that my end is near, I shall pass it on to a dear friend, who will find an editor and allow it to entertain those who still live.

I suppose that it all started because John Millais, the famous painter, was too pig-headed to take the advice from my brother and me. If we had not gone out with him that night, perhaps my life might have been quite different.

But let me tell you what happened.

It was a dark and stormy night, as Dickens' friend, Bulwer-Lytton, once wrote at the beginning of *Paul Clifford*, his bestselling book at the time. The wind howled and the rain, that had fallen continuously during the last three days, continued to pour down from the heavens and the streets of London were flooded. Here and there the storm had brought down those plane trees which had been planted to beautify our streets and they lay across the roadway, stiff and heavy, broken from their roots, blocking the traffic and emptying the busy London roads. There was no chance of getting a cab on a night like this, but my guest John Millais, the painter, after he had dined well and partaken of the wine, perhaps slightly too well, refused all my mother's offers of hospitality in her house at Hanover Square and said that he would walk back to his parents' home in Gower Street.

'We'll go with you, won't we, Charley?' I said to my brother.

'Never let it be said that we sent a guest out alone and unprotected to drown on the streets of London!' I, too, had imbibed
plenty of wine and now the sight of the wild night outside
filled me with excitement. It would, I told myself, make a
good scene in a novel which I was writing. Charley, as usual,
was amenable to any suggestion of mine and so we pulled on
heavy coats, tied scarves around our necks and fastened our
leather hunting caps and went out into the storm.

After that terrible summer of heat and stench from
the River Thames, the summer that was now known as the
'Summer of the Great Stink', there was something about this
early springtime storm that exhilarated our senses. The three
of us staggered along, sticks in hands, heads bent against the
wind, driving rain stinging our faces as we shouted and laughed
at each other's jokes.

And then it happened.

We were passing along a suburban street, a street lined on
either side with row upon row of small villas, all newly built,
all with 'For Sale' signs fastened to the gateposts. Ugly little
houses with the typical parsimonious gardens, prim concrete
path, iron gate and mean windows, I looked at them with
disdain and kept my attention on the magnificence of the
stormy sky and the strange shapes of the clouds that flew
across it.

I was just about to point out a cloud that looked like an
enormous celestial bat to Millais when we heard, in a sudden
cessation of the wind, the sound of glass breaking and crashing
down up the pathway.

And then, above the noise of the storm came an almost
unearthly scream, shrill, full of fear, enough to curdle the
blood. I stopped instantly and shouted to Millais and to my
brother.

'Look!' I said to them, yelling above the noise of the storm.
'Look up there at that window. The window is broken. See
the moonlight on it. There's a woman there. I can see her hair.'

At that very moment, there was a sudden gust of wind,
stronger and shriller than we had yet experienced, then a
loud, creaking noise and with no more warning, a plane tree,
planted at the edge of the pavement, just inches away from

us, swayed, and then crashed to the ground. The moon flared briefly and disappeared behind drifting cloud.

'Oh, my God, Collins, for Jesus's sake, don't delay,' shouted Millais. 'We'll get ourselves killed.'

'We must turn back to our mother's house,' screamed my brother Charley. 'Quick, Millais, come back with us. Hanover Square is not too far. We might get ourselves killed if we go on. Come on, Wilkie.'

It made sense. We did not know what lay ahead, but it had not been too bad between Hanover Square and this spot in Charlton Street. I watched them turn, watched their bent backs as they trudged back along the pavement strewn with twigs and broken branches.

But as I hesitated there came another scream. A woman's scream, certainly. A plea for help. Then a sudden lull in the wind, that dangerous moment when a storm appears to gather its forces, almost as if it drew breath before a sudden and violent assault. And into that moment of silence came the heartbroken sobbing of a child.

I delayed no longer. The gate was padlocked, but the padlock was probably a cheap one and it yielded to a vigorous shake. I crunched through the splinters of smashed glass on the pathway and came up to the door. Another scream from above punctuated the child's wailing. A woman's scream without doubt. I looked up, but could see nothing, no light, just the evidence of the broken window and the sobbing from above.

The front door was locked. I slammed and slammed the door knocker against its metal plate, but there was no more sound from above, only a sudden silence as though a hand had been placed over the child's mouth. Somehow that silence was full of more menace than the screams and the sobs had been. I hesitated no longer, but bent down, unlaced my steel-capped boot and then, standing awkwardly, with the damp seeping through the sock that my mother had knitted so carefully for her son, I attacked the door panel with all the vigour that I could muster.

It didn't take long. These cheap villas, run up by speculators for the delight of city clerks and shopkeepers, were not well built. The costs were calculated with great care and the wood of the panel was probably less than half an inch thick. Three blows from my sturdy steel-capped boot and I heard the delightful sound of splintering wood. Three more blows and I had removed the top panel.

No light within. No moon, either. The wind howled even louder, but there was an ominous silence from the woman and child.

'Don't worry. I'm a respectable person,' I shouted as loudly as I could and then waited, but there was no sound. I thrust my hand inside, fumbled for a minute, moving my glove up and down the frame of the door. Yes, a bolt, a heavy iron affair, but new, like the rest of the building and it slid back easily. I gave the door a vigorous shake, but the lock still held and a few blows from my iron-capped boot had no effect upon it. A sudden and quickly smothered wail from upstairs lent an urgency to my usual hesitant nature. Quickly I replaced my steel-capped boot and holding the door knocker firmly with one hand, I swung my right leg and vigorously kicked the bottom panel of the door. Now I could hear no more from upstairs; my ears were full of the sound of heavy blows and the encouraging noises of splintering wood. For a moment I quailed at the thought of a policeman passing. He could not fail to hear the din I was creating, but then I told myself that no policeman would be out on a night like this and so I continued, drowning any fearful thoughts with the thunderous noise of the vigorous blows I was inflicting upon the shoddy wood of the door.

Once I had a hole broken through the bottom panel, I paused, still holding onto the door knocker, my breath panting like a steam engine. The storm had slightly died down, though the wind still ruffled the trees, but the flashes of lightning had ceased, and I stood in complete darkness.

And then in the silence came a voice from above, a woman's voice, a voice broken with terror. 'Quick, quick!' it said. 'Whoever you are, please be quick. He'll be here soon, and he will beat us with a poker if he finds you here.'

These words brought back my energy. I was small, barely five-and-a-half feet high, with tiny delicate hands, and I didn't

feel up to confronting a brute wielding a poker. No more rests.
I should continue to kick that door until I had a space large
enough to insert myself into the hallway.

Four more vigorous kicks were all that it took. And my
first piece of luck. A rumble of thunder and then a flash
of lightning lit up the small hallway. Tiled floor, small
table. And on that table I could see a candle in a candlestick and some matches. In a moment I had managed to
squeeze my head and my torso through the broken panel
and then my legs followed. I pulled myself to my feet.
Moved down the hallway, fumbling my way with a hand
on the wall until I felt the edge of the table against my
hip bone. And then I laid my hand upon the matches. A
second later, I had one lit. It trembled in my hand, but I
managed to steady it enough to apply the small blaze to
the candlewick. Now I could see the gas meter beside the
front door, but I dared not touch it. I began to climb the
stairs, candlestick in hand. A new house, not long occupied,
I thought. The wood on the stairs was fresh from the
sawmills, almost white in colour and there were no stair
coverings, no carpet or stair treads. The howl of the wind
seemed to lessen and through the broken panel of the front
door I heard a familiar sound.

It was the sound of a metal gate. I had left it open, but now
some force had clashed it shut against its iron frame. The
wind, I hoped, but I dared not trust to that thought.

I looked back hesitantly and then turned. There was a door
at the top of the stairs, partitioning the top half of the house
from the lower end. A house meant to hold two flats, I thought
before lowering myself to be able to speak through the
keyhole.

'Is your door open?' I said the words, placing my mouth
against the edge of the door, rather than shout them. The storm
still raged, but I feared the sudden arrival of the poker-wielding
monster.

'It's locked. We're locked in.' The voice was frightened, but
there was a certain sweetness in it which aroused my curiosity.
The voice was that of a young woman, I thought.

'Stand back,' I said bravely.

I heard her repeat my words to the child and I waited for a few seconds while gathering my strength and resolution. 'Don't be frightened,' I called out as steadily as I could as I placed the candlestick to the side and then I lifted my foot and kicked at the bottom panel. Once, twice, three times. Success! A crackling sound, almost as though I had set the panel on fire, a strange creak and then the clatter of wood falling upon the floor. I stopped for a moment to get my breath back, picked up the candlestick, put it on the floor inside the door and then inserted myself through the gap and straightened up. I could see a passage and beyond it was the open door to a bedroom.

I saw the child first. Quite little, about five years old, I guessed. My heart melted as I noticed that she looked up at me with the same expression on her little face as my beloved little dog Tommie, such a trusting look as though she knew that I would look after her. I held out my arms to her and in a minute was holding the soft, warm, little body and feeling the child's arms around the back of my neck.

And then I looked at the woman. She had picked up the candlestick and was holding it in front of her, looking at me by its light. Very pretty, a pale face, a pair of frightened blue eyes, about my own height, a mass of soft golden hair, not tied up, or plaited, but streaming down her back in pale gold ringlets.

'Quick,' she said, and her voice trembled. 'Quick, the storm is dying down. We must get away.'

She was right. When I came to know her better, I knew that she was always right. I had been so immersed in my efforts to break the door to the passageway I had not realized until this moment that the noise of the storm, the claps of thunder, the howl of the wind had begun to melt away and the ordinary sounds of the night were taking its place, wafting up to us through the broken front door. In the distance, I thought that I could hear the clip-clop of horses' feet and feared that her bugbear, the man with the poker, was on his way to slaughter us all.

'Take the candle,' I said. 'You lead the way.'

She did not hesitate. She swept down the stairs and had

turned away, going down the back passageway by the time
that I, carrying the child, had stumbled to the last step. She
was making for the kitchen, and I felt the cold night wind
ruffle my hair as she opened the back door.

'Look after me, won't you?' I whispered to the child and
she giggled. I held her tightly against my chest as we went
through the kitchen and then out through the scullery door,
out into the dark chill of the wet and stormy night.

But we were too late. There was a sound from the road, a
sound that penetrated through the noise of wind and rain. It
was the clip-clop of a horse's feet and then a pause and then
that sound again. The trap had stopped outside the gate but
was now moving off. The moon was emerging from its bank
of clouds and the carriage lamp illuminated the wide-open
gate. There was a shout of anger. The broken padlock had
been discovered. And then another shout, even angrier. He
had found the smashed front door and he yelled, a harsh, brutal
sound that sent shivers down my spine. My blood ran cold.
The man, the brute was shouting for the cabbie, going to send
him for the police, I reckoned. He must have discovered that
his prisoner had escaped. There was no chance of someone
like me, burdened with a woman and child, being able to
escape these two men.

'Cabbie!' came the shout again.

And then, in despair, I acted.

'Wilkie, dear old Wilkie, Wilkie the tortoise,' my friend,
Charles Dickens used to say. But the nickname never bothered
me. While Dickens strode impatiently through busy streets, I
was often the first to reach our evening's rendezvous. I had a
trick up my sleeve, a piece of cunning. I understood cab drivers,
understood how to get a cab when others were fuming and
shouting. Still carrying the child, I turned back from the shelter
of the garden and came right out to beside the wall, beneath
the gas lamp, waving a glittering gold sovereign high above
my head, just where it caught the light.

And, of course, the cabbie reacted instantly – they always
did. His horse responded to a touch of the whip. The cab door
was opened just beside us. I almost threw the child onto the
back seat and the woman joined her immediately.

I took the front seat and handed over the sovereign. He bit it with an almost automatic gesture, whipped up the horse and we went clattering down a narrow side street, an old street with none of those plane trees that had been planted so profusely in the newer parts of London housing estates.

I looked back once or twice, but there was no sign of the man, no shouts for the police, no lights showed from the damaged house.

'You all right, little Tommie dog?' I said over my shoulder and the child giggled. My heart warmed at the sound. A courageous child!

'Is Tommie your dog?' She sat forward and thrust her little face close to my shoulder.

'He's my little boy dog. You can be my little girl dog,' I said, thankful that the child sounded so relaxed. I had thought to hear a sob from the woman, expected to have frightened appeals for speed, requests for help poured into my ear, but she said nothing. I looked back once at her, but she was not even looking at the road behind us, not checking whether there was pursuit, but was staring straight ahead. A courageous woman!

'Where to, governor?' asked the cabbie. He sounded quite casual as though things like that happened to him every night of his life.

'Howland Street,' I said decisively. I had lodgings there which I used from time to time and the landlord did not live on the premises. My mother was easy-going, but I did not think that I could bring a stray woman and child into her house at this hour of the night.

'Howland Street, it is, governor. Terrible storm, wasn't it?' he added. 'No need to go too fast is there, now, sir?' He glanced over his shoulder and I followed the direction of his stare.

'No need,' I said tranquilly. 'You take your time, cabbie. You'll want to watch out for fallen trees or loose slates flying down from roofs.'

'Or bad men with pokers,' said the child and my heart lifted to hear the amused note in her voice.

'Oh, don't worry about bad men with pokers; I know what

to do with them,' I said in a careless way and immediately the little face appeared at my shoulder.

'What do you do with them?' she asked eagerly.

'Can you keep a secret?' I asked.

'Of course! I'm five now, not four anymore!'

'Are you really?' I said respectfully. 'Well, I know I can trust you then.' I lowered my voice and whispered in her ear: 'I kick bad men with pokers into the coal-hole, and shut the door on them and guess what I do then?' I waited dramatically for a moment and then said impressively, 'You'll never guess what I do then; I throw away the key.'

She giggled at my joke. 'That's good,' she said.

I wondered about her briefly. Despite her mother's apparent terror, the child was calm and unafraid, rather like one of my friends' children. How had her mother managed to shield her if there had been a genuine threat?

But that was not the immediate problem. The cab had turned into Howland Street and I pulled my key from my pocket. I was out of the cab and had the gate opened before any inquisitive questions could be asked by our driver. I motioned to the sovereign in his hand. 'Keep the change,' I shouted, and he was off almost before the words left my mouth.

They both followed me without question, but when I had inserted the key into the door, I thought I should clarify matters before I met one of the neighbours or even the landlord himself.

'You don't mind if I say you are my housekeeper?' I asked hurriedly and in a low voice. I could see her plainly now and she was startlingly beautiful – huge blue eyes and hair of pale gold. 'There is a bedroom for you. You and little Tommie will be safe there.'

She looked down at the child and then back at me. I thought her eyes were extraordinarily beautiful, so clear and so very courageous.

'I'm an extremely good cook,' she said, and she said it in such a brave manner that I had to restrain myself from giving her a kiss.

'Excellent,' I said in a businesslike way. 'Now come and see the room. It's beside the kitchen.'

It was a miserable-looking place, that room for the servant, I thought, looking around it. Still there was quite a large bed, and an enormous linen closet furnished with a hot water cylinder next door to it. And there was a stove in the kitchen next door and a hatch that led to the coal-hole. When that stove was lit, the rooms would be warm. The landlord had left a pile of sticks in a basket and I snatched a newspaper from the pile that he had stacked beside the fireplace.

'You tear that into strips for me and we'll get a blaze going, little Tommie,' I said and the child, with the enthusiasm of her age, began vigorously shredding the newspaper. I crumpled the pieces, stacked the sticks, and piled pieces of coal on top of them. Once I got some sort of fire going, she clapped her little hands with joy. 'That's nice,' she said. And then she said with a grimace, 'I'm not really Tommie, you know. My real name is Harriet, but I don't like it very much. Will your dog be upset if I borrow his name?'

I sat back on the heels. 'He might be,' I said, biting my lip and frowning thoughtfully. 'Now that I come to think of it, he might be cross. And I don't like him being cross with me. It makes me sad. Why don't you like the name Harriet?'

'Sounds like a boy's name,' she said in her decided way. 'I'd like to be called Caroline, but that's my mama's name and she won't lend it to me.'

'I'll tell you what, I think I'll call you Carrie – rhymes with Harrie, and Carrie is a pretty name, and it suits you,' I said after considering the matter solemnly while I poked more sticks into the fire and managed to get a magnificent blaze going. The chimney had been recently swept, so the landlord had assured me when I gave a deposit for the rent a few weeks earlier. I would be extravagant with the fuel and get the place warmed up. It was, I thought, a nice little kitchen, and in a fit of enthusiasm when I took over the lodging, I had shopped for tea and biscuits and some vegetables and fruit – and quite a lot of beer and wine. I had pictured myself having little dinner parties, but after the first one where I had invited my brother and some of his friends, it had all seemed too much trouble and so I had reverted to trading upon my mother's hospitable nature. But now I was pleased that I had those stores.

I sat back on my heels and looked around. The landlord had recommended a cleaner and a washerwoman and a boy to run errands, had even written names and addresses upon a card which he had left upon the mantlepiece and which I was sure I must have put somewhere in a safe place. If this Caroline really was a good cook, I might be very cosy here and even bring the real Tommie over to play with the child. With a good cook I could hold dinner parties after my own careless fashion where none of the guests need wear starched linen and uncomfortable collars. I, as the host, would set a good example by receiving my guests clad in my best dressing gown.

'Let's all have some supper and then it will be time for bed,' I said, still speaking to the child.

'Where am I going to sleep?' she demanded and then she looked at her mother and a shadow came over her face. 'Do I have to be put into the attic?' she asked.

'Certainly not,' I said, pretending to be stern. 'No one, ever, ever, ever is allowed to put anyone in an attic in my house.'

She watched me carefully. 'Are you sure that you own this house?' she asked, scrutinizing my face with a cautious air that seemed too old for her years.

'Of course I'm sure.'

'And no one makes you do bad things?' She said this with a sidelong glance at her mother and I was sorry for the woman.

'I'm too tough,' I said. 'And I've got lots and lots of money so I can take care of a little girl and her very nice mama.'

Oddly, that reassured her. She danced up and down. 'Lots and lots of money; are you sure?' she queried, but in a happy way.

'Lots,' I said firmly. 'And now finish up your milk and your biscuits and you and your mama can go off to bed. And I'll lock all of the doors and here's a key to your door so the two of you are as snug as two little bugs in a rug.'

I handed the key to Caroline and they both went off looking quite relaxed and happy. I spent some time checking locks on doors and windows and went to bed eventually, but I took some time to go to sleep.

What would happen if that angry man turned up and demanded his property?

TWO

When I woke up next morning, there were the usual traffic sounds from outside my window but not a sound from within my own apartment. I began to think that I must have dreamed the whole affair. It almost, I thought sleepily, seemed more likely than the idea that I, Wilkie Collins, the most indolent and peace-loving of men, had actually kicked down the front door belonging to a perfect stranger and gone off with what might well be his wife and child. No, I must have dreamed it!

And then I sat bolt upright in bed. A knock on the door, an extremely soft knock, but unmistakably my door. Quickly I got to my feet, dragged on my dressing gown, crammed my feet into my slippers, crossed the floor and threw open the door.

No one was there, but on the small table outside the door to my room was a tray. Coffee pot, smelling deliciously, cup and saucer, small side plate, a rack filled with crisp gold triangles of toast, a bowl of sugar and a dish of marmalade. And in a small round dish there was the butter carefully shaped into small balls. I didn't even know that such an instrument for making butter balls existed in the drawers of my kitchen. And beside the tray, well covered, there was a large jug of boiling water.

Breakfast and shaving water. All delivered to my door.

This was luxury indeed.

'Thanks!' I called out and heard a slight giggle from a child. So, I hadn't dreamed it all, I told myself, but despite the toast, despite the coffee, despite the shaving water, I still felt as though I were living in a dream. I looked down at my boots, untidily sprawling on the rug beside my bed, picked one up and examined it. Yes, there were scratches on the metal toecaps. So I did kick in a door with those very boots. Even so, it still felt like some sort of dream. No one, I thought, not even my younger brother, Charley, who normally listened to all of my tales with great respect, would believe me if I told him what I had done that night after we had parted. I could hardly believe it myself. Or that my household now consisted of three people.

They were there, however, when I came out, fully dressed and ready for what the morning would bring. The child was bouncing with excitement, the woman hesitant and with black shadows under a pair of the most beautiful eyes.

'Thank you for my nice breakfast. Just what I like: coffee and toast,' I said, and she smiled in a tentative manner, looking at me with those lovely big blue eyes. There was something about that look, something perhaps of that frightened puppy that I had once rescued from a gang of hooligans, that made me feel very protective about her. I longed to take her in my arms and reassure her, but I knew that I would have to be most careful and so I just smiled back. I would have to buy her a comb, I decided. Her hair was lovely; it looked so incredibly soft, so fine, like a glimmering sheet, pale blonde in colour, but its ringlets had tangled during the night and she had tied it back from her face with a small piece of string. I would have to give her some money to buy the necessities for herself and for the child, but when I took a note from my pocketbook and suggested, in a businesslike way, that she might like to pop out after breakfast in order to shop for a few necessities, she shook her head in terror and clasped the child to her.

'No, no!' she said, her voice just a whisper, and the child looked up at her in a frightened way.

I would have to reassure both. Go very gently, I told myself.

'Never mind,' I said cheerfully. 'You two stay nice and warm and safe here in my house. I'll do the shopping. My mother says that I am the worst person in the world to be trusted with shopping for a lady, but I'll do my best. Would you give me a list of what you want? There's a grocery and a ladies' shop beside it just down the next street.'

I handed Caroline a notepad and two envelopes. She might, I thought, be shy of writing female requirements for my eyes.

'What about you, little Carrie? What can I do for you, my lady?' I was glad that the child was there. She took some of the tension from the atmosphere. I was fond of children and always enjoyed talking to them. Deliberately I turned my back on her mother and proceeded to enjoy a conversation with her little daughter.

'I'd like a bed of my own,' said the child in her decided manner. 'I'm tired of sleeping with my mother. She twists and turns too much, and she wakes me up by crying in her sleep and then she makes me go into the attic. Have you got a bed for me? And a room of my own, please. Not an attic. I hate attics.'

A determined and self-assured little lady. Whatever had happened to the woman, she had managed to shield the child from much of the terror that she had experienced. This little Harriet had been frightened, but not too badly, I guessed. She would recover and perhaps forget her bad experience. I would make sure that she was happy and that would help to reassure the woman. I beamed a smile of relief at the little girl and assured her that I would find a bed for her in a nice shop. As for a room, that was a puzzle. These were lodgings for a single gentleman, I told her, and she nodded slightly impatiently and repeated that she needed a bed of her own and that she would really, really like a room, even a very little one.

'I've got an idea,' I said with sudden inspiration. 'Come and see my idea.'

Followed by them both, I went into the little passageway from the kitchen and opened the door to the linen room. It was a fair-sized room. Even had a small window. My possession of linen was very scanty and consisted of little more than a few pairs of sheets and pillowslips and two rather worn tablecloths, all of which had been bestowed upon me by my generous mother when I had first hired the lodgings. There certainly was room for a little bed for the child and the empty shelves could hold her clothes and her toys. I was most pleased with myself, though the child shook her head wisely.

'Bedrooms have closets and dressing tables and things like that,' she said severely.

'Harriet! Be quiet! Stop asking for things. You don't need a bed. You can sleep with me.' The woman was distraught and turned angrily upon the child. She seemed on the verge of tears, I thought, and hastened to bring a little lightness into the atmosphere.

'The bed will be a little present. She can be my godchild,' I said. 'I became a godfather last weekend, you know, and I really enjoyed the whole day. Except,' I said to the child in a stage whisper and from behind my hand, 'that baby was drunk. Would you believe it? Not able to stand up straight, making strange sounds, waving arms in the air and dribbling! I told all the guests that I was sure he was drunk and most of them believed me – all the men, anyway. Of course,' I said with mock solemnity, 'he was a boy, and I don't like boys much. I prefer little girls. They don't get drunk, do they?'

'So, I'll be your girl godchild.' She nodded her little head. 'And I never get drunk! Never ever!'

I was enchanted by her, and while I was fetching my hat and stick I planned with pleasure a few little surprises for her after I had bought a little bed and some bedclothes. I wished that they could come with me and we could do the shopping together, but the terror on the woman's face had been too stark, too real, for me to suggest such an expedition again, even under my protection. What had happened to her? My novelist's imagination began to work overtime. But in the meantime, I, the most unpractical of men, had to work out some solution to this problem which I had landed myself with.

'I'll tell the landlord that I have a housekeeper; I'll drop into his house on my way into the town,' I told her. 'He won't trouble you, but you can bolt the front door after I leave and there is a good solid lock on your own door. You have the key to your own room, don't you?' I had handed that key ceremoniously to her the night before so that she didn't suspect me of anything, but I thought that it would be good to remind her. I didn't want to see that look of terror come back again.

She nodded and produced a slight smile, more to reassure the child who was watching her anxiously than to express any relief or amusement, I thought.

'And the man in the next-door house is a policeman. He works by night so he will be sleeping, but if you open the window and scream, you'll wake him up,' I said, trying to sound as reassuring as I could. It was a lie, of course. I had no idea about the man next door, did not know his name and hadn't the slightest idea of what he did for a living. The woman was in my thoughts as I walked through the streets. She puzzled me. There was something so withdrawn, so rigid about her. One expected a girl as pretty as that to smile and toss her head and use the beauty of her eyes to engage attention, but this Caroline looked at me with eyes that showed nothing but a secret terror. It worried me.

I enjoyed shopping for the child. And the shop had just the thing. A small bed, not much bigger than a baby's cot, with pretty, pale pink sheets and a cosy pink eiderdown embroidered with small rosebuds. The assistants bustled around me, entranced by my fluent story of a parentless godchild who had just arrived from India lacking all sorts of necessities. My latest book, *The Woman in White*, was selling extremely well so I acted as though money were of no object and the shop assistants loved me, persuaded me into a pretty, little, pink bedside mat and a large fluffy teddy bear. They rushed up and down the stairs fetching small-sized nightdresses, dressing gowns and little slippers, all for me to choose from. When Caroline's fears had subsided, I planned, I would give her money to buy proper clothes for herself and the child, but in the meantime my new godchild could have a nice little nest to give her a pleasant night's sleep.

My next visit was to a toy shop where I purchased and arranged for the delivery of a Noah's Ark with its boxful of animals and a bucolic-looking Noah with a fat wife wearing a workman-like apron. When I came out of the shop I met Dickens in the company of a youngish man, about my own age, I thought, and he hailed me instantly.

'Just the man I wanted to see!' he said with an effusiveness that surprised me as Dickens wasn't usually effusive. 'My dear Collins, let me introduce you to Mr Joseph Bazalgette, an engineer who has more ideas in a second than most men have in a lifetime,' he said. 'Bazalgette, this is Mr Wilkie Collins, the famous novelist – I'm sure that you've read that wonderful book *The Woman in White* – pure genius.'

Bazalgette and I shook hands, both of us slightly embarrassed by our introduction; in all probability, he had never read my book, and for my part, I hadn't the slightest interest in engineering and would certainly not be able to assess the worth of any engineering idea. I knew Dickens, though, and was not surprised when he said, artlessly, 'What would you say to Bazalgette and myself coming around to see you this evening, Wilkie? I'm sure that you could manage to get that excellent cook from Haddisons to dish up a few tasty chops – my domestic arrangements are a bit churned up at this moment in time, Bazalgette, but Wilkie is a wonderful host.'

Bazalgette looked even more embarrassed. The whole of London knew the story about Dickens' domestic arrangements and about the huge row with his wife who had accused him of all sorts of things when he took the young actress, Ellen Ternan, under his wing. The letter that he wrote to *The Times* had informed the world of his side of the story, detailing his wife's 'peculiarity of character' and 'mental disorder' writing of these things which had led her 'to relinquish all care for her children', castigating 'two wicked people who coupled his separation with the name of an innocent young lady' – well, of course, this letter, as anyone could have told him, had only worked to trigger a tidal wave of gossip about Dickens himself and about the unfortunate girl, whose relationship to himself he would not publicly acknowledge in order to protect her actress mother. Now there were a whole batch of words like 'actress', 'bedroom', 'wife' and 'newspaper' which everyone tried to avoid using in the presence of Dickens.

I hastened to relieve the tension.

'No need for Haddisons,' I said loftily. 'I've a new housekeeper, Dickens – just as you advised, and she is an excellent cook. What about seven o'clock? Would that suit you both?'

'Yes, indeed.' He wasn't curious about my sudden acquisition of a housekeeper. I was lucky there. Dickens liked people to follow his advice and he had often told me that at my age, and with my newly acquired source of money, I should be setting up a home of my own, with a cook and a housekeeper rather than drifting back to the greater comfort of my mother's hospitable house. So now he was pleased that I had done what he had told me to do. We parted amicably and the three of us agreed on meeting again at the hour of seven that evening.

Caroline was taken slightly aback at the news that she had to cook for guests on that very evening, but the little bed and the bedclothes arrived soon after I had told her the news and, in the bustle and excitement of setting up the little room in the large linen cupboard as a bedroom, she became natural and very practical, consulting her little daughter on all details but managing to make a pretty little bedroom out of the linen cupboard, even suspending a tablecloth over the top shelves of the cupboard and arranging the Noah's Ark on the lower shelves. While little Carrie was tucking her enormous teddy bear in under the bedclothes, she found a notebook in the kitchen, its first few pages filled with my scrawls of items to be purchased and then abandoned when I realized that housekeeping was really beyond my capabilities. She had written a neat list of foods while I was being persuaded into bestowing a goodnight kiss upon the teddy bear.

'I thought that I wouldn't do chops,' she said, when I came out into the kitchen. 'If an extra guest turns up that mightn't work out. I know a recipe, something I've cooked when I was a girl – Goulash of Beef. I've made it before, quite several times, and each time it turned out very well. That's if you will trust me,' she said in an anxious way.

'I'm sure that it will be wonderful, but, in any case, they won't be fussy,' I said reassuringly, making a mental note to praise the meal to the skies once the guests had gone. 'Don't worry. I'll open a couple of bottles of wine and I'm sure that everything will be excellent.' I wondered whether to call her Caroline – after all she had offered no other name, but I decided to wait until after the dinner and so obediently wrote down as many items as she wanted.

I would get that boy from the landlord, I thought. Someone who could do the heavy scrubbing and lifting and who would be available to run errands for my little household. I was beginning to get quite excited at my first dinner party. I

was filled with energy. I would be a reformed character, would
work hard at my writing, perhaps even devote regular hours
to it and would produce a novel to rival anything that Dickens
or Thackery could write, would become famous and spend
my life doing something I enjoyed, and not revert into that
slough of laziness, where I had played at studying the law and
lived upon the money which my hard-working father had left
to maintain his wife and his two sons. So off I shot, down the
street to the landlord, and less than an hour later, the smart
boy dressed in pitiable rags, though his face was looking
scrubbed and neat, was delivered to my hands for a wage of
half a crown a week. His name was Francis and he seemed
willing to do any jobs that were allocated to him. I sent him
down to the shop with Caroline's list and then went to look
at my stock of wine.

By the time that I emerged from the small cellar, with a
pair of bottles in either hand, little Carrie was waiting for me
and followed me into the dining room and stood, frowning
slightly, watching as I poured the contents of the first two
bottles into my pair of decanters.

'Well, what can I do for you, little lady?' I asked as I
tipped a few spoonfuls from the bottoms of the bottles into
a glass and sipped it appraisingly. It was good, I thought,
and I prided myself on being able to assess wine. Carrie was
frowning at me in a most serious fashion, so I put away the
glass and sat on a chair to listen to her. Another teddy bear,
perhaps, was needed. But no, I did her an injustice. Carrie
was always a little manager and she had seen something was
wrong.

'He needs clothes, that boy Francis,' she said imperiously.
'He's got holes in his trousers and in his jacket. You must
buy him some clothes. I'll come with you and help you to
choose. He's in the kitchen, come on, be quick, now, no
dawdling!'

I was delighted with her. If only her mother could be as
straightforward and candid, we would all get on very well
together.

'You're quite right,' I said humbly. 'Men are bad at clothes.
You'll have to help me.'

We went straight into the kitchen. If Francis was there, unloading his messages, then the conversation with Caroline would be easier. I had already noticed how at home with the boy she was already and how, though polite, she had issued orders to him in the manner of one who was used to dealing with servants.

'I think that you need some new clothes if you are going to be our messages boy,' I said to Francis as soon as I came into the kitchen. 'I'll take Carrie, too, to help us choose the right things for him,' I said over my shoulder to Caroline who was kneeling on the floor, with her head in a cupboard, sorting out tins and saucepans.

A bit abrupt perhaps, but I was determined to get little Carrie at least out into the spring air in a natural fashion. She, I thought, must have an opportunity to forget the past as soon as possible and so steering the two children to the door, I gave a shrill whistle to a passing cab and popped the two of them into it before any objection could be lodged.

The cabbie was immediately helpful, in the way that cab drivers usually are and knew of a shop that sold boys' and men's clothing in Euston Road, less than five minutes away. He had cast one glance over his shoulder at Francis and made an astute choice, as the shop he brought us to was obviously designed for working men and boys. I tipped him well. It was honest of him, I thought, not to drive us all over London and then drop an ignoramus like myself in front of some high-class purveyor of fashionable clothes for young gentlemen.

Carrie took her duties very seriously and decided that Francis had to have two sets of clothes, one for everyday and one for Sundays and going out to parties, according to her. A rather supercilious assistant wanted to throw away the boy's original clothes, but I thought that was too high-handed and demanded a bag and handed the rags back to the boy himself, who looked smart and respectably dressed in ordinary working clothes with a warm jacket, while Carrie, with great pride, took his Sunday clothes and said she would keep them safe for him on a shelf in her bedroom. Francis, himself, seemed a bit bewildered so I decided that we would walk back, since it was quite a short distance and that we would do a bit of shopping on the way. On an impulse, I stopped at a flower shop and bought a bunch of red geraniums. These, I knew, were Dickens' favourite flowers and I wanted his approval of my new cook and housekeeper.

THREE

Caroline was right when she said that a goulash was a better idea than chops and she certainly proved that it was wise to make provision for extra guests arriving. Yes, there was a third guest. When the doorbell went, I opened it myself. There was Dickens, and slightly behind him was Joe Bazalgette, but beside him was Henry Austin. So, we would be four at table, not three.

Now, I knew Henry Austin – he was, after all, Dickens' brother-in-law, married to Letitia, the younger of Dickens' two sisters, and he also, like Bazalgette, was an engineer. I wasn't pleased to see the man, though. I didn't like Henry Austin very much. For one thing, he was one of those people who were always so sure that you want to hear about their health. One of those people who will answer your perfunctory greeting of 'how are you?' with a long description of their health, incorporating minute and often disgusting details of the sort that only an adoring mother would want to know. It may, of course, have been his bad health, or his perception of bad health, but he always seemed to be in poor humour and to feel that you should be giving him something, either advice, physic, or even the offer of employment. He was, I often thought, a hopeless sort of man. Someone who was always looking to extract value from his acquaintances – either to gain money or information.

Dickens was patient with him for his sister's sake, but he had often cursed the man for the poor quality of his work. I had watched with amusement when Dickens had drawn sketch after sketch of the cold shower which he wanted built in his new house, but in the end the overworked novelist had had to stand beside his brother-in-law, the engineer, and, step by step, coach him through the piece of plumbing which Dickens deemed was necessary for his health and his feeling of well-being – even to the extent of dictating the size of cistern which would be required in order to have the requisite strength in the flow of the water. Henry Austin could not see why the original three-hundred-gallon cistern should not be enough, but Dickens insisted upon a four-hundred-and-forty-gallon cistern and when all was done held a small party to demonstrate to everyone his splendidly torrential shower. I had noticed with amusement on that occasion how Henry Austin had typically taken full credit for the strength of the water and how Dickens had had difficulty in hiding his irritation with him.

Nevertheless, Dickens took responsibility for his family seriously and quite quickly I could see why Henry Austin had been dragged along.

He was a great man, Dickens. There were times when he annoyed and distressed me, especially recently after his outbreak of temper against his wife, but there were far more times when I loved him for his generosity of spirit and his burning ambition to do good to the world. All in all, I esteemed him more highly than any living man. So now I looked resignedly at his brother-in-law, invited all three in and poured the wine with as hospitable a hand as always. And then I went to the kitchen to tell Caroline the news that an unexpected visitor had turned up. I thought that she would take it as a joke and I told it like that, teasing her that it was an admirer of hers – stupid of me, but my relations with women were always like that. I joked, teased, they laughed, and we always got on very well together.

But Caroline was different.

It was stupid of me to pretend that Henry Austin had come on purpose to see her. She panicked. I literally saw the whites of her eyes. She had heard of Dickens, had seen his picture in the newspaper and she had heard of Bazalgette, also. His picture, too, had been in the papers and she remembered the unusual name. I think she was quite resigned to both of them, but now this extra man that she had not even seen, nor even heard his voice had turned up. The name, Henry Austin, meant nothing to her, but she was frightened of some man. This man was bringing that terrible look of terror to her eyes. Even the information that Austin was married to Dickens' sister didn't seem to calm her initially. The child, who had been playing with the Noah's Ark toy, stopped what she was doing and watched her mother with widened eyes and a white face.

I kissed her. It was the only thing I could think of doing. Her lips were soft and trembled. 'Don't worry, Caroline,' I said hastily. 'You do the cooking and I'll do the serving. You have everything ready. I can see that. Leave the dishes ready in the oven and I'll come in and take them. You and the little girl will be quite safe in your own room. You can lock the door, if you wish.' I filled a glass with wine, made sure that she drank it and then took the two of them into the servant's room, carefully carrying the Ark and as many of the animals as I could scoop up in a hurry. Carrie followed me, still saying nothing, and when they were both inside I heard the key turn in the door.

There was a protest from the child. She wanted her teddy bear, but I did not want to interfere. It had shaken me, somewhat, to see how ill poor Caroline had looked. Her fear of this mysterious man was very real, and I would have to be careful about unexpected guests turning up.

I went back to the guests. The table was laid, everything was ready, very fancy, I thought. She had even prettily arranged the geraniums in small vases, red flowers alongside sprigs of crisply green parsley in a row down the centre of the table.

'My new cook has an artistic side,' I said to Dickens as I caught him admiring his favourite flowers. He was bound to approve of a cook with such good taste. If it had not been for her terror at the idea of a fourth man, I would have risked taking him into the kitchen to meet her, but in view of her panic, I knew that I would have to give her time and privacy.

The soup was excellent. There was no bread with it, but next to the tureen there was a dish piled with tasty croutons, fried to perfection, crisp on the outside with soft centres which soaked up the soup and made them incredibly delicious to crunch between your teeth. I carried both in on a tray and ladled out the soup with a confident flourish. I could tell by the tasty aroma that we were in for a treat.

'Splendid,' said Dickens, swallowing a spoonful and crunching a crouton. 'Just the way that I like my soup. My dear fellow, I have to congratulate you on the new member

of your household. My goodness, Collins, this cook of yours
is excellent! How pleasant this is,' he went on. 'The clink of
busy spoons against plates, the smell of oxtail soup and the
meeting of minds. Let's drink to it.'

'Hear, hear,' I said. 'Have some more wine, Dick. And you,
Bazalgette. And what about you, Austin. Is this wine to your
liking?'

It was no good, though, for me to try to change the subject.
Dickens, though he could talk endlessly about food, could
make a nation hungry with a chapter in *The Pickwick Papers*,
was, himself, not a big eater and now he had something other
than dinner upon his mind. He scorned my efforts to quieten
him and turned to Bazalgette.

'Such a treat for penpushers like myself and Wilkie, here,
to meet two such technical minds, two engineers like yourself
and my brother-in-law Henry Austin. In fact, I dared to bring
him along tonight because he was so interested in the conversation which you and I had this afternoon as we both stood
outside the Houses of Parliament and remembered the horrors
of the summer that has gone by, of the heat and the dreadful
stench from the river and our unfortunate Members of
Parliament, trying to serve their country with all the zeal and
wisdom at their command while holding pocket handkerchiefs
to their noses and doing their best not to retch from the
appalling odours. I remember how they hung sheets dripping
with lime in front of the windows, but to no avail. No lime
could avail against that disgusting odour from the river, from
our cherished Father Thames.'

Then Dickens, having set the ball rolling, picked up his
spoon with a satisfied air and proceeded to finish the last drops
of the oxtail soup.

'It's the fault of Parliament,' said Henry Austin gloomily.
'Things were not so bad when every newly built house had
to have its own cesspit. Every man had to cope with his own
problem. That was the law.'

'Nonsense, man,' said Joe Bazalgette sharply. 'London has
got too big for that solution. You know, you must know, how
cesspits overflowed, how pipes were laid so badly that the
waste waters flowed back into the houses or into the streams

that emptied into your Father Thames. Of course, the pipes were not being properly laid. That's what happens when you allow each man to make his own arrangements and trust him to pick a qualified engineer instead of the cheapest man in the neighbourhood. You wouldn't believe it, Collins, but nine out of ten engineers, applying for the job of surveyor, had no idea what a spirit level was, no idea why it was important to get your levels correct, no idea of making a pipe leakproof! If I had my way, I would insist that every pipe in the country was made from Portland cement.'

I had no idea what Portland cement was or why it was superior to other cement, but after a quick glance at Henry Austin's inquisitive nose trembling with curiosity, I decided not to ask. Dickens, of course, had no compunction about milking one of my guests for the enlightenment of the other.

'Why Portland cement?' he asked casually.

'Just cement, stuff you use to make concrete,' said Henry Austin. His tone seemed to imply that Bazalgette was being pretentious, and I hastened to distract attention by collecting the soup plates and laying out the dinner plates in readiness for Caroline's goulash and whatever else she had cooked for us.

'What is cement, exactly?' I asked while stacking the plates. I could see a look of slight annoyance on Joe's face as he looked across at his fellow engineer.

'An ingredient of concrete – pipes are made from concrete and if you make sure to get your cement from Portland in Dorset, you get a nice blend of shale and limestone. I always insist upon it, otherwise the concrete crumbles and the sewage spills out onto the ground, gets into the drinking water pumps and finds its way back into the houses, kills thousands and thousands of Londoners, most of them children – nearly fifteen thousand of them last summer. So,' Joe Bazalgette continued as he turned toward Henry Austin in an irritated fashion, 'you are a builder, I seem to recollect. Well, you would do us all a favour if you made sure to use Portland cement when you were mixing concrete for your pipes.'

'Yes, but the solution to the problem . . .' Henry Austin was not too bright. Dickens often swore when he repeated to me stories about the troubles he had with him during the work

on Tavistock House and had once confided in me the extremes
to which he found himself forced to employ with his brother-
in-law. 'You wouldn't believe it, Collins, but every note I
write to him, I print on the bottom of the page the words
"DO YOU UNDERSTAND?"!' I had enjoyed that story, but
now I did not want my dinner party ruined by any display of
bad temper.

'I positively forbid any more talk about sewage,' I said
with mock severity. 'Tell me, Dick, have you seen Macready's
King Lear? Magnificent, wasn't it? Which did you think was
the best scene?'

That worked. Peacefully I finished collecting the soup plates,
piled them and the jug onto the tray and as I left the room,
Dickens was reciting a quote from *King Lear*: '"O, reason not
the need! Our basest beggars. Are in the poorest thing
superfluous."'

The goulash and the vegetables were a huge success. I
kept refilling plates and kept the conversation firmly on the
famous actors, managing to start Dickens on one of his
monologues while everyone else enjoyed the main course of
Caroline's dinner.

The kitchen was still empty when I came in. I set the dishes
into the sink with a slight clatter and then went to her door
and called out quietly, 'It is I, Caroline. And how is Mr Teddy
Bear, little Carrie?'

There was a giggle which warmed my heart. At least the
child was happy and at home. Now I had to reassure the mother.
I shot the bolt between the dining room and the kitchen premises, making as much noise as I could. 'Just me and the door
is locked,' I said cheerfully. 'Come and show me this pudding,
Caroline.'

She came after a moment's hesitation. Little bright-eyed
Carrie behind her, clutching the enormous teddy bear. I wished
her mother could look so happy. There was a frightened look
about the blue eyes that touched my heart. She took the pudding
from the oven and placed it on a warm plate. A lovely oval-
shaped pie, smelling deliciously of almonds and warm apples.

'I've been a bit extravagant with it, I'm afraid. I've used
butter for the crust, and I moistened the flour with four yolks

of eggs,' she said hesitantly, looking into my face with slightly frightened blue eyes as though she dreaded a blow.

I kissed her forehead. 'I'm sure it will be absolutely delicious, and I feel like eating it all myself,' I said lightly.

'That would be very greedy,' said little Carrie, so I gave her a kiss and another to Teddy, just for good measure. And I wished my visitors to Jericho so that the three of us could sit down at the well-scrubbed kitchen table and devour that succulent-looking pudding.

When I came back into the dining room with my tray of food, Henry Austin was discoursing on the enormous prices that could be got for loads of sewage and putting forward the rather controversial viewpoint that if you allowed only fresh faeces into the River Thames, it would help to breed fat, healthy fish.

'No more! Not a word more about sewage! I can't bear it!' I put the tray down upon the side table and covered my ears in a theatrical fashion. Dickens, I was glad to see, was frowning at his voluble brother-in-law. He, according to Dickens' plan, was here to listen to the expert, but it was turning out that it was the expert who was too modest to press his views upon his fellow diners while it was the numbskull – Dickens' description of Henry Austin, not mine – who was holding forth and delivering a mixture of his own views and others that he had picked up.

I was determined to have no more of it, though. The scent arising from the apple pudding was worthy of respect from a man like myself who loved his food. I went around the table, refilling glasses and then placed the pudding in front of Dickens and invited him to divide it up between the guests, while I bestowed the cream boat upon Henry Austin and handed a dish of spice-smelling little shapes to my other guest. I could see a look of relief upon his face, and I guessed that my arrival had come just in time for him.

'By Jove, Wilkie, that's a splendid cook that you've got for yourself,' Dickens exclaimed after he had chewed a few mouthfuls. 'Bet she costs you a fine sum,' he said after another mouthful, and then, when his plate was half-empty, he sat back with a sigh, wiped his mouth with his napkin and said decisively, 'I must have a word with this woman before I go. I'd love to know how she makes pastry like that!'

'Certainly not,' I said sternly. 'I know you, Dick. You'd be offering to double her wages and would steal her from me. I'm not putting up with that.'

And then to divert his attention – no one was quicker at sniffing out a mystery than Mr Charles Dickens – I turned back to Joe Bazalgette and asked him about his engineering practice in Great George Street. He was voluble and enthusiastic about this. An old warehouse, he told me and added that his landlord had gone into the housebuilding business as that was more lucrative than warehouses and so he had let the young engineer have it at a bargain price.

'Got windows on the north-eastern side, a whole wall lined with them, up high so they don't get in the way of the work benches and the machinery, but we have plenty of light and plenty of privacy as well. Just the one window at ground level and we've white-washed that. No small boys flattening their noses against the windows and putting themselves in danger if one of the machines go wrong. Most of my stuff is second-hand, of course. I'm good with my hands so I can repair most things,' he said, without a trace of false modesty, 'and so I can pick up plenty of stuff that others would put on the scrap heap. Got lots of room, of course. A huge place, big as a church, high ceiling. Myself and my workmen even built a little gallery halfway up one of the walls so that if we are doing a dangerous experiment, we can watch the result from a safe little nook up above, can test all sorts of materials and devices.'

Dickens, I noticed, was listening with great interest. I half smiled to myself. His latest novel, *A Tale of Two Cities*, set in Paris as well as London, had been published to great acclaim and was earning him large sums of money. Now his mind was in that fertile state where ideas for new novels slid in and out of his busy brain. Anything new and different interested him intensely now. I wasn't surprised when he said in his most charming manner, 'I'd love to see your workshop, Bazalgette. We must have a talk about that. Great George Street, you said, near Parliament Square, just off Horse Guards Road. I know it well.'

'Now you must all have a glass of brandy and some cheese,' I said hospitably, seeing that the plates were bare. I was half sorry that I had not asked Caroline to cook some biscuits, or even a cake, but perhaps that was enough for the moment. I smiled to myself with pleasure as I thought of the weeks and months to come, if only she would stay with me. As I deposited the plates and the empty dishes on the kitchen table, I was planning hard. Soon, I hoped, she would begin to trust me, would confide in me details about the man who had frightened her so badly and who had kept her a prisoner. I smiled at the thought of peaceful evenings by the fire. I would find a good school for the clever little child, I promised myself. Somewhere with a good and kind teacher and other children to play with little Carrie. And her mother would be safe and happy. Perhaps I would employ a housemaid, also, so that Caroline could bestow all of her talents on the cookery and running my little establishments. Smith and Elder had just made a bid of five thousand pounds for my next novel. Five thousand pounds for nine months or a year's work! I was going to be enormously rich. I would be able to afford a whole new house! Not in the country like Dickens, I had no interest in the country, but a house in town. A place where I could entertain friends in my own fashion – no ceremony, no starchiness, just good wine, good food and a happy relaxed attitude. And a beautiful, blonde-haired, blue-eyed woman for my housekeeper. No fear that any wife of mine would dislike having such a beautiful woman for a housekeeper. I was completely resolved to eschew marriage at all cost. I could see what it did to friends, how it altered their social life, curtailed their liberty.

I would have more dinner parties, I decided. Choose an interesting mix of people who would discuss the burning issue of the day. Nina and Frederick to discuss music – I would have to buy a piano – I thought. No evening would be complete without listening to Nina play. She was, I thought, without match in the whole of the United Kingdom. Perhaps also some engineers, though I had never taken any interest in such matters in the past. But what a feather in my cap if it could be said that it was at Wilkie Collins' dinner table that the first seed of the solution to the terrible problem of the polluted city and of the polluted magnificent River Thames was sown! In the meantime, I resolved, I would have to protect Joe Bazalgette from the cross-questioning of the persistent Henry Austin who was determined to squeeze information from someone with a better brain than he possessed. I promised myself, though, that I would go and see the warehouse which he had turned into a workshop. I was fascinated to hear his plans for the future of London.

FOUR

I t must have been about four or five days later that I met Big Ben in the company of my friend Charles Dickens.
I had not seen Dickens since the night of my little dinner party. Strictly speaking, I was employed by Dickens as a journalist, employed to work upon his magazine *Household Words*. However, Dickens and I, though two quite different people, had come to a very amicable arrangement about my terms of work. When it came down to the result, Dickens had decided that he did not really care whether I worked for two hours or four hours in the day. Neither did he care whether I did that work under his eye, or under the eye of his manager, Wills, at Wellington Street or whether I did it at home. I don't think that I ever let him down even if it meant staying up all night when publication day was coming dangerously near.

So, when we met on that sunny breezy day in March, on the pavement leading to Westminster Bridge, he greeted me with great amicability and introduced me to his companion Benjamin Hall, an immensely tall man, known as Big Ben, now towering over Dickens and probably making me look like a misshaped dwarf.

'Well met,' he said with great warmth. 'Well met, indeed, my dear Collins. Oddly, I was just talking about you. But let me introduce Sir Benjamin Hall; I'm sure that you have heard of him, Chief Commissioner of Works, and look up there, the great bell of Westminster, now and forever named after this gentleman, Big Ben it is, engraved upon its copper sides. And Big Ben will sound all over the city of London, thanks to this gentleman and his department. Sir Benjamin, this is Wilkie Collins, the well-known novelist.'

He was indeed 'Big Ben', but I wondered, while shaking hands, whether having a bell named after you was a great honour or not. I bit a smile from my lips as I imagined a few jokes about him that his friends could make. But then I became serious. Dickens had that intense look in his eyes that showed he was planning something.

'I was telling Sir Benjamin about our pleasant little dinner party at your house last week. So enlightening. And what a brilliant setting for the technical minds of our troubled times to open the storehouses of their knowledge,' said Dickens in one of his grandiose moods when his utterances were liable to take on the cadences of blank verse.

I was a little taken aback. Was I supposed to invite this stately Member of Parliament, member of the aristocracy, knighted by the queen herself, to my lodgings, to a dinner cooked by a woman who came from nobody knows, who was assisted by a little boy named Francis? If Dickens wanted to entertain this magnificent gentleman, why didn't he invite him to Rules, Dickens' favourite restaurant?

So I smiled uneasily and rapidly changed the subject. 'I was on my way to look at Mr Bazalgette's work premises,' I said. 'He had a lot of interesting ideas, I thought. Was even thinking that he would be an interesting character to put in the novel that I am writing . . . am about to write,' I added quickly as Dickens often scolded me about my haphazard methods of authorship. He, himself, once he had decided upon writing a new book, was meticulous about sitting down to work at the same time every morning, at nine thirty precisely and then working steadily until two in the afternoon. It suited him but it wouldn't suit me. He planned scrupulously; I allowed a new novel to float around in my subconscious and like a man with a shrimping net, occasionally landed a prize idea.

'Great George Street, wasn't it?' Dickens, as usual, was on the alert. 'Only a stone's throw from here. What do you say, Sir Benjamin, shall we accompany my young friend? Should give you food for thought.'

To my initial relief, Sir Benjamin looked a little uneasy, pulling out a large pocket watch and comparing its face with that of 'Big Ben' far above us. But then, to my annoyance, he nodded resignedly. Like most others of my acquaintance, he found it easier to give in to Dickens than to argue.

'Very well then, but I don't have very much time,' he said.

'I'm sure that you will find it to be of immense interest to you.' Dickens, of course, was always sure about everything. And normally he managed to get his certainties accepted by his friends and acquaintances. But then he added meaningfully, 'I'm sure that the queen will be most interested and most grateful to you for taking such an interest.'

The queen – well, if Queen Victoria was interested, that was a different matter, I thought. Joe Bazalgette would be hugely grateful if this informal visit by two powerful men resulted in his ideas being adopted.

'It's only about five or six minutes' walk from here,' I said to him consolingly and steered them both across the road. When we landed safely at the other side, Dickens bustled ahead at his usual rapid pace and Sir Benjamin slowed down to accommodate himself to my short legs.

'Don't think I am ungrateful, Mr Collins,' he said with an earnestness which impressed me. 'Something must be done for this distressful city of ours. We cannot allow our great River Thames to turn into a stinking sewer, we cannot allow cholera to stalk through the lanes and back streets of the town and fill the overflowing graveyards with children who should have had fifty years of health and industry ahead of them. We must do something. If I had my way, it would be top of the government's business on every day that Parliament sits. Ah, here we are, I see the name. Bazalgette. An unusual name. Grandfather was French, I believe.'

Bazalgette's premises were not very imposing. Rather a dirty-looking warehouse with just one visible window, placed just beside the door with most of its surface smeared with a light skim of white powder or perhaps paint to prevent anyone from looking in. It didn't stop small boys from standing there, spitting on the glass and rubbing it hopefully with the ragged sleeve of a jersey or a torn jacket. They didn't accomplish anything, but when a loud explosion came from inside, they thrilled with excitement, jumping up and down and trying to see inside these exciting premises. Sir Benjamin came to an abrupt standstill, but Dickens was made of sterner stuff. He made straight for the door, tried the handle and when it did not respond, knocked hard and authoritatively upon the shabby door with its peeling paint. Sir Benjamin and I followed him.

'I hope that we won't get blown up,' I whispered to him, and he gave me a delightful smile.

'I'm sure that you will make an exciting story out of this, Mr Collins, and let me say that I am a great fan of your work and enjoyed your last novel enormously.'

I glowed at his words and resolved to be as helpful as possible to him. The queen, I had heard, listened only to Lord Palmerston and it was probably quite difficult for someone like this unassuming man, Sir Benjamin Hall, to get his ideas endorsed by her.

The door was opened by a boy, not unlike my latest recruit, Francis, in appearance. He seemed to expect a delivery and had his hand stretched out to receive a parcel. Dickens was not at a loss, of course, but instantly tore a small sheet from a pocket notebook and scribbled a message upon it.

'I've signed your name to it, Collins; he'll be expecting a visit from you. I overheard him press you to see his warehouse,' he said casually as he handed the slip of paper to the boy. He stood back then and allowed the door to be closed in our faces.

'Let's hope nothing else explodes when we go in,' he remarked and then used the time while we were waiting to walk along the line of little boys at the window, asking each of them whether they had ever been to school. The answers he got were probably not too enlightening, as the children, receiving no hint of the right answer from his impassive face, tended to answer 'yes', or 'no' completely at random. Nevertheless, every one of them received a penny and my heart warmed to him. I had seldom been in the company of Dickens, in any part of London, where he had not found some children to bestow his pennies upon. He always kept a bagful. He told me once that his tailor, who cleaned his suits, was annoyed by the way that the pockets sagged in such an ugly fashion.

Bazalgette was at the door a couple of minutes later. He looked quite disconcerted when he recognized the man who came with us. Indeed, Sir Benjamin Hall, by reason of his height and his broad shoulders, was one of the most well-known men in London. I could see him searching for words and casting worried glances over his shoulder.

'It's not the best of times,' Bazalgette said in a hesitant way.

'We're in a bit of a mess in here. Just testing something.' From over his shoulder we could see that his assistant had extracted from one of the machines something that looked like an immense dog's bone with knobs on both ends. He gazed at it with satisfaction and came over to show it to Bazalgette, who was dressed similarly in powder-stained leather trousers, well tucked into iron-capped boots and wearing a leather apron. They exchanged smiles of sheer satisfaction and I guessed that if unexpected guests had not arrived that both would be cheering. 'We're in the middle of experimenting, you see,' Bazalgette added in a tentative manner, looking apologetically at Sir Benjamin. 'And then, well, well, it's a success . . .' He looked at the other man. 'This is my assistant, Andrew Wainwright.'

Quite a Lancashire name, I thought, but certainly not a Lancashire face. This Andrew Wainwright looked as if he were half Indian. He had jet-black hair, dark brown eyes and despite the long, wet winter, his skin was deeply tanned. He spoke perfect English though and seemed quite self-possessed. He and his master seemed to be on extremely good terms, both about the same age, I guessed. Joe was explaining that Andy was invaluable to him and had taught him a lot about working with steam. 'Great training, out there in India – wouldn't mind sending one of my sons out there to join the Indian police, or the Indian army, and get that sort of training,' he said with a nod at his assistant.

'But what brought you to London, Mr Wainwright?' asked Dickens, as always interested in people whose way of life was somewhat different to his own.

'I like London,' said the young man. 'I went to school here in London, myself and my twin sister. She stayed on in London, works as a clothes model in a shop there, but I went back to India, to my parents, and joined the Sappers as soon as I left school. Learned a lot there, but somehow, never satisfied, that's me, I yearned after London, came back and got a job with Joe here.'

'Taught me a lot,' repeated Joe generously.

'Including all the Indian rules about how to keep your workplace neat and tidy. Ah well, no man can get everything right, isn't that what we always say when things go wrong,

Joe?' said the assistant with a laugh and Joe laughed, also.
They were, I thought, more like a pair of students than master
and man.

'Well, impossible to have a hundred per cent success all the
time,' Bazalgette said in an easy fashion. 'You're very keen
on that, Andy, aren't you? Learnt it when you were a Sapper.
Some old Indian saying, isn't it? Sorry we didn't know that
you were coming, Mr Dickens. We'd have tidied up for such
a distinguished guest, wouldn't we, Andy?'

'Your name sounds Lancashire, Mr Wainwright,' stated
Dickens with his usual air of certainty and the young man
smiled.

'You're right, Mr Dickens. My father came from there.
Trained as an engineer there and then went off to India to join
the Sappers. Saw my mother, fell in love and they got married.
So, myself and my twin sister were born in India. Sent us
back to England for an education and that was a mistake, I
suppose, because we've both stayed there. I went to Lancashire
for a while but came back down to London.'

'So, what brings a man from Lancashire down south to
London?' Dickens had taken a fancy to the man and was eager
for all details.

'Brass,' said Mr Wainwright with a grin. 'We have great
engineers up north, the best in the country, but you have the
brass down south. Follow the money, that's an old saying and
a good one, Mr Dickens. Came down to join Joe here when
he came into the brass, had money left to him by his old
grandad. Helped him to spend it wisely. Best machines in the
country. Come and have a look at them. I can guarantee you'll
find nothing of this sort in any other engineer's premises in
your city of London.'

'Wish we were a bit tidier. We were in the middle of something, you see . . .' Oddly Joe Bazalgette, despite being the
owner, did not have the same confidence as his assistant.

'Nonsense, man. That's what we've come to see. A workshop
that is working.' Dickens was having none of this diffidence.
In a moment, he had us all inside and the boy, with an almost
comic air of satisfaction, was shutting the door in the face of
some peering urchins. Dickens looked around with wide eyes.

'Lord bless my soul; what an interesting collection of machines,' he said with such unaffected pleasure that I saw Bazalgette's worried face relax into a smile.

It was an immense old warehouse. About forty feet in height, I would guess. The windows on the ground floor were coated with paint and covered with iron mesh, but the ceiling, thirty feet above our heads, was intersected with sheets of plain glass and the warehouse was filled with light. Despite the muddle of machinery and tools the place was clean and well-swept. There was an expanse of empty floor and the three walls lined with machinery. Here and there upon the stone floor were a few heavy wooden tables and a few piles of sand stacked against the wall with an ominous-looking fire extinguisher beside one of them.

'I love that desk,' I said.

It was shaped like an ordinary writing desk, with a fold-down top, but this top was raised just now, and I could see that every inch of it was filled with screwdrivers and chisels of every shape and size. The hutch was formed by two narrow cupboards each with storage space for a variety of different sizes and shapes of saws and at the back of the hutch were steel drawers, each tightly shut. I went across and looked at it. There was no end to its ingenuity. Even the seemingly solid sides opened to reveal row upon row of tools, most of which I had never seen before – and had not the slightest idea of what they were used for. I was like a child with a new toy for Christmas, like my little Carrie playing with her Noah's Ark.

Dickens, in the meantime, was cross-examining Joe Bazalgette about the explosion that we had heard but was not getting too coherent a reply. A man with only one matter on his mind, Joe was still fondling the dog bone shape, stroking its smooth sides.

'Not a crack, Andy, is there?' he was saying to his assistant while Dickens looked with bright and interested eyes from one face to another.

'There wouldn't be – I told *thee* that.' With that answer, mimicking the Lancashire accent, Andy took up a large magnifying glass and examined the dog bone shape with immense care. 'Not a crack,' he said eventually.

'Why is that?' Dickens put in his question rapidly before they wandered away from him.

It turned out to be the correct question.

'Because of the cement, you see; we made the shape from the cement that we were testing,' said Joe and there was an exultant note in his voice.

'Portland cement,' said Dickens with a nod and I tore myself away from the splendid desk to admire the encyclopaedic memory of my friend. Now that he mentioned the name, I vaguely remembered some talk of Portland cement during our dinner party. The name of Portland had caught my attention. Chesil Beach in Portland was a favourite place of my brother Charley who had sailed there with a friend.

'It's the sand,' said Dickens with another nod. 'It's the lime—'

'That's right!' The Lancashire man interrupted Dickens with the informality of his countrymen. Held a hand up to check the famous author, while explanation poured from his lips. 'You see, Mr Dickens, you see, Sir Benjamin, the production of crystallization leads to more and more calcium silicate hydrate forming and thickening until the water molecules' path is blocked and there are no longer any empty, weak spaces in the mixture. This results in a very low porous, and therefore very strong, structure when you use Portland cement in your concrete.'

It was interesting, I thought, how the slight Indian accent and intonation disappeared once he got involved in a technical explanation. Words like 'crystallization' and 'silicate' were all pronounced as a Londoner would say them. A man of three accents – Lancastrian, Indian and London.

I saw how Dickens listened to him with interest and I reckoned that he was more interested in the man than in the engineering science. It was, I thought, most likely that Andrew Wainwright could have had a good future working as a Sapper in the Indian army or the Indian police service, especially as his father, before him, must have reached quite a high office in India to be able to afford to send daughter and son back to England for an education. That sounded like officer class to me, but his son had rejected India and come back to London and so had his daughter. I mused briefly upon the strength of inheritance but then discarded those thoughts for speculation about what young Andy's sister looked like. Dark hair and dark eyes. Probably, like her brother, she spoke good English. From time to time there had been an Indian intonation, but that vanished when he was talking about technical or engineering matters. The sister, I thought, would be immensely attractive.

Sir Benjamin appeared to be listening to both speakers with interest, but Dickens as usual was the one who put the question and he addressed it to the master, not to the man.

'Tell me, Mr Bazalgette, why is it so important that the concrete is strong?'

'Leakage,' said Joe impatiently. 'If the concrete cracks between the bricks of a house, well it doesn't matter too much. Send a man up a ladder with a bucket and palette knife and he'll mend the damage in ten minutes. If the concrete in a sewer cracks, no one knows about it for days, weeks, or even months. But the sewage keeps seeping out, widening the gap, forming puddles, contaminating any nearby stream or river. You know what happened five or six years ago in Broad Street, before that doctor, that Dr John Snow, took the handle off the water pump? Remember that, Andy, don't you? He did it to stop that deadly outbreak of cholera in the district. Clever man. Used his head. Noticed that the only ones in the neighbourhood who didn't get cholera were the workers in the brewery. They had enough sense to drink the beer and leave the water alone. Didn't go far enough, though, did they? Should have investigated where the contamination was coming from. And now you ask me why it matters to have the strongest possible concrete when you are cementing the bricks to make a sewer.'

'We won't ask you again,' said Sir Benjamin with a smile and Dickens gave a sharp look from one man to the other as if he had lots more questions to ask. It occurred to me then that the most interesting people to meet were people who held strong opinions, people who would argue, would justify their actions, would have intense interest in what they did, whether it was for work or for play. But, of course, Sir Benjamin was the one that had the power. The man who had access to the queen and to Parliament.

'Just come and have a look at this,' said Joe and he took us to the back of the warehouse, casually naming his machines, just as a proud father might name his children: The Centrifugal Governor; The Double-Screw Toggle Press, which had the nickname of The Boomer; and his crowning glory, Richmond's Patent Differential Telescopic Hydraulic Lift, which he gazed on fondly and even stroked as he told us what a bargain he had got when he went to the sale of a bankrupt engineering company up in Scotland.

'What do you use it for?' I thought it was time that I asked a question and he smiled on me approvingly.

'You're quite right, of course,' he said, somewhat to my bewilderment. 'I don't use it much just now. But when I'm good and ready, this will be wonderfully useful for checking.'

I said nothing, glad that I had sounded intelligent, though I was quite out of my depth and was happy to remain so. Dickens, however, was made of sterner stuff.

'You still haven't explained why you need Portland cement for concrete – why concrete for pipes? What's wrong with cast iron?'

Andy Wainwright gave a short laugh at that, almost a snort, but at a look from his employer he left us abruptly and went back to work on a lathe where we heard him shout a command to one of the young apprentices – something about not sanding down a piece of iron in a place where a chip might land in the blades of the lathe. Despite his young age, he had an authoritative way with him. He would be a good manager of apprentices for Joe who was a young man himself, I thought. They were an ambitious pair and knew that mistakes could be fatal. Andy was now telling the lad about how someone could lose an eye if the machine spat out that piece of iron.

'Rust,' Bazalgette was saying briefly in answer to the question. 'Rust is what is wrong with cast iron pipes. Come and see my little model of what a sewage pipe should look like. It's just down here.'

He led us to the back to the huge warehouse, drew open a curtain and there was a little tunnel built from bricks, just about ten foot long and standing upon the stone flooring of the ware-house. It was beautifully built, very carefully done with a curved top and every single brick cemented into place with snowy white concrete and its top covered with a layer of the same concrete.

'Children would love to play with that; it's like a little bridge in Toyland,' I said, thinking of little Carrie and wishing that I had her with me. A child would be fascinated by this place with all its strangely named machines and little models here and there. Not safe, of course. Most children liked to experiment, and these machines could be fatal.

'A tunnel made from bricks to carry the sewage. It would have to be built on the spot, wouldn't it?' Sir Benjamin sounded interested but slightly sceptical. 'The roads would have to be dug up and stay dug up for months. Think of the traffic, man!'

'Yes, of course. But what's the inconvenience of a few months if you get something that will last many lifetimes? I could lay a bet with you, Sir Benjamin, if you and I could come back into the world in a couple of hundred years, these brick-built tunnels, coated with Portland cement concrete would still be beneath the ground of London town. Look at that machine, there.' He seized a large poker and pointed. 'That's what we call a Coal-Brook-Dale. We've had that pumping water over those bricks for a solid week. You can see how we built it inside that old tank, and you can see the hole that we made in that wall beyond it. Well, we had a second tank on the other side of the wall, right below it, ready to catch any water that leaked out of it. Pumped away for the whole week. Andy and I kept coming over and looking at it and not a leakage to be seen. We'll go on with the testing, of course. That's the name of the game. Test; think; test; think, retest and so on. London has been doing things the easy way for too long. Allowing the rainwater to flood out the cesspits, allowing the sewage to drift into the rivers and streams; allowing those polluted rivers and streams to drift into the Thames and we end up with a "Summer of the Great Stink", and, worse still, we end up with fifty thousand children in the city dying of cholera. It's worth taking the time, gentlemen; worth taking the time and getting things right. What we need now is not a "Summer of the Great Stink", but a "Spring of Hope".'

Dickens, I could see, was impressed. But Dickens, like myself, was an ordinary citizen. A glance at Sir Benjamin's face showed me that he was still sceptical, and I could see why. Instead of the usual make do and mend, the city would have the enormous expense of building these brick pipes or little tunnels, coated in their special Portland cement concrete. And where was the sewage to end up eventually? At the moment it flowed into the River Thames which hopefully absorbed it all and carried it downstream to the Thames Estuary where the river met the North Sea, between the counties of Kent and Essex. But that system which had worked in the past was beginning to fail now. And the Summer of the Great Stink had marked its demise. A situation like that could not be allowed to occur every hot dry summer when the feeder streams and even the great Thames itself began to run short of water and sewage still flowed from houses equipped with new-fangled flush systems at ever increasing numbers.

I could see the thoughts racing through the great man's mind and he gave a sudden and an abrupt nod.

'Food for thought, food for thought, gentlemen!' he said and then turned and thanked Joe Bazalgette, but rather abruptly, ignored Andy Wainwright and without waiting for Dickens and myself, strode towards the door, casting keen glances at all the strangely named machines and the tools that lay so neatly to hand.

I lingered for a moment, waited for Dickens to make his adieux and give his thanks, and then I shook very warmly the hand of the engineer.

'That was one of the most interesting mornings that I have ever spent,' I said to him and knew that my sincerity rang from my voice. 'I would love to know more about your ideas. Would you come and have dinner again with me on some evening?'

'Indeed, I will. I would enjoy that immensely.' He also sounded sincere.

'May I send you a message? I shall have to consult my new

cook. Is there any particular evening that doesn't suit you?' I asked.

I had a little plan in the back of my mind, but I didn't want to say anything about it until I had arranged the details.

'I'll come any evening you wish,' he said enthusiastically. 'Your cook is a wonder. That was a magnificent meal. I stay up in London during the week and my evening meal is usually just something from a chop house. So, send me the word when you arrange the evening and I'll be there.' And once again we shook hands, and I left the warehouse and re-joined my companions on the pathway outside.

'I was just telling Sir Benjamin about the pleasant little evening we spent at your lodgings the other day,' said Dickens as soon as I came out. 'In fact, I was remarking that I might be able to persuade you to hold another little soirée. Sir Benjamin was very interested to hear about that, and it chances that he has a free evening next Friday. And he knows a couple of men, Hope and Napier, who have an interesting scheme. You wouldn't mind including them on your list, would you, Wilkie, old friend? And I'll bring a case of wine. Just got it and I can tell you that it is of superb quality!'

There was nothing I could do. No one could resist Dickens when he was in an organizing mood. I might as well hand over the whole affair to him and concentrate on coaxing Caroline to cook an extra-special meal for us all on the appointed Friday evening.

FIVE

had a busy few days before my dinner party, 'The Engineers'
Conversazione' , as I called it to myself, to avoid naming
it 'The Dinner of the Great Stink'.

On Thursday I went to a bookshop and bought a copy of
the latest edition of Maria Rundell's cookery book, beloved
of my mother, and filled with delicious-sounding dinner
recipes. And then, when I delivered that to Caroline, I went
to see my landlord and wove an ingenious tale about a gang
of international 'book thieves' who were determined to steal
the works of my brain, my next novel, after the huge success
of *The Woman in White*. He was most excited about the matter.
Not a reader himself, he explained to me apologetically, but
like everyone else he read the newspapers and had gobbled
down the inflated figures supposedly paid to me because of
the ridiculously huge number of the copies sold, and doubtless wanted to share in the probable earnings of the lucky
author.

'I can buy a safe,' I told him. 'I can even have it fastened
to the wall, but they may break in and torture me to reveal
the combination number,' I told him, confessing sadly that I
was not very brave and holding out my very white and unusually small hands to him as an indication of my total inability
to withstand torture.

He was immensely pleased to be asked; quite excited by
the matter. He dismissed the police with a contemptuous shrug.
'Useless! Useless!' And then set his mind to work. I was
interested to hear, in the light of my own experience of housebreaking, that he had no great opinion of bolts. Easy enough
to cut through a normal panel of wood with a special saw
which he described to me with such detail that I half-wondered
whether he, himself, went in for a spot of housebreaking on
moonless nights. But, he said, a couple of panels of steel,
fixed to the top and to the bottom of the door and then a bolt

screwed on to them should do the trick. It might be worth, he thought, despite the uselessness of the police, greasing the palm of the local constable to keep an eye open for any strangers inspecting the house, and I promised I would attend to that matter. And then I went home and explained the whole matter to Caroline and wove a long and complicated story about buried treasure for little Carrie.

Caroline, I was puzzled to see, had no fear of the strange men tramping in and out of the house, hammering, sawing, shouting orders and making quite a mess. She was even happily supplying them each with a mug of tea and a slice of cake when they came to fit bolts and metal sheets to the insides of the doors. Her fears, I had noticed, were quite specific – not young men, but an older man. I noticed how she froze at the sound of some voices from the street outside and how other London voices of young men, even when loud and threatening, did not affect her in the least. She cooked a delicious lunch for me, and I could see that I would soon need a new suit of clothes if I went on gobbling my food in that fashion. I had built up the pleasant custom of giving her a kiss after each meal, straight after bestowing a kiss upon the child, thereby making believe that they were as one.

When the men had finished and had been paid for that ring of steel that they had put to guard my lodgings, I went out again, this time to the bookshop. I bought another cookery book for Caroline, this one written by Mrs Eliza Acton, full of delicious-sounding recipes, and I also bought a picture book for Carrie. I dropped into my landlord, engaged a girl to wait on table and arranged that the handy boy, Francis, was to become a permanent member of my staff.

And when I came home a note from Dickens lay upon the hall table.

> Dear Friend,
> All is fixed up for our pleasant little evening. Here is the guest list: Sir Benjamin Hall (Member of Parliament); Benjamin Disraeli (Member of Parliament); Engineers: Mr Joe Bazalgette; Henry Austin; William Hope; David Napier; and John Phillips.

Much obliged for your hospitality and I remain, my
very dear Collins, your grateful friend . . .

And then there was Dickens' signature, the usual distinctive
scrawl with the famous flourish to round it off.

I should, of course, be angry at the way that he so light-
heartedly exploited me, but I wasn't.

I was, in fact, quite thrilled at being involved in these
discussions. If a solution could be found to the stinking
streets, the polluted water from pumps, the terrible deaths
from disease – more than half of all babies dying before they
reached their first birthday was a statistic which shocked and
sickened me – then we will have achieved something momen-
tous. We could have done without the two Members of
Parliament, I thought initially, but then rejected the thought
when I remembered Sir Benjamin's earnest and interested
face as Joe Bazalgette showed off his equipment. The baronet
had access to Queen Victoria. Goodness only knew how
useful that could be to a young engineer. I was still somewhat
overwhelmed at the amount of machinery that Joe had
collected. I guessed that the legacy from his grandfather that
he had mentioned must have been a substantial one and
that every penny had been spent upon these machines with
strange names – machines that would help in the testing of
materials and theories. Disraeli, also, was a rising man, a
protégé of Lord Palmerston, the queen's advisor. Two powerful
men and my friend Dickens might have done a great service
to humanity by bringing these two groups, politicians and
engineers, together under my roof.

'Money is no object; we have a knight of the realm coming
to have supper with us,' I told Caroline, then hoisted little
Carrie into my arms and whispered in her little ear, 'Do you
think that the queen will make me a knight?'

'With a sword?' she enquired. Earlier, when she and I had
sat together on a comfortable easy chair before a blazing fire,
I had read to her some stories from a child's book and the
one about King Arthur and his knights was one of her favour-
ites and she went around the house reciting lines like: 'The
wind is sharp as a two-edged sword.'

Intelligent little child as she was, she had thrilled to the music of the words and had taken from it whatever a clever little five-year-old could take, but now her small face was clouded with anxiety.

'Yes,' I said solemnly, feeling her anxiety as if it were my own. 'Yes, a very sharp and a very, very, very long sword.'

'Better than a poker?' I had known that question would arrive, and I was ready with my answer.

'Fifty times better, fifty times longer, fifty times stronger than a poker,' I chanted, and she snuggled into my waistcoat. Over her head, I smiled at Caroline who was busily studying Mrs Eliza Acton and her recipes for a successful dinner party. Caroline, however, did not lift her head and did not return my smile. A shadow had come over her face and I resolved to keep away from any mention of pokers and intruders in the future. Let her take a silent reassurance from the locks, the bolts, the tread of the well-bribed police constable outside the basement window, the steel shutters and the plates of steel fastened to front and cellar doors. Soon her anxiety and that of the child's would become a thing of the past.

It was pouring rain on the day of my little dinner party, but that did not matter. Once coats and umbrellas were shed, the guests crowded into the dining room and exclaimed at the heat of the fire, the excellence of Dickens' wine and the beauty of the long table with its starched white drapery illuminated by small vases filled with brilliantly red geraniums, its silver cutlery, borrowed from my mother, and a new service of Willow Pattern crockery that I had just purchased. There was an additional guest. Bazalgette took me apart and whispered into my ear that his landlord, a Mr Bob Smith, had begged to be included and given all the man's kindness and his forbearance in the matter of explosions, Bazalgette had not had the heart to refuse him. I assured him that the more the merrier.

Soon everyone was seated. I looked around the table with a sense of satisfaction and pride. I had purchased a set of dinner table place cards and, watched by Carrie, had carefully inked the name of each guest upon them, rapidly doing

an extra one, marked Mr Robert Smith, Patron of Engineers
– something that amused the genial old landlord. In fact, he
was an asset to my little party, decked out as he was in his
sumptuous tweed suit with elaborate tiepin. He was even
sporting many rings including a large gold signet ring – with
a made-up crest, I had to assume – along with another ring
that seemed to sparkle as it caught the light. Convivial and
curious as a child, he mingled instantly with the guests,
cross-questioning every man about his place of work and his
facilities for experimentation and the room was soon full of
animated conversations. I would have many of these little
dinner parties, I planned. This band of people, practical
people, engineers, with knowledge of how the world worked
and how man could harness nature to his needs – 'this happy
breed of men', I thought, remembering the words from
Macready's performance of *Richard II* which I had watched
again and again in Drury Lane Theatre. Well, from *this* happy
breed of men, here around my table, fortified by my well-
cooked food, warmed by my fire, and enthused by Dickens'
wine, perhaps the solution to London's troubles would come
from them on this very evening.

'Gentlemen, I give you "Engineers and All who work with
them"!' I said, getting to my feet after the soup had vanished
and all had been served with a bumper of Dickens' inimitable
wine. The toast was drunk and the conversation became even
more animated.

'What's all that I hear about you two wanting to transport
the contents of the cesspits by train to Essex?' I said to Napier
and Hope who were sitting opposite to me.

'Only on Sundays!' said Napier, holding up his hands in
defence. 'No interruption to the working gentlemen travelling
to their city jobs.'

I laughed. There was something quite comic about the
picture of trainloads of pin-striped gentlemen carrying
umbrellas, walking sticks and newspapers on the working days
of the week; and then being replaced by loads of sewage on
a Sunday.

'Absurd,' said Henry Austin. 'Utter nonsense. We need a
converging system. Pipe the sewage to four reservoirs in

Belgravia and build a pumping station there and pump the sewage out for use in agricultural areas.'

'What would be the cost of that scheme?' asked Disraeli with a slight sneer. I had the impression that he took a malicious satisfaction in asking that question. None of the suggestions so far had ever mentioned a sum of money for their construction. I didn't care for Disraeli much. Never had, in fact. He had stopped appearing in public wearing green velvet trousers and his hair was no longer in long ringlets dangling over a ruffled shirt, but he had pretensions to being a writer as well as a politician and he had been rude about a previous novel of mine, *The Unknown Public*. Considering that he was not much of a writer himself, judging by his novel, *Tancred*, I found it hard to forgive him his remarks.

'The farmers will pay for it,' retorted Henry Austin.

'I'd estimate the cost to be in the region of a good half a million pounds,' said John Phillips. 'What farmer is going to pay for that, or rather how many farmers are you going to get to pay for it? And remember you are going to have to build new pipes to take the stuff out into the countryside. Unless, of course, you think that the farmers will collect it for themselves in their little wheelbarrows.' He had a sneer on his face. There was, I thought, a lot of enmity amongst these engineers and I began to regret the size of my dinner party – perhaps I should have made it bigger, had other friends, people who painted, someone like Fredrick Lehman who was a musician. Austin and Phillips were obviously at daggers drawn. I should never have agreed to the addition of Disraeli to this dinner party, I thought sadly, looking around at the tense and ambitious faces. It had been a mistake to invite that overbearing politician. Plans were in those men's minds, but some, perhaps the best eventually, were not ready to be publicly aired. I had thought of the night as a meeting of minds, but it appeared to be turning out as a clash of ideas. I shouldn't have agreed to this crowd of men. Well, there I was, weak as water, as usual.

'The Great Stink of London!' Disraeli, the politician, pronounced as he wrinkled his long nose and took a moment to stir the 'Beef a la Mode' into long streaks on his plate.

Then he continued in his pretentious way, 'Something has to be done, gentlemen. The stench in Parliament last summer was like a Stygian pool reeking with ineffable and unbearable horror. Never again can we go through that experience.'

'We had to hang sheets dripping with lime between the windows and the odours from the river last summer.' Sir Benjamin Hall's voice was as loud as his namesake, the bell at Westminster, and the sound of his words, matching his height and size, took the attention of everyone at the table.

'I am convinced that not one half of the entire filth produced in the metropolis finds its way into the sewers; that has to be remedied before any more grandiose schemes,' said Joe Bazalgette quietly.

I saw Dickens look at him with one of his sharp, quick looks and guessed that he thought this was a man who knew what he was talking about. Remembering his experiment with concrete made with Portland cement, I agreed with my friend. Bazalgette was a man ready to abandon past practices and come up with a completely new solution. And I could see his point. Sewers were needed and they had to be resistant to all possibilities of leakage. Wherever its contents were flowing, those contents had to stay safely enclosed in the sewer with no possibility of leakage, no matter how great the force of a downfall of rain. The drinking water for the city had to be kept as pure as possible.

I looked around at the troubled faces and decided to introduce a new subject. 'What did you all think of The Great Exhibition?' I enquired. Even to myself this sounded a little lame. Seven or eight years had gone by since The Great Exhibition and the machines that we had seen at Bazalgette's workshop had not been, as far as I could remember, featured in Prince Albert's ambitious dream.

Nevertheless, Dickens took up and embellished my feeble effort. 'Wonderful demonstrations of cutting-edge technology of the day, including electric telegraphs, microscopes, a prototype facsimile machine, a revolving lighthouse light and an early submarine!' His words flowed enthusiastically, but no one else followed his lead. I tried to think of something to add to it, but the submarine only reminded me of the tons and tons of sewage that was lodged beneath the water of the River Thames.

There was a moment's silence, but then the conversation resumed.

And, of course, we had to talk about the 'Great Stink' – right in the middle of dinner. Civil engineers, mechanical engineers, and every other kind of engineer – they all had a view on what was best to do with the sewage produced by the vast amount of people now living in London.

We were in the middle of a delicious dish, chunks of succulent meat, and hunks of vegetables floating on a thick gravy when John Phillips, who had drunk more than his fair share of the wine, got to his feet and held up his hands in a demand for silence.

'Gentlemen,' he said, with that sort of solemnity that men affect when they have a suspicion that they might be sinking into drunkenness. 'Gentleman, all, I am of the opinion, like our esteemed friend Bazalgette here, that much of the filth that is produced by our inhabitants is retained in the cesspools and drains in and about the houses, where it lies decomposing, giving off noxious effluvia and poisonous sulphuretted hydrogen and other gases which constantly infect the atmosphere of such houses from top to bottom, and which, of course, the inhabitants are constantly breathing. There are hundreds, I may say thousands, of houses in this metropolis which have no drainage whatever, and the greater part of them have stinking, overflowing cesspools, and there are also hundreds of streets, courts and alleys that have no sewers. How the drainage and filth are cleaned away and how the miserable inhabitants live in such places it is hard to tell. The stench and the poisonous gases are almost impossible to bear. These pipes that are supposed to carry away the overflow from the cesspits just don't seem to work unless you have a downpour of torrential rain. Otherwise, the filth just piles up.'

'That's not the worst of it,' said Bazalgette quietly. 'The worst is after a downpour occurs and then the sewage in these pipes is pumped into the Thames.'

'Best place for it. The Thames!' Henry Austin gave him a belligerent look.

'I disagree,' said Bazalgette.

'So do I!'

'No, you are wrong!'

'What's needed is a better pump. Twice as strong as anything that we have now! Pump it all into the river.'

'No! Create a market for the sewage. Stop all this talk about buying in guano. Use our native by-products. Three million people in London and each of them excrete every day of their lives.'

'If they are lucky,' put in Dickens with a comical expression. As most of his acquaintances knew, he suffered badly from piles and was always seeking new remedies for his condition of chronic constipation. I thanked him in my mind for injecting a little humour into the conversation, but it was no good. Henry Austin and John Phillips agreed with the estimation of about five hundred thousand pounds revenue from the sale of sewage to farmers and vegetable growers. It seemed ridiculous to me, but I was the host and could not contradict a guest.

So, there we were, the nine of us, sitting around my table, drinking wine and talking so hard that it was not surprising no one heard the door open, and no one noticed a small figure creep into the room and stand at the bottom of the table, nibbling at some nuts. Disraeli was the one who noticed her first, pointing a disdainful finger and enquiring, 'Who on earth is that?'

Little Carrie noiselessly and rapidly disappeared. I blinked hard and wondered whether I had imagined the child. I looked around my guests, some of whom had resumed devouring their dinner, others lifting their glasses in silent tribute to each other, or a few looking vaguely around the room.

'I saw a child, a little girl. Just down there, beside you, Dickens. You must have seen her,' said David Napier. He stuck his head under the tablecloth and the more sober of the company followed suit. I sat very still. I had taken no part in the conversation and so I was probably slightly more drunk than the others. I didn't feel that I could lower my head and cover my eyes without becoming sick and dizzy, but Disraeli was braver. His long, pointed nose was ideal for ferreting out a disappeared child and he let out a shout of triumph.

'There she is,' he shouted. 'Just beside your knee, Dickens. I don't for the life of me understand why you can't see her. Come on, child, come out of there. Come out immediately, I say.'

Dear little Carrie. She was a brave and resolute child. She came out straight away and stood there, looking coolly around at the company. Small for her age at that time, the top of her head was not much above the table. She stared courageously around the room and a lump in my throat prevented me from coming to her aid.

'God bless my soul,' said Dickens, in his usual firm and authoritative way. 'What are you talking about, Disraeli? That's the butler. Isn't that right, Collins? Your new butler.'

He stared belligerently around the table and such was the force of his fame and of his personality that no one said anything. Even Disraeli bore his usual slightly anxious look of having just missed a joke. And so, after a quick look around the table, he said nothing. Just looked at Dickens rather uncertainly. The child, herself, nodded in an important way. Children live in a world of make-believe, and I had mentioned jokingly to her mother Caroline earlier on in the day that we might think of getting a butler. She drew herself up to her full height and looked Dickens straight in the face.

'That's right, sir. I'm the new butler,' she said with dignity and then walked out of the room to a great shout of laughter.

And it was at that auspicious moment that Sir Benjamin Hall got to his feet and made his announcement.

I think that if he had not done so, I would have followed little Carrie from the room. There had been something in her eyes, a look that I had not seen since that night when she and Caroline came into my life. A courageous child. But no five-year-old little girl should have to hide her fear, conceal terror from those closest to her, show a false face to the adults who were supposed to be caring for her, looking after her. That child had looked deeply frightened, but at the same time, she was resolute in hiding her fear to the best of her ability. I should, I thought afterwards, have gone after her and found out what had frightened her.

But I was, after all, the host here at my own dinner table.

And when the most distinguished guest in the room got to his feet and tapped one of his wine glasses with his fork, no host could do other than turn an attentive face towards him.

'Hear! hear!' announced Dickens. He was always good on these occasions. An acclaimed public speaker himself, he was immensely courteous to others who took to the floor after the wine had flowed freely. A quick look around the room, an exaggeratedly listening aspect, and the room immediately became silent, every eye turned to Sir Benjamin Hall.

'I think that I may be permitted to use the name of Her Majesty's government to thank Mr Collins for hosting this very pleasant evening,' he said in a slightly pompous fashion.

'Hear! Hear!' Dickens led the loyal chorus.

'The queen, God bless her!' I said with a moment's inspiration and rose to my feet, glass in hand.

'And also, to thank you all for coming here tonight.' There was now a slightly perfunctory note in Sir Benjamin's voice as we had all re-seated ourselves. And he swiftly went on without allowing a moment for any further comments or cheering.

'I have been today in the company of Her Gracious Majesty; Our Queen Victoria, and we were discussing the terrible summer that we have all endured. Her Majesty related to me how she and Prince Albert had to turn back from a proposed evening trip on the river because of the terrible stench. Her Majesty was most upset at the disappointment of her subjects who had waited for hours in the heat and the disgusting odour without having the chance to greet her with loyal cheers.'

This little anecdote was received with a blank silence, so that Sir Benjamin after a quick glance around the room came swiftly to the point.

'Her Majesty is so concerned about the situation that she has determined on announcing a money prize for an engineer who comes up with the best solution, as judged by a board of distinguished experts, headed by my humble self. And . . .' he proceeded, lifting a hand to halt any efforts at cheering, 'the successful candidate will be knighted by the queen.'

That did it. Dickens led a rousing cheer and glasses were raised. 'I give you Her Majesty,' said Dickens, always one,

when in public, to praise the queen highly, though in private
he confided in me that she was totally boring to talk to, and
during a long sought-after interview with the man whom she
had designated as her favourite author, her choice of topic for
conversation was the servant problem, on which, said Dickens,
she felt that she was an expert. And, indeed, she was most
fluent on the subject.

I, like the others, raised my glass and purposely caught the
eye of Joe Bazalgette. What a wonderful thing for him to win
it. Everything that I had heard tonight told me that he had the
best of ideas and had the equipment to test his ideas before
implementing them. He had said very little during the dinner,
but I knew that his scheme was well worked out and that
the experiments with this Portland cement would set him on the
track to win this money prize and the knighthood to boot.

I mouthed, *How much?* to Dickens but he shook his head
at me, so I guessed that the queen, notoriously parsimonious,
had not actually come up with a sum. Still, Lord Palmerston,
who had great influence over her, would make sure that it was
a respectable sum. And a knighthood! That would be a
wonderful feather in the cap for a man as young as Bazalgette
and would be of prime importance for future employment, not
just in England, but also in the great cities of Europe, all of
which had problems with their rivers and their drainage.

And then, for the second time on this exciting evening,
someone else got to his feet and tapped his glass, his ring
glinting off the crystal. It was Bazalgette's landlord, Bob Smith.

'Gentlemen, I want to thank Mr Collins for allowing me to
come here tonight. I don't think I've ever spent a more enjoyable night,' he said, bowing politely in my direction and looking
brightly around the table of faces.

'Hear! hear!' said Henry Austin, taking the opportunity to
swallow down more of the wine.

'Well, the queen, God bless her, has offered a wonderful
incitement to one of you talented people here and I would like
to do my bit. You will have heard talk about Mr Bazalgette's
workshop that he has set up in my old warehouse. And much
impressed I am with what he has to show there. So impressed
that, in the name of public good, I will take no more rent from

him for the next month or so while he is working on his scheme. And . . .' The old man paused here and looked around at the rest of the faces. 'Gentlemen, I have another warehouse standing empty, ready to be let, and I propose to offer this warehouse to any of you talented engineers as a space to experiment. I'd suggest that you fill it with machinery, just like our friend, Mr Bazalgette. What were they? Those machines? Lathes, toggle presses, centriful . . . whatsoevers – whatever you can buy, beg or borrow, and if you are short of the odd bob, well, Bob Smith is your man. And just to set the ball rolling, how about us all going out one day next week to have a look at these Maplin Sands where these two gentlemen propose to cart our sewage where it can turn something useless into good agricultural land? If the idea appeals to you, I'll stand the cost of hiring a whole railway carriage and though I can't give you a great dinner like we've just eaten, I'll get one of my men to fill the racks with Fortnum & Mason hampers. What do you say to that, gentlemen all?'

There was a great burst of applause. I went around with a carafe of dessert wine and Dickens followed me with another. We drank his health, we drank success to the lucky winner, we drank to London when the 'chains of disease' should have been removed from the River Thames by the new system – I think we drank to everyone and everything we could think of. And then my guests went home, and I walked with Dickens back to his house across London to Tavistock Square.

SIX

Dickens and I always walked briskly, but never parted at his door without a long talk. We had a lot to discuss this night. He was filled with a certain excitement about the possibility of being involved in finding a solution, not just to the unpleasant stench, but more importantly to him, to the terrible pollution of London's drinking water. The well-off, like ourselves, drank wine, and boiled water for our tea and our coffee; the working classes with jobs stuck to beer, but the poor and the destitute, and their children, drank water straight from the street taps. And the water which they drank came from the most polluted river in the world, our mighty Father Thames. No wonder there had been over ten thousand deaths from cholera already this year. Something had to be done to save the unfortunate poor and their children. And Dickens, dear fellow, I could see from his animated face, was determined to do everything in his power to solve the terrible problem. So, we stood, and we talked, and we discussed the ideas and the personalities and the expedition next week to Maplin Sands.

Which meant that, by the time I got home, it was almost midnight.

I inserted my key in the door, turned it and pushed. No result. I pushed again and again, retried the key, but no result.

And then I realized what had happened. Perhaps Caroline had, by mistake, forgetting that I was still out, locked the door with those two sturdy bolts that I had installed to reassure her. Well, there was no help for it. I wasn't going to spend the night out of doors or awaken the neighbours with thunderous blows to the door. I went down the basement steps, into the little area outside the kitchen, and knocked on the door.

No answer. There seemed to be a dead silence within the house. No sound, no lights, almost as though the place was empty. I knocked again, more loudly this time, but still no result. I bit my lip with a mixture of annoyance and puzzlement. What was I to do? I could not spend the night out of doors in this chilly weather. Dickens, who was the soul of hospitality, would by now be in his bed and I could not rouse his household. Reluctantly I went to the window of Caroline's little room, quite high up, just above my head. The carpenter, at my request, had screwed four bars across its glass, so that she would feel safe, but I had to wake her and so I tapped loudly on the window, using my signet ring to make the small, enclosed space resonate with the sound.

No answer. I swore silently. By now I was tired; that lovely tiredness that comes after a good evening filled with wine and laughter and rounded off with a brisk walk and pleasant conversation. I wanted my bed and felt filled with anger. Why, on earth, did she not wake up to that sound? I knocked again. Still no answer.

At that my patience exploded.

Beside the steps into the area there was an empty half barrel which had once held beer. I dragged it over, endeavouring to make as little noise as possible, then picked up a brick from the ground, took a firm grip of the windowsill, clambered up on top of the barrel and peered into the room. No light. No movement. I tapped once more and called her name. It was useless, though. I dared not shout. Any moment now a prowling night watchman would pass the house. As carefully as I could, I pushed with the brick, broke one of the small panes of glass and then reached in, pulled back the bolt and opened the window.

There was a muffled scream. So, she was there.

'Snakes alive! Caroline!' I exclaimed. 'Will you let me in? Didn't you hear me knock?'

She was beyond reason, weeping hysterically. I cursed, but silently. There was no mistaking the sheer terror in those gulping sobs. I couldn't see her, the gaslight did not penetrate the room, but by the sound of the sobs I guessed that she had the bedcovers over her head.

There was no help for it. I would have to penetrate these woollen wrappings, penetrate the fog of her terror. I could not climb in. My workmen had done their work too well. Even

this small window was well barred. I dared not attack the
screws with my brick. I had neighbours on either side, and
one was bound to awaken and call for the police, but my voice
should be less alarming than a loud hammering sound.
'Caroline,' I said. 'It's me, Wilkie. Let me in, Caroline.'
And then, in an effort to penetrate her consciousness, I
added, 'Caroline! I'm freezing cold. Let me in!'
And at those words, something happened. The door to the
little room which housed the hot press opened and out came
a small figure in that pretty nightdress which I had bought
for her. Child though she was, and terrifying though the
experience of being woken in the middle of the night was,
Carrie, as always, was in control of the situation. Braver
than her mother. Always was, and always will be. Dear
Carrie!
'Don't cry, Mama,' she said in her sensible manner, her
clear, child's voice sounding determined and very calm.
'Mama, stop crying. It's only Mr Wilkie.' She gazed up at me
and then said, very firmly, 'You are too fat to climb in.'
'So I am,' I said thankfully. 'Do you think that you could
be a clever little girl and let me in through the cellar door?
Your mama is a bit upset.'
She looked at me rather dubiously and then across at her
mother.
'How is Mr Teddy?' I asked, determined to be patient.
Something terrible had happened to the woman and child and
so I could not push either beyond the limit where they felt
safe.
'He's very well, thank you,' she said sedately. The little
exchange seemed to reassure her as she took a candle from
her mother's table and brought it and a bag of matches over
to me and placed both on the windowsill in front of me.
'I'm not allowed to light candles,' she explained, 'but I am
allowed to carry one if I am very, very careful.' She sounded
calm and self-possessed, and oddly the little voice penetrated
the terror-stricken woman on the bed. Now that I had lit the
candle on the windowsill I could see more clearly. The heap of
tumbled bedclothes stirred, and the light caught the sheen of the
blonde curls.

'Would little Carrie be able to open the door for me, Caroline?' I asked in a polite and relaxed tone. 'Or would it be better if you did it yourself? Just the cellar door. I'll be inside in two shakes of a monkey's tail.'

That feeble joke made little Carrie laugh and suddenly the atmosphere seemed to lighten. Caroline sat up, pushed back the bedclothes, gathered her disordered curls at the nape of her neck and came forward. She was, I noticed, fully dressed. The child took her by the hand in an almost motherly fashion. 'It's only Mr Wilkie, Mama,' she said in a comforting manner. She then added, 'He's got a sword, but he hasn't got a poker.'

Her mother made no response to this. She went from the room, carrying the candleholder by its handle and leaving the child and me looking uneasily at each other. But a minute later there was a sound of the well-oiled bolt sliding back.

'See you soon, as the fork said to the spoon,' I said gaily, and Carrie laughed again. There was, I thought, despite the laughter, a tinge of strain in the child's voice and I felt sorry for her.

I came in through the cellar door, trying to assume a matter-of-fact manner, making a big show of checking the bolts and the lock of the door by the light of my candle. Then I took the box of matches from the hall, pulled the little chain of the gas lamp and when the gas was flowing freely, I lit that. Somehow, its clear, strong light made quite a difference. I saw how little Carrie looked around with a brightened face and even her mother seemed to straighten her back and breathe more deeply.

'Let's have a midnight party,' I said. 'Biscuits and milk for everyone. Come and help me, Carrie.'

I cheated by pouring wine for myself but gave the child and her mother a glass of milk and some of the biscuits that had come from the nearby bakery. Little Carrie relaxed, leaning against my shoulder. Replete with milk and biscuits, the child's eyelids drooped over her eyes and her head sank down on the plump arms crossed upon the table. I picked her up in my arms, carried her into her small, warm bedroom and tucked her in beside her teddy bear. That small room, that linen cupboard, was snug and cosy, and I looked around me with satisfaction. I kissed her and by her instructions kissed Mr Teddy as well. And then I went back to her mother.

She had not moved since I had left her. Still sat there, but now her head was in her hands and a few soft sobs came from her hidden face.

I took a small comb from my pocket and, one by one, I gently combed the dishevelled and tangled ringlets. Her hair was very soft and the pale gold strands were warm to my fingers.

'Come and see little Carrie,' I said.

She said nothing, so I went on combing. She just sat there, very quiet, very removed from me, but she allowed me to do my will. And then, almost reluctantly, she got to her feet and went to look at her child.

Little Carrie, worn out by the excitement and emotion, had fallen asleep. We both stood looking down at her for several minutes, but she did not stir. In the way that children do she had fallen into a deep and dreamless sleep.

Caroline and I looked at each other. And then we went back into the servant's room. There was a gaping hole in the window of her bedroom and the damp March air poured in. It was safe; the bars were still in place and nothing bigger than a kitten could have slid between them, but the air was already damp and chilly. I scooped up the bedclothes and pillows from the bed, gathered them into an enormous bundle and carried them from the bedroom. I dumped them on the couch in the living room and then sat down at the table.

'Tell me what happened?' I kept my voice low and unconcerned and concentrated on filling two clean glasses with some red wine.

'Harriet, Carrie, came into me, just when I had finished dishing up the dessert and she told me that *he* was here, there in your dining room.'

'*He?*' I exclaimed. I allowed my voice to rise high with a note of incredulity. I knew perfectly well what she meant by the pronoun. 'Don't be ridiculous, Caroline,' I said. 'There was no mystery villain here tonight. All perfectly respectable gentlemen. All guests of mine.' I laughed, but in a kindly way,

I hoped. My role now was to soothe her fears, not to ridicule them.

I slipped more wine into her glass, waited until she had taken a sip and then sat back. 'Which one did she describe? Who did she imagine was this mystery man?' I swallowed some wine and sat back and waited for her response.

'She didn't know. She had just heard his voice.' Her own voice was low, very hesitant. After a moment she said, 'I've never allowed her to see him. I locked her in the attic every time he came. I frightened her. Told her stories about his poker. Told her that she had to be as quiet as a little mouse.'

This was getting more and more complicated.

'He didn't live in the house, then, did he?'

She shook her head. I reached over and treated myself to a couple of biscuits. 'So, he came to . . . to visit you. Is that right?'

She nodded. This was turning into a one-way conversation.

'Tell me about him,' I said, endeavouring to make my voice firm and friendly.

'I can't,' she said.

'Just a simple description. Tell me what he looked like.'

'I don't know,' she said in a helpless manner. 'I think that he wore a mask.'

Stranger and stranger. I ignored the mask. 'What did his voice sound like, Caroline? A big, deep voice, like this? Or a high, squeaky voice, like this?'

'I don't know,' she said helplessly. She was on the verge of tears, but I had to get the truth; I had to find out the form and substance of her fear before I could begin to endeavour to release her from it.

'But you must know, Caroline,' I said softly, 'a mask doesn't disguise a voice all that much.' I picked up a cloth napkin and tied it around my face. 'Now listen to this – doesn't this sound like Wilkie Collins?' I said, exaggerating the rather high pitch of my voice, but she did not smile.

'He mesmerized me.' She spoke after a moment's silence and I could see how her eyes sought my face as though to endeavour to study my response.

'Mesmerized you!' I repeated the word 'mesmerized' with a feeling of shock. I knew all about mesmerism as my friend Charles Dickens was a believer.

On the fourth of January 1838 Charles Dickens had walked from his house at 48 Doughty Street to University College Hospital, some twenty minutes away in Gower Street. There he had witnessed a spectacle which changed his ideas, his fiction and his life. Soon afterwards Dickens told a friend, 'I am a believer.' He used the same words to a doctor in America. So, what did Dickens see that made such an impression on him that day? The answer is mesmerism – hypnosis as some call it.

Dickens, I knew, not only became a fervent believer in mesmerism, but he also learned the technique himself and mesmerized his wife, his sister-in-law and several friends – though he would never submit to being mesmerized himself. I remember that he wrote, in his usual bombastic way to a friend, Emile de la Rue, 'I have the perfect conviction that I could magnetize a frying pan.'

The story of Caroline and the evil man who mesmerized her in order to satiate his own sexual desires would, I thought, really appeal to his imagination. One day, I thought, he might even write a novel where a young girl was hypnotized by a man who wished to be her lover and to banish from her mind all thoughts of her first love. I would suggest the idea to him, allow him to turn it over in his mind, to incubate until eventually it would rise to the surface as a Charles Dickens masterpiece. I smiled a little to myself at the thought.

Then I turned my mind away from Dickens' experience of mesmerism and back to my poor, frightened Caroline.

'Tell me all about it,' I said softly.

'He met me in the street. I was hungry. I had no money. We were alone and I feared for my child. I wanted her to have milk, to have food, plenty of food. I didn't want her to die, also. I . . . I . . . I don't know what happened. He told me to look at his ring. It was . . . I've never seen a ring more beautiful, a huge stone, a strange colour. It was blue, but when he turned it under the gaslight it flashed like moonlight, like rays of moonlight. I couldn't stop looking at it. I just stood there, and the rays seemed to go into my brain.'

I waited. There was something very strange about her, almost as though even the very memory of that strange jewel had mesmerized her again. Her eyes were blank, looking ahead, but I knew what they saw now. Once again, I stroked her hand gently. It was stone cold, and I enclosed her fingers within my own warm hand and stroked the back of her hand with a finger and waited.

After a few minutes, the gentle rhythm seemed to work and her eyes sought mine, now so full of pain and distress that I almost resolved to give up my questioning. There were, however, a few details that I had to know, and I tried to sound as reassuring as I could.

'What did he look like, that time, that first time that you saw him, Caroline?' I asked gently. 'He wasn't wearing a mask out in the road, was he? Not the first time that he met you, was he?'

She hesitated. 'I don't think so. I can't really remember. I think that he had a beard. I'm not sure. I just remember him telling me to look at his ring, to keep on staring at it. He said that it made wishes come true. So, I looked at it and wished as hard as I could that we would never be hungry and cold again. I don't know what happened next, but I found myself in a house, a new house, the one where you found me. My little Harriet was with me. We were sitting in the kitchen and there was food on the table and milk and even some chocolate. Harriet was eating chocolate. I remember that. I remember that he wasn't there, then, but there must have been something in the milk, because Harriet fell fast asleep, very, very deeply asleep. I couldn't wake her up. I can't remember what happened next. I think I fell asleep, too. But I remember saying to myself, or perhaps I remember him saying it, but whichever it was, I knew the truth: we could never leave. I knew that. I felt as though I were tied with an invisible rope by that ring.'

I waited for a few moments and then asked, very gently, 'Did you stay in the top part of the house? Or did you ever try to get downstairs?'

She almost seemed as though she could not understand the question. Just sat there, very quietly. Just sat and stared across the room with a slightly bewildered expression upon her face. And yet, there must have been more to relate. She had told me that she had never allowed the child to see the man who had imprisoned them, but his voice had been heard. Carrie had told her tonight that she recognized the voice of one of my guests. But was it when Carrie was hiding under the table that this man had spoken?

How long had they stayed there, locked up in that house? The questions flooded into my mind, but I said nothing. Soon, I thought, she would learn to trust me and then some more details should come out. I was beginning to discount the child's alarm. She was, after all, only about five years old and had been through a strange and traumatic time. Perhaps now it almost seemed like a bad dream. Certainly, she appeared happy and mischievous. Perhaps, I told myself, she had told that little story in order that her mother would not scold her for going into the dining room when I was entertaining guests. That was it, I told myself. After all, Carrie had been matter-of-fact, and even helpful, when I found myself locked out of my own home. It was her mother who now needed care and time to recover from whatever strange experience she had suffered before I rescued her from that man who had imprisoned her and her child.

Caroline, I thought, as I mused over her story, was already reassured by my quiet and attentive reception of her tale. And the child was sleeping peacefully. Poor little things, I thought compassionately. I would not bother Caroline anymore. That story about a man with a wonderful ring, a ring with a blue diamond jewel streaked with moonlight which had been used to hypnotize her, might or might not be true – I suspected that it was a tale, but I would not cross-question her anymore. Instead, I stretched out my arms and took her into them. Who was I to judge? My own life had been full of events that the censorious world could look upon with a critical eye.

I took no further notice of the child's story. By her mother's account, she had never seen the man, had been sleeping in her mother's arms when first they met, and I doubted whether someone of little Carrie's age would distinguish between one man's voice and another.

'It's all just a bad dream,' I said reassuringly. I got to my feet, still holding her within my arms. Then I released her and, stretching my arms above my head, yawned loudly.

'Well, I'm off to bed,' I said. And then, on an impulse, held out my hand to her. 'Come and see my room,' I said quietly. There would be no pressure, no coaxing even. The decision must be hers. She stayed where she was for a moment, looking, not at me, but at her plate and the half-eaten biscuit.

'Are you married, Wilkie?' she said after a minute, saying the words in a low voice and still without looking at me.

'Married!' I gave a half laugh and withdrew my hand. 'Me! My dear girl, I'm the biggest opponent of marriage in the whole of London. Marriage is something that I will never indulge in. I don't approve of it. It's a leg-shackle for a man, but for a woman it's worse – a legal pretence which makes sure that her body, her soul, all her possessions are no longer hers but now belong to a man. Never get married, Caroline. That's a piece of good advice that I can give you.'

She smiled at that. It was the first time that she had smiled at me and I thought that it was a lovely smile.

'I have been married,' she said. 'I was married to Harriet's father, little Carrie, as you call her.'

I had not thought about that and it gave me a slight shock. What if there was a man who reckoned he owned her, who would come looking for her?

'He's dead,' she said, as though she had read my thoughts. 'He died when Harriet was a baby.'

'I see.' I felt relieved, but the next move was up to her and so I meditatively chewed a biscuit and waited for a couple of minutes. She bore the look of a woman who was confused, who found it difficult to make up her mind, and so I changed my own. It was too much to ask of her to lead the way and so I went around the room, turning off the gas lamps and then, before extinguishing the last one, I lit a candle and handed the candlestick to her, opening the door and standing back politely. Once she was through the door, I led the way to my own room. No curtains had been drawn, and the streetlight from outside threw a faint, dim gleam over the bed – neatly made – and the bedside table with its one candle set in the centre of a wide metal plate with a big handle – a present from my mother who dreaded fire in bedrooms. I lit this candle and blew out the match, then, sitting on the side of the bed, I bent down and unlaced my boots. The laces were tight, and I took some time over them. While I was working on the second boot, I felt the slight movement of the mattress.

'Have this pillow,' I said gently. I would not force her. She had to be one that made the movement. I waited, smiling to myself in the darkness.

I would never marry. I had decided that a long time ago. Marriage, I thought, was a form of slavery for a woman and of domination for a man. Caroline was pretty, grateful, needy and without any links, any vows, any legal bindings, she and I would do well together. And I vowed that I would care for her child.

As for the past. As for this mysterious stranger who had, supposedly, mesmerized her, kept her and her child in custody, I would never again allude to that story but would allow it, in an atmosphere of security and peace, to die a natural death.

And as for this mysterious stranger being one of my guests that night, well, I discounted that absolutely. These people at my dinner table, two Members of Parliament, two well-known authors, the rest all engineers, were esteemed in their professions. There was no chance that any one of them had surreptitiously engaged in midnight terrorism of an unfortunate woman and her child – whether by brutality or by this new-fangled mesmerism. Mentally I glanced though my guest list. There was Dickens and myself. Sir Benjamin Hall and Disraeli, well known and esteemed Members of Parliament. And then there were the engineers: Bazalgette; Henry Austin, Dickens' brother-in-law; William Hope and David Napier; John Phillips; and lastly Bazalgette's landlord, Bob Smith. The more I thought through my guest list, the more I was convinced that every man upon it was a hard-working, genuine man who was determined to solve the terrible problem of one of the world's greatest cities, which was now so polluted by sewage that it was a huge danger to all who lived with or near to its precincts.

It was, I believed, imperative upon me, and upon Dickens, to do our best to solve this terrible problem and I vowed that I would not allow myself to be side-stepped by the terrors of a child. Even a child who had experienced a life that should never have been inflicted upon any child, not to mind a clever, sensitive one like little Carrie, who, with her pretty mother, now seemed as though they were going to be part of my life and responsibilities.

I lay there, very still, keeping well to my own side of the bed, but when, after about ten minutes, I stretched across to make sure that the eiderdown covered her completely, I felt a warm hand seek out mine and, completely of her own accord, she turned towards me and crept in close.

When I woke in the morning, she was gone. I half sat up in bed but there were voices in the kitchen, the child, high-pitched, laughing and then, the first time I had heard it, the sound of the woman laughing in return. I lay down again. Some joke about the big teddy bear, I thought. I lay there, half asleep, drowsy and contented. It seemed a very pleasant thing not to be alone, not to have to make my own coffee, see to my own breakfast. The fire in the little grate had been lit and the shaving water had been brought in and stood, keeping warm, upon the hotplate. After a luxurious few minutes, enjoying the feeling of being looked after, I slid out of bed and put on my dressing gown. I shaved meticulously and thought, not for the first time, of growing a beard. I rather fancied myself in one of those flowing beards, like a prophet of old, and resolved after a few days to consult Caroline about it. Some women, I knew, liked beards, but others disliked them.

And then I dressed. She would prefer that, I guessed. For the sake of the child, our relationship would have to be secret for the moment. After a while she could think of an explanation, but it might be best to allow the memory of the man with the mesmeric powers and the heavy poker to fade before she told the child about sharing a bed with another man.

And so, when Charles Dickens, bright and energetic, arrived at my front door at half past nine in the morning, he was ushered into the dining room by a respectable, be-aproned woman and I was sitting, fully dressed and neatly shaved, in front of a breakfast of coffee and eggs.

'Not still at breakfast, are you?' he said. And then with a change of voice, added, 'Where's the butler?'

I was bewildered and so was Caroline, but a little voice piped up, 'I'm here!' from so near to the keyhole on the door that I guessed a small ear had been placed to it. Dickens gave a grin and opened the door quite carefully.

'So, there you are,' he said. 'You should say, "I'm here, sir!" The butler always says "sir".'

'I'm here, sir,' she said, her little face shining with amusement.

'Been polishing the silver, I suppose,' said Dickens, producing a piece of chocolate. 'Well, butlers must always have a piece of chocolate to get their strength back after polishing silver.'

'Thank you, sir,' she said, accepting the chocolate. 'It's very hard work. I feel quite exhausted! I'll just go and play with my Noah's Ark and get my strength back.'

'Just the right thing to do!' he said approvingly. 'Better go quickly before they find you any more tasks to do.' He glanced meaningfully at the apron-clad Caroline and the little girl slid away. I expected him to share a smile with the mother, but he did not, just looked her up and down appraisingly.

Caroline, I noticed, was uneasy in the presence of Dickens. She gave him a shrewd glance. Obviously he was not the poker-wielding bogeyman, but she was mistrustful of him. He was friendly and affable with the child, but it was obvious that he mistrusted the woman.

'Are you at liberty this morning?' He asked the question of me rather abruptly and once again his eyes slid towards Caroline.

'Yes, of course. I'm giving myself a few weeks off before I start my next book,' I said. I felt rather surprised by his question as I had told him that the previous night and Dickens always had a great memory for what was said to him. In fact, he had replied by saying that he was in the same boat and perhaps we might go sailing. I noticed the frowning glance he gave Caroline and she picked up the rest of the plates and went off to the kitchen, closing the door, gently but firmly, behind her. The useful boy Francis had arrived. I heard him

cheerfully talking to my little Carrie and then another voice.
So, the housemaid had arrived also.

'Setting up quite an establishment, aren't you?' Dickens
was always alert.

I shrugged. 'Time that I left my mother. She wants to sell
that house. It's too big for her.'

He dismissed the matter. 'Sir Benjamin wants me to accompany him this morning to have a look at one of Bazalgette's
proposals,' he said. 'We'll meet there. He's anxious to be able
to explain it to the queen as she prefers an oral explanation to
reading lots of dull engineering notes,' he explained. 'I thought
that you are good at this plain, simple English and could make
a good job of an interesting narrative for Her Majesty.'

I resisted the temptation to say that Her Majesty should
perhaps hand it over to someone who would be competent to
judge engineering notes, but I resisted the temptation. Dickens
was always respectful towards Her Majesty, though I had
heard that he had declined a knighthood. In any case, I liked
Bazalgette and was pleased to have the opportunity to see
him again.

'I'm your man,' I said cheerfully. I decided on an overcoat
and a warm scarf to shield against the river breezes and then
called out cheerfully, 'Be back late afternoon, Caroline. Dinner
at six, I suppose.'

He watched me carefully and when we were out in the
street and he had refused my suggestion of looking for a cab,
he couldn't contain his curiosity anymore.

'So, tell me all about your mystery lady,' he said. 'She is
the one that you met on that stormy night, isn't she? Now
don't try to fob me off. I heard the whole story from John
Millais. Met him this morning coming out of the British
Museum. A beautiful woman with long golden hair, leaning
out of a window, crying for help and Wilkie Collins goes to
rescue her. What a story, Wilkie. You'll have a new novel out
of this. Now, tell me all.'

And, of course, I did. I suppose that I was a bit under his
spell, or else the story was so strange that I had to share it
with him. I didn't, of course, tell him of the child's words,
didn't tell him that the villain might have been at my little

dinner party, but I told him the rest. And the bit about mesmerizing took his attention, as I knew it would.

'What a story!' His eyes were fired with interest. My story
had intrigued him so much that he had stopped dead and had
stood there, in the middle of the pavement, throughout the
whole recital, slightly opened-mouthed. Even when I drew my
story to a lame conclusion, he did not move but fixed me with
those very sharp, very intent eyes of his.

'You know the one that I am most sorry for in this strange
story of yours, Collins,' he said in his peremptory, authoritative manner. 'Well, it's not you or your Caroline – I have
no doubt that you are, or soon will be, happily tucked up
together. No, it's that poor child. Lovely little girl.' He tapped
me hard somewhere in the region of the middle button on
my waistcoat and fixed me with a penetrating eye. 'When
I came out to see you this morning, Wilkie, my three
youngest boys: Alfred, Sydney and Henry, were out in the
garden. They had begged some pruned branches from
the gardener and had built themselves a wild Indian wigwam,
and when I went through the gate, bless their hearts, they
were having a wonderful time shooting each other. Now
that,' said Dickens, 'is what I call having a happy childhood.
That little girl of yours, cooped up in your lodgings, no one to
play with, stuck indoors on a fine, breezy, spring morning
like this. Let's go back and get her. A bit of fresh air by the
river will do her a world of good. We'll take a cab – a bit
far for little legs – and then she can play and chase birds to
her heart's content while we listen to these engineers. Let's
fetch her.'

I gave in. I always did when Dickens took that tone with
me. By now I knew that if I gave in on a major point, he
would allow me to sort out the minor details myself.

'Good idea,' I said. 'Wait for a moment, Dick, and I'll
get her.'

'She needs a coat,' he decided the moment I returned with
the child in my arms. 'Cabbie!' In a moment he had us into
a cab and was directing the man to take us to a shop whose
name and situation he had off-pat. Ten minutes later we left
the shop with my little Carrie swathed in a fur-trimmed scarlet

cape with hat to match. I paid, of course, but I didn't grudge
a penny of it. The delight on the child's face was enough for
me. Dickens looked at her with satisfaction when we got back
into the cab.

'Always like bright colours on children; remember that,
Wilkie. You can keep an eye on them better,' he said with the
authority of a father of ten. There were times when I found
this self-congratulatory mood of his rather tiresome, but now
he embarked upon a story about how a puppy, belonging to
his two enormous Newfoundland dogs, had swam rather too
far out and the puppy's father had come down onto the bank
of the river, had looked out at his son, then plunged into the
water, swam out, seized the puppy by the ear, and towed him
back to dry land. Carrie was enchanted with the story.

'He didn't beat his puppy, did he, though?' she asked
anxiously, when she had finished laughing over the description
of the dripping puppy shaking himself.

Dickens looked at her and I was glad to see the gentleness
on his face. 'No, no beatings in my house,' he said firmly. 'If
anyone does something wrong, they just have to put it right
again.' Probably not quite correct, but it had been the right thing
to say. Her face brightened again, and I was glad that we had
taken her.

SEVEN

Joe Bazalgette was waiting for us on the shore of the River Thames near to Westminster when we arrived. At almost the same time, the cab bearing the tall figure of Sir Benjamin Hall, drew up at the pavement beside the embankment. He got out with the slow pace that befitted his stature and his dignity and when Dickens went across to greet him, I went down through the sand to Bazalgette.

Joe was not alone. His amiable landlord was with him, wearing a massive pair of boots and looking eagerly around the sands, his eyes shining like a child expecting a treat. He greeted me with a nod but said nothing, as if determined not to be in the way of the professional engineers. The others arrived soon after: Henry Austin with John Phillips; Frank Foster, Engineer to the Commissioner of Sewers and John Grant, Assistant Engineer to the Metropolitan Board of Works, neither of whom I had met before; and then William Hope and David Napier.

To my relief, little Carrie showed no signs of any unease in their company and happily began to chase seagulls, egged on by Dickens who promised his little friend the butler a thruppenny bit for every bird that she captured. She made a pretty sight with her golden curls flying behind her as she raced down the sand and I was absurdly proud when Napier came up to me and admired her.

'Your niece, is she? Is that right?' he asked in a casual fashion, but that stiff, white, curly beard of his seemed to jut out with curiosity.

I hesitated. It occurred to me that I had not requested Dickens to keep the story of Caroline to himself. It was, after all, quite a fantastical story. I did not want anyone laughing or insinuating a disgraceful secret if her name came up. She was to be my housekeeper as far as these casual acquaintances were concerned. Carrie brought a complication into the matter. I could hardly claim her to be a niece, not even a goddaughter if she were the offspring of my newly acquired housekeeper. The sound of Dickens' voice in the distance rescued me. And, as often, I borrowed his imagination for my own purposes. I turned an amazed face upon Napier.

'My dear fellow,' I said with mock astonishment, 'didn't you hear Dickens? That's my new butler.'

And then, happy to have put him and his inquisitive beard in his place, and swinging my stick merrily, I strode down the wet sand to have a look at the work in progress as I waited for Carrie to return.

It was a fine morning. The River Thames did smell, but not too badly, and I hoped that the brisk north-westerly wind which wafted the odours away would last for another few weeks. I didn't like to even think of the stenches we would experience during the summer to come and began to plan a move to Broadstairs with my newly acquired housekeeper and her little daughter. I could write just as well, if not better, when by the sea and I could take some summer lodgings for a couple of months. The thought cheered me immensely and I looked around with a smile. I wasn't the only one who had sidled away from work. Bazalgette's landlord, rightly determining that there was going to be no excitement until all was unpacked, was chatting to the skipper of a schooner tied up to the bridge. Something about a trip to Belgium, and wanting a full load, I seemed to make out. The man, of course, I seemed to remember, made his money from building as well as by letting out warehouses and dwelling houses. Bricks, I thought vaguely, were imported from Belgium and Holland and perhaps London exported something in return. With interest I watched. Britain, I knew, had been nicknamed the workshop of the world. I wondered whether the landlord's interest in these engineers might lead to him purchasing some machinery and exporting it in return for an import of Flemish bricks. Bazalgette, I gathered, had invented and manufactured the machine that they were going to use for dredging up some of the river water. Holland, I remembered, was a country crisscrossed with canals which drained the land and were used as we used roads in England. If Bazalgette were to be successful, his new model dredger might have great sales in that low-lying land.

Everyone else was engaged in unpacking sheets of thick board, made from elm wood, from a cart drawn by some enormous horses of the sort used for bringing the beer from the breweries. The board looked immensely heavy and certainly not something that someone of my build and fragility could easily carry, and so, on the pretext of looking after Carrie, I removed myself from the workforce and left them all working hard, while amiably teasing David Napier about being the only engineer in London who had managed to blow up two ships on the River Thames.

Carrie wanted nothing to do with me. Dickens' offer of a thruppenny bit for a seagull had excited her and she was determined to catch at least one of those annoying birds who were feeding from the rubbish on the sands up to the moment when she came within a few feet of them. She sent me off with the crisp admonition to go and do my work and to leave her in peace to do her work. And so, I left her and went back to the men, smiling to myself.

When I reached the men, the wood was all unloaded, but they were still discussing an exploded ship on which the unfortunate David Napier had spent a morning repairing a boiler.

'And that was the second ship that he blew up,' Foster said to me. 'He's going to specialize in exploding ships. A new line, but it might be profitable.' He put his hand to his mouth in an exaggerated gesture. 'Someone told me that he has gone into insurance as a sideline. They say that marine insurance is a great way to make money.'

Napier gave a grin but didn't acknowledge the insinuation. An easy-going fellow, I thought him, though I was a little sorry for him to be the butt of the other engineers' jokes.

'Best to let these things burn out once they start,' said Bazalgette with a nod at Napier. A nice fellow, Bazalgette, I thought, and wished that I, also, could say something in support of the man.

'So, when he saw pieces of metal fly up into the sky, he just shrugged his shoulders and went off home to his secret mistress. He keeps her locked up in a tower,' said John Grant.

'Secret mistress? That sounds interesting,' said Dickens, and he cocked one eyebrow in such a quizzical fashion that everyone burst out laughing.

'That's right; none of us have ever seen her as he keeps her sealed up in a secret room somewhere in the suburbs.' Grant gave an amused nod.

'A secret mistress,' I said, pricking up my ears. 'That does sound interesting.' I did not meet Dicken's eye, but I knew that he would not betray my confidence. My thoughts immediately went to Caroline's story. I looked with interest at Napier. I wondered whether he and I shared a history. Had he, also, rescued a beautiful girl kept captive by that monster and his mesmerizing finger ring? Or was there a more sinister background to those words spoken so lightly by the young engineer?

Napier and Hope were partners but quite dissimilar in age. William Hope was a very young man, a good ten years younger than me, according to something that Dickens had said, but David Napier was certainly not a young man. He was a good twenty years or so older, even than Dickens, I would have said, putting him well into his fifties or even more and so was more like a father than a partner in age to William Hope, the young hero, decorated by Queen Victoria for gallantry. Napier had white hair and a white beard and certainly at this moment was wearing a rather bad-tempered expression. Could he be the one that the child had overheard when she had hidden under the table in my dining room? Perhaps the man was warped in some way and instead of enjoying a mistress openly and, of course, rewarding her generously, like any other man of my acquaintance, he liked to imprison her, frighten her, make-believe to mesmerize her, or even to be one of those people who can truly mesmerize, and who use mesmerization for their own wicked purposes and satisfaction. I looked at him dubiously. Nothing too strange or different about him. He had conquered his annoyance and was laughing now, not in a forced way, but with what appeared to be genuine merriment.

'I do like a man who is good with explosives,' said Frank Foster, punching David Napier amiably on the arm. 'With you on the team, the problem of getting rid of the sewage will be no problem. We'll just turn you loose and after an hour or so you will manage to blow a giant hole in the river and then we can get Bazalgette's new pump and use it to empty all that stinking stuff into it and it should sink into the sand. And then, Bob's your Uncle! Problem solved!'

'Oh, shut up,' said Napier, but he said it in an amiable manner with a grin on his face.

I began to envy these engineers their camaraderie, their sense of fun, and above all that companionship between young and middle-aged that came from having a shared aim. I knew many writers, but none of us had fun with each other like that. There was always a tincture of envy, an unwillingness to discuss a work in progress for fear that ideas could be borrowed, could become stale through over usage. The engineers weren't like that. They discussed methods and machinery with the air of men who were enjoying the feeling of exploring ideas. There appeared to be a sense of adventure among them, like explorers in unknown territory. Even now, the joke turned to semi-earnest as they began to exchange ideas on the strength of explosives and how, if possible, that strength could be used to lend extra energy to a pump.

I noticed that now they had stopped teasing David Napier and were listening to his ideas with interest. He had even made a few notes about what had gone wrong – something which surprised me. A novelist, certainly I, myself, who senses that he has written a bad book tends to burn it or shove it into an obscure drawer and endeavour to forget it as soon as possible. But engineers, I thought, were, from what I could make out, not at all like that. They took failure as a learning process and David Napier now became a valuable witness in the process of understanding explosives by these eager minds. Words like 'ammonium nitrate' and 'oxygen' and others were flying between them, sentences left unfinished as nods showed comprehension until eventually they turned back to the problem of the sewage. And then the disagreements began all over again.

'Dig deep enough into the Thames and bury the stuff,' said Phillips with renewed energy.

'And then, of course, you will be the first to drink the water from the Thames on the day after it all seeps out and goes to the surface,' said Bazalgette with a measure of sarcasm in his voice. He was, I noticed, considerably less carefree than the rest. He had an intent and serious look upon his face and his lips were set in a tight line of resolution. 'Let's get these timbers up before we waste any more time,' he said with the air of a man who had a lot on his mind.

Even while he was organizing the carrying of the heavy slabs of timber down to the water's edge and handing out some spades to volunteer diggers who materialized as though by magic, I could see that Bazalgette was thinking hard. There was a frown between his brows and a certain impatience as he bellowed orders. I cast a quick eye in little Carrie's direction – she was obediently keeping well back from the water and running in pursuit of the seagulls who descended in flocks in order to pick through the rubbish and crowd around the giant holes where the contents of the sewers of London carved a channel down the sand and emptied into the sea. The child, I was glad to see, was staying quite near to us, coming up to me from time to time to reassure herself that I had not departed. I took her hand in mine, felt it to make sure that she was not cold, but the new cape had kept her warm. She did not pull the hand away, but stayed there beside me and, once again, I worried a little about her, worried about the slight look of tension that came over her little face when any of the engineers came near. She seemed now to be listening hard to their conversation as they shouted against the engine noise of the boats and lapping of the waves and the strange sucking noise as the tide began to turn.

'What are they doing?' She whispered the question into my ear as I sat upon the sand and held her hand.

'No secret; you don't need to whisper,' I said. 'I'll tell you what I think they are doing. You see, they want to build a giant pipe under the water and then the stuff that comes out of those pipes will go across to the other side of the water where not so many people live.'

She nodded, quite satisfied with my explanation. She said no more, but I got the impression that she was still listening intently to the voices. David Napier, as if goaded by the taunts of being the only man to blow up two ships on the River Thames, was working extremely hard, directing the insertion of the great planks of wood into the riverbed, shouting loud orders to the workmen. There were about ten yards of a pathway framed by these slabs of elm by now and already it seemed to be excluding some of the river water. Bazalgette's workman wheeled down a load of bricks, some already cemented into three-foot-long sections of piping, and a sack of his Portland cement. John Phillips and Henry Austin were assembling the pump and, when they were ready, they gave a great shout.

'Now comes the test,' I said to Carrie. 'It's so very, very exciting! It's a race between the men and the river. Can they build their pipe before the river floods the space between the boards? We'll cheer for the men, shall we?'

'I'm going to cheer for the river, and you can cheer for the men,' she said, independent as always.

'I think that you and the River Thames are going to win,' I said after about five minutes. No matter how energetically the water was pumped out, no matter how fast the men cemented the sections of bricks to form a rough pipe, the water crept back into the space. The race against the power of the river seemed doomed to be lost by the men no matter how well the Portland cement worked, no matter how strong a pump was used.

'I think that Henry Austin, for once, has backed the right horse,' said Dickens in my ear as he lowered himself onto the sand beside me. 'Best to build the works inland and then find some way of pumping the stuff into the Thames Estuary. There's nothing for it but to dig up London's roads again. As for John Phillips, his scheme of having a set of pipes crossing the Thames eleven times carrying sewage to Eel Island and then eventually dumping it on Plumstead Marshes – I can't see that working, can you?'

'You'd certainly need an army of men to build the pipes,' I said, taking a neutral view. Despite my doubts, I was

impressed to see how fast the men were working and how
they had now managed to achieve a short length of piping,
holding the water away by means of the great slabs of elm
and the fast pumping. I lifted little Carrie onto my knee, feeling
her hands again to make sure that she wasn't cold. She
leaned her cheek against my shoulder and snuggled into me.
My little godson always had a midday nap and I wondered
whether she might sleep there. She didn't, though. Too tense,
I thought. Every shouted word made her stiffen and I wondered
what notion she had got into her little head on the night of
my party. I was glad to have her there in my arms, though. I
had worried about her when she was running on the sands,
but now she was safe and I could turn my mind to the problem
of the Great Stink of London.

On this spring morning with a strong wind from the south-
west blowing the stench of the river away from us, the smell
was quite bearable, but once summer arrived, London would
become unbearable again. And in the meantime, the poor who
were dependent upon drinking water from this polluted river
would continue to die in great numbers from cholera, polio,
typhoid, even from dysentery. Dickens and I discussed the
problems in low voices, and I was impressed, as always, by
the amount that he knew and by the strength of his feeling
for those who had to live precarious lives in slum housing and
who did not even have pure water to drink.

'If we have a chance in our lifetime of remedying the matter,
I'd say Bazalgette, that young man with the outlandish name,
will be the one who will save us,' he said. 'Imagine it, Collins.
Fish leaping in the Thames, pure water for the poor to drink.
London smelling of sweet flowers, a pleasant place for all
who dwell within its ancient walls,' he finished, looking with
distaste at the sewage that flowed into the water a few yards
down from where we sat. I nodded agreement. This enterprise
to divert the sewage from the River Thames, to run it in pipes
beside the river, but not into the water, until the pipes reached
the Thames Estuary, that was a magnificent scheme and I
wished Bazalgette all the luck in the world.

The tide was coming in fast now and I could see that the
men in the water were beginning to give up their efforts. Sir

Benjamin Hall who had retired to his cab for a quick cigar now came down to the edge of the water and waved an arm, summoning them back. They had, I thought with a tinge of admiration, all shown a bravery and a dedication to their trade that should earn them praise from Her Majesty and Her Majesty's government. Dickens got to his feet and went down to join them, but I stayed where I was. The little bundle on my knee had become heavier and while Dickens and I had been talking in low voices, she had fallen asleep.

I held her carefully and took an oath that I would not turn out this waif and her mother from the comfort of my lodgings. They would find refuge with me. I would never marry; I had sworn to that again and again, and so there was no one in the world who could validly object to my way of life. My mother, I knew, was too wise a woman to interfere in matters that she would deem were none of her concern. I was in my mid-thirties, far beyond a mother's control, in easy circumstances as the fortunate possessor of a substantial sum of money from my hard-working father, who had churned out paintings faster than I wrote chapters. But I was improving at my trade all the time and now earning potentially great sums by way of my pen. Soon, I hoped, I would be as wealthy through my pen as my father had been through his paintbrush.

Caroline and her little daughter, Harriet, my little Carrie, would be cared for by me for as long as both wished to stay. In the meantime, I would do everything that lay within my power to help these men to solve the terrible problem of this great city of ours.

Suddenly I seemed to feel a responsibility for the poor and the outcast and wanted to bear my share in remedying their living conditions.

Dickens had read my thoughts. When he came back, he sat down beside us and bit his lip thoughtfully, looking out at the brave crowd of men, battling the water. If it worked, this under-the-river piping of the sewage, would certainly take the stink from the River Thames and, perhaps, its advocates were right. It might at least pay for its building and its upkeep by selling the manure to the farmers. It was not, though, an ideal solution. Sooner or later, I felt, the River

Thames would win. The pipes would need continual maintenance – pipes always did – and that would be immensely
difficult if they were underwater, instead of, as was the present
position, underground.

The engineers and their workers were coming back up,
just ahead of the fast-rising tide, as the edge of the river
began to creep over the sand. Sir Benjamin was finalising
the arrangements for the train journey to Maplin Sands and
Bob Smith, Bazalgette's landlord, was reminding everyone
of the Fortnum & Mason hampers which he had promised
to provide. 'Not just wine and lunch,' he said, 'but a splendid
dessert as well. Don't turn your noses up at good food. You
all deserve the best as you have worked so hard.'

'"Dost thou think because thou art virtuous there shall be
no more cakes and ale?",' quoted Dickens.

During his entire life, my friend Dickens had borne a slight
regret that he had not been a famous actor like his friend
Macready and there was little doubt that he had a magnificent
voice and now as hc looked around the company with a theatrical air, it boomed over the sands. Wet and disheartened as
they were, most of the engineers laughed at the aptness of the
Shakespearean quotation. The noise woke little Carrie and she
straightened herself sleepily in my arms and sat up, looking
around at all the men.

'And there is something else that I would like to say – my
pennyworth, so to speak,' continued Bob Smith. 'As you
know, I'm keen to do my bit for this great enterprise. I've
said how impressed I've been with how Mr Bazalgette has
turned my warehouse into such a great workshop, and I've
offered the use of another of my warehouses. Well . . .' The
landlord paused and looked around. 'I will offer very good
terms to any gentleman, or group of gentlemen here, if they
want to hire it. Half price and use the place as you will, and
you'll get no complaints from me. I can't say fairer than
that.'

There was a scattered round of applause and shouts of
'hear!' 'hear!' from all.

The noise, I suppose, slightly alarmed my little Carrie. I
felt her arms go around my neck and she whispered in my

ear, 'I don't like all these peoples. I want to go home, back
to your house.'

'And so you will,' I whispered back. I felt a thrill of pleasure
that she should call my lodgings her home and vowed to make
some more purchases to change the place and make everything
warm and inviting for the new members of my family. 'You'll
have to tell your mama what a nice day you had. Tell her
that and I'll buy you some sweets,' I said in her ear. I felt
somewhat ashamed of myself to be bribing a child, but I
wanted, very badly, for these two waifs to find shelter with
me. I had never seen anyone as ethereally beautiful as Caroline
with her blonde curls and her immense blue eyes, and as for
her daughter, Harriet, my little pet Carrie, I wanted to do the
world for her. A good school, a happy home, love and understanding. She would have the best of everything. I swore that.

As for the man who had frightened and mistreated the two
of them, well, hanging was too good for him. If ever I found
out who it was, I would, I swore, hand him over to the police
and make sure that he was never in a position to terrify another
woman and child again. I scrutinized my companions, one by
one. I didn't want to put any ideas into the child's mind, but
she had twice reacted to the sound of the voice of one of these
men and I wished that I knew which one of them had sounded
like the man who had locked up her mother and kept her as
a slave. After all, apart from Dickens, I knew very little about
any one of them.

I was musing upon this idea when Phillips came up and sat
beside us. Dickens looked at him with sympathy. Another man
might have stayed silent, but Dickens was nothing if not courageous and instantly he hastened to give the man an opportunity
to talk about his failed plan. This, after all, was the kernel of
Phillips' scheme. His plan involved crossing the Thames with
these underwater pipes, not once but with a total of eleven
pipes. By now he must have seen the impossibility of his
dream.

'Are you disappointed in the results, Mr Phillips?' he asked.

To my surprise, the man shook his head. 'Nothing ever
really disappoints me, Mr Dickens. I'm not made like that. As
soon as one scheme doesn't work, I just shift it to the back

of my mind and move another one into its place. Funny, looking at your little girl, there, on your knee, Mr Collins, well, it brought something back to me and it's given me an idea. I'm from the country, originally, Mr Dickens, west of London. Well, I wasn't much older than that little child, but I was working in the brick works and when I was coming home one day, tired out as you could imagine, I was called over by a crowd of men. They were road makers, and they were hired to make a bridge over the river. Big piles of stones there, all cut into slabs, but they were having awful trouble making the foundations. You could imagine what it was like, after watching those lads trying to put a pipe down under the water, well, every time that they dug a hole for a foundation slab, the water rose from the ground and filled it. I was put standing in the hole with a bucket and my job was to ladle out the water as soon as it began to rise. But it was no good, of course, Mr Dickens. These were ignorant country folk, no brains, even at five years old I could have told them that the land beside the river would be full of water and that no matter how hard I worked to clear it of water, that hole would keep on refilling. Anyway, they tired of it all after an hour and stood around talking, so that I was able to have a rest. I can tell you that my legs were trembling.

'And then along comes an old fellow, white hair, white beard – plenty of brains, though. Well, he looks at the hole that the men had dug, then he looks at me with my bucket, looks at the pile of stones, looks at me – and I didn't amount to much at that time, small, skinny little fellow that I was – and when he looks at me, a big smile comes over his face. "Well, my lads," he says, "the Bible tells us that it took Almighty God to divide the waters of the sea, but you think that you can do it with a puny little lad like this." He said some words then, this old country man – they meant nothing to me, but I remembered the sound of them, and I looked them up twenty years afterwards when I had learned to read and this is what they said: And thou didst divide the sea before them, so that they went through the midst of the sea on the dry land; and their persecutors thou threwest into the deeps, as a stone into the mighty waters. "You'll have to think again, lads," said this old man. "Give the river its way. It's on a little hill here. Let the river go down the hill and build your bridge in a new place on this new road of yours. When everything is right, you can bring the river back. And so they did as he told them, gentlemen. The ground was soft and wet, and they dug that new channel for it in half an hour, diverted the river down, cut off a bend, easy as anything, joined it up on the meadow and then built the bridge on dry land. Of course, when the cement was dry and the bridge had settled, then it was the easiest thing in the world to dig a new channel and to funnel the river water back under the bridge. A year or two later no one who didn't know the story could have told what had happened.' He brooded for a moment and then repeated: '"And thou didst divide the sea before them, so that they went through the midst of the sea on the dry land; and their persecutors thou threwest into the deeps, as a stone into the mighty waters."' Have I got the words right, Mr Dickens?'

'You have indeed got the words right,' said Dickens in low and solemn tones. 'And I have seldom heard them more movingly pronounced and more appropriately quoted.'

There was something about this elderly and indomitable man that moved my friend, and I could see the interest in his eyes as he looked at him.

'You said, Mr Phillips, that when a plan failed you were not disappointed, just moved it to the back of your mind and brought another forward to fill the space,' Dickens said after a minute's silence.

The elderly man smiled at him. 'Yes, indeed, Mr Dickens, and it's simmering away up there in my head. I shall have to keep it there until everything comes right for me, but I'll give you a hint. That story I told you has helped me. Five years old, I was, but I never forgot how easy it was to build the bridge first and then to turn the course of the river. Just a different way of looking at things, but that was what made all the difference. Now I'll wish you gentlemen a good day and I'll be off back to the drawing board – back to the drawing board, Mr Dickens, that's my watchword!'

And with that he was off, and Dickens looked after him in

a thoughtful fashion. After a moment, he shook his head sadly. 'That's an indominable man, Wilkie, my friend, but I fear that in this case the race is to the swift. I think Bazalgette's plan will be the one that wins the golden prize.'

EIGHT

On the morning of the expedition to Maplin Sands, I woke late. I had been vaguely conscious of Caroline sliding out of my bed at some time around sunrise, but had just sighed happily and gone back to sleep. When I woke again, the sun was shining directly into my face through a gap in the curtains and I said sleepily to myself, 'Dickens was right; the day is fine.' And then I repeated 'Dickens!' I took my watch from the bedside table and looked at it with horror. I washed and shaved as fast as I could, making a deal of noise about the procedure, I guess, because when I came out, there was hot coffee and toast waiting for me and my little Carrie was already wearing her gorgeous, new, bright scarlet cape and carrying the little fur cap that went with it.

'She said that you promised to take her.' Caroline looked from one to the other with a worried frown and the child stuck her chin defiantly in the air. I hesitated, but I had glimpsed a tear forming and I had not the heart to refuse. After all, she had been so good and most obedient on the day when we were down by the river.

'You'll have to stick like glue to me because I'm afraid that I will fall into the marsh and get lost for ever,' I told her, and she nodded solemnly. Caroline, to my surprise, said nothing. I would have expected to be deluged by anxious questions from a mother of a five-year-old child, but she seemed too frozen within herself to assert any authority over the child.

Dickens, however, gave an anxious stare when I arrived at Liverpool Station holding the hand of the child. 'Good God, Collins, you are not taking that small child to Maplin Sands?' he said in an undertone as she gazed around the busy railway station with delight. 'Don't you know that the grave-yard there has over a hundred bodies, sucked down into those sands and drowned before they could be recovered?'

He spoke in a low voice, but she was quick and sharp and picked up immediately.

'Don't wowy,' she said, that enchanting 'r' lisp making me smile despite my anxiety. 'Don't wowy. I'll look after Mr Wilkie. I'll hold his hand vewy tight.'

She was, I thought, anxious to placate him. I had not heard her lisp before, and I guessed that she had picked up the note of anger from his voice and it had brought to the surface that nervous unease that lay beneath her rather grown-up manners. I looked at Dickens with annoyance. Why did he always have to be the one who knew what was best for everyone? Luckily, there was a big fuss going on about the safe loading of the two immense Fortnum & Mason hamper baskets provided by Bob Smith and so Dickens, who couldn't bear not to be in the forefront of any organizational matter, left us abruptly and went to give instructions to the men.

'Let's creep into the second carriage,' I said to her, making a conspiracy out of the whole matter as we slipped into the other reserved carriage. I was glad to be away from Dickens in any case. He was the best of fellows, but he did like to organize train journeys and keep everyone busy playing word games. Myself, I preferred to doze off and I guessed that the child beside me would soon tire of looking out of the window and would also fall asleep.

When we arrived at the railway station at Southend-on-Sea, there was an assortment of cabs lined up ready to convey us to Maplin Sands. Refreshed by my sound sleep on the train, I cheerfully questioned our cabbie about this fortitudinous abundance of cabs and was informed that one of the gentlemen had wired a message to the railway station at precisely seven thirty a.m. in the morning. I did not need to ask who that gentleman was, and feeling rested and looking forward to the day, I eyed my friend with affection. What a man, I thought, and knew that I would never approach his efficiency in any respect. Still feeling cheerful, I joined Joe Bazalgette and the friends/partners David Napier and William Hope and listened with interest to stories about the history of Maplin Sands. Some of them were quite blood-curdling though and I began to feel worried about having brought my little Carrie. She was unusually quiet, stayed snuggled into me, hiding her face in my waistcoat, but after a few jolting miles she had dropped off to sleep again and I looked down at her flushed face and wished that she were back home with her mother. Perhaps Dickens was right. Perhaps it had been stupid to bring such a small child to this dangerous spot.

After a few minutes, my silence was noted by the company and David Napier leaned across the gap in the cab and tapped me on the knee.

'Don't worry about your little goddaughter,' he said. 'There's a lodge there, just where the cabs will drop us off. I know the woman well, Mrs Taylor. An extremely nice woman. Has grandchildren of that age.' He nodded in Carrie's direction. 'Keeps toys in the house to amuse them when they visit. I'll take you over there as soon as we arrive. Give her a shilling and she'll look after the child while you have a look at the marshes. Nice little girl, isn't she? Full of imagination, like all children of that age. I remember my own children. The stories they used to make up. But, of course, they have a will of their own at that age and so she will be better off left with Mrs Taylor than running around on those dangerous sinking sands.'

I thanked him very sincerely and thought what a nice and considerate person he was to have noted my unease and diagnosed it so swiftly. He was as good as his word once we arrived, and while all the talk about the hampers was going on he took me across to a small, neat cottage and introduced me to a sensible-looking woman, not too old, despite being quite lame. She told me that she was a grandmother and very used to children. She admired Carrie's cape enormously, made her turn around and twirl to get the full benefit of the fur-edged skirt and then said cheerfully, 'I'm so glad that you have come to visit me. You see, I need a bit of help. I have to bake a cake for my husband when he comes home tired and wet, and you look to be just the sort of girl to help me.'

Carrie was flattered but wary. She looked across at me and then from the woman back to me again. I cursed myself for bringing her. One glance at that immensity of shimmering sand, with the threatening billows of waves on the horizon, and even a childless person like myself knew that this was no place to have brought a self-willed, five-year-old little girl.

'I'll help you when I come back,' she promised, 'but now I have to go for a run on the sand. I want to chase some birds.'

I looked helplessly at David Napier and he gave a faint shrug of his shoulders. My business, not his, the shrug said. 'I'd better be getting out there,' he said. 'Will Hope is waiting for me. I think I hear the arrival of the experts from the Essex Agricultural Department. We have to convince them that our plan will work – and convince Sir Benjamin, of course.'

There was a prospect of a large sum of money and a knighthood for these two men all hanging upon the possibility of impressing Sir Benjamin, and Her Majesty, of course, with this solution to the terrible problem by conveying the sewage from the northern side of London by a forty-four-mile culvert to Rawreth in Essex and then via two branches to Maplin Sands, where it would be used to reclaim an area of about twenty thousand acres from the sea on either side of the estuary of the River Crouch. It would, of course, only get rid of less than half of the sewage, but half was better than nothing. And the Napier/Hope scheme would not involve digging up the streets of the city of London and of Westminster – something that everyone dreaded, given the enormous amount of traffic on the roads of these central and southern districts. If this scheme could be demonstrated to be workable today and Sir Benjamin were to recommend it to the Queen, then David Napier and his partner would become rich and famous. Napier looked from Carrie to Mrs Taylor, shrugged his shoulders and left to join William Hope.

The problem of a self-willed child was mine and Mrs Taylor and I were left looking at each other across the head of a determined child. I put down the shilling on the edge of the table and turned towards the door. But it was no good. Carrie's little hand slid into mine and she also turned, resolute to accompany me.

Quite frankly, I did not know what to do. Perhaps, I thought, Dickens was wrong. Perhaps the child would be quite safe with me and would hold my hand in a docile manner. But then I thought of that cemetery and of those hundreds of bodies, sucked down into those sands and drowned before they could be recovered. I opened my mouth and then shut it again. What was I to do?

Luckily, the lady of the house had more brains than I. 'Oh, that's a shame. Still, never mind,' she said in an agreeable fashion. Then, just as though it were an afterthought, she added, 'Before you go, would you like to have a look at the doll's house that my husband has made for my granddaughter, a little girl just the same size as you? And do you know, it's even got a little staircase with a tiny carpet on it. And little beds for the dolls in the bedrooms. Would you have a look at it and tell me what sort of curtains it should have on its little windows?'

That was irresistible. Carrie dropped my hand instantly and held out her hand to Mrs Taylor. I waited a few instants, listening to the enraptured and excited tones of the child and then I slid out of the front door, closing it very quietly, but quite firmly, behind me.

I crossed over to the sands where Dickens had taken over the two picnic baskets and was busy supervising the placing of the bottles of white wine in a hole by the edge of the sea. I shuddered when I saw how quickly the prints of his boots had filled with seawater and determined that nothing would persuade me to wander around those treacherous sands.

But when the lunch was over and the cloths, the napkins, the plates, the glasses, the bottles and the small wicker containers were all piled back into the baskets, Dickens was on his feet.

'We'll leave you gentlemen to your scientific and engineering experiments,' he said cheerfully. 'Collins and I, as novelists, cannot resist a stroll across the Broomway. I've had a chat with the man who helped us to unload, and he assured me that it was quite safe if you keep to the path marked out by those broom trees out there. Come on, Collins, let's make for the pathway. Don't worry, man! I'm quite assured that it is safe, and I have checked the timetable and have found that the tide does not turn until four o'clock – and by five o'clock the cabbies will be back to take us to the station and soon after that we will be on our way back to Liverpool Street Station. Come on, Collins.'

And I went. Dickens had a way with him that made it almost impossible to refuse him, but I put in a stipulation. 'Just half an hour, Dickens, and we turn back,' I said. 'Half an hour out and half an hour back. You can go on if you like, but I want to check on Carrie.'

For a moment I saw him hesitate and I thought that he was going to suggest taking her with us, after all, but then I saw him looking out at the miles and miles of sea, saw him scan the path, looking at the frail and battered specimens of wind-torn barren sticks of broom that indicated a safe passageway, but did not shield it or enclose it in any way. No place to take an active, self-willed child!

'Very well,' he said. 'That's a bargain. Let's go, Collins. Bless my soul, this is one of the strangest places that I have ever seen.'

And so, we went. From behind us I could hear the booming voice of Sir Benjamin, delivering a speech to the agricultural experts whom he had assembled. 'Gentlemen,' he was saying, 'the links between our excrement and our food have been fundamental to human survival as long as our species has existed. In hunter-gatherer and nomadic societies, human excrement nourished wild plants. The Book of Deuteronomy instructed the Israelites, "when you relieve yourself, dig a hole and cover up your excrement", a measure that reduced disease and recycled waste. In settled agricultural societies, the excrement of humans and other animals helped maintain soil fertility and crop yields. In early towns, many townspeople had plots of land or kept animals, so using excrement continued to be part of everyday life. As towns grew, so did urban-rural manure trade . . .'

As we got further along, the voice began to fade and was eventually lost in the immensity of the sand and seascape which surrounded us. I could see now why Dickens was so determined to go on this walk. If there were speeches to be made, he would probably have preferred to make them himself. But now, he felt quite strongly, was not the time for speeches, but for solid, uninteresting testing of the soil and for the verdict of experts. They had brought with them some ominous-looking barrels and I guessed that a certain amount of practical work would go on which would have spoiled the remaining savour of our excellent lunch.

And he was right. This landscape was the strangest that I had ever seen.

Strange, I thought, was an inadequate word.

The Broomway, as the man had called it, snaked across the vast sand flats and mud flats that stretched as far as the eye could see, certainly for miles. The tide, I thought, must have gone out at Foulness Island, and it seemed to have gone out a great distance, uncovering an endless stretch of sand – an immensity of flat surface which could form no obstacle to an incoming tide. The sand looked, I thought, eyeing it nervously, packed hard enough to support the weight of a walker, but I could imagine that when the tide turned it would come in at a frightening rate, probably spreading over those flat sands quicker than my short legs could run.

'Are you sure that it's safe, Dick?' I asked the question in as steady a fashion as I could manage but could not help a slight quiver in my voice.

To my surprise, he did not reply instantly, did not, as he usually did, scoff at my fears and sweep away all doubts with an assurance that he knew best. He just stood very still, looking all around him. There was, I noticed, a glitter in his eyes and an air of pent-up excitement about him.

'Lummy,' he said, taking to cockney slang, as he always did when he was excited. 'My God, Collins, this is a place. We'll have to keep a sharp look out. See the way the land dips around the edges of the sand. I'd reckon that the tide would slide in and circle you before you knew where you were. We could very easily be trapped upon this splendid path and then all the stone in the world underneath our feet wouldn't prevent us from being swept up and sucked back out into the ocean.'

Disorientation, I thought, could be a danger as well as inundation; the sun had faded and there was a slight mist in the air. In rain or fog, I thought, as soon as we left the pathway outlined by these barren sticks of broom, it would probably be easy to lose direction with shining sand extending in all directions.

'Better leave our shoes at the top of the path, before we go onto the sands; there's mud beneath that sand and we could ruin our shoes,' said Dickens, still in that excited tone of voice. 'Don't worry, Collins,' he added, misinterpreting my horrified expression, 'they won't be lost. We'll retrieve them before the tide comes in. We'll put them under that last broom bush, and I'll tie my scarf to it so that when we turn back, we can make straight for the right spot.'

If the fog doesn't thicken too much, was my thought, but I was ashamed to voice my terrors in the face of his excited relish of the eerie place. Left to myself, I would have just gone to the top of the Broomway, had a good look around at the ghostly landscape, made a mental note to tell my brother that it could make a wonderful picture if he lugged his easel and paints down to this spot, and then returned happily to dry land and listened to the engineers making their plans.

At the end of the causeway, as we stopped to take off our shoes, I found a large heap of cockleshells and nervously filled my pocket with them. I would, I planned, drop one every yard or so and then pick them up again on our way back, as some unknown walker or walkers had probably done some time ago. The evidence that he had returned and left his pile of cockleshells for the benefit of another adventurer somewhat cheered me and I stepped bravely off the end of the causeway and felt my bare feet sink into the sand and sensed the soft mud beneath it.

'That's the mud that our friends, Hope and Napier, want to convert to fertile land for farmers to grow their vegetables for the London market.' Dickens bent down and scraped out some black sludge and held it out for my admiration. Somehow, I didn't think that I would enjoy vegetables from the unappealing mixture of that stuff and the sewage from all the cesspits and lavatories in north London, but I held my tongue. After all, those healthy vegetables which I purchased and imagined coming from the idyllic surroundings of rural Kent, might well spring from a similarly unappetising source. I turned to look over my shoulder. The tide, in that sneaky way that tides seemed to adopt when you take your eyes off them, appeared to have crept a lot nearer towards us.

'Let's go back,' I said to Dickens. 'I'm worried that our shoes will be swept away.'

'Don't worry, Collins; if your shoes are swept away, you will be swept after them,' he said in his bracing manner.

Out and on we walked, barefoot, over and into the mirror-world. I glanced back at the coast. The air was very damp and there was certainly a bit of a sea mist. From time to time, I looked over my shoulder and was reassured by the sight of the weird, other-world aspect of the barren stumps of broom. A few cottages, blurred and indistinct, showed on the shoreline. Every few hundred yards, I dropped a white cockleshell and I hoped fervently that I would be picking them up again before long.

Suddenly I heard the eerie, melancholy sound of a foghorn. It gave me a start and I stopped dead and looked all around me as though expecting to see something from another world loom up in the distance. I wiped my glasses free from the spume and mist and when I replaced them, I saw the light-house – like something from another world. Not the usual lighthouse, not a tall, conical, snow-white tower such as I had seen when sailing in the civilized waters in the English Channel, but a strange, almost crab-like structure, a tiny tower on top of a cluster of bent iron rods.

'Built that about twenty years ago,' said Dickens. 'Had the devil's own job with it. Kept falling down – the whole structure – kept being swept off by the tide. They had to keep hammering in new rods.' There was a note of admiration in his voice. Dickens was a great believer in the virtue of tenacity and no man exemplified these principles more than he. Now, though, I was in no mood for heroics.

'I'm going back,' I said firmly. 'I'm not going to be respon-sible for some poor devil of a fisherman, with ten children to support, being sent out to rescue us – at the risk of losing his own life.'

To give him his due, Dickens always knew when I had reached the end of my tether. Perhaps, too, the solemn, bovine note of the foghorn had entered his subconscious.

Whatever it was, he turned without a word and led the way. I followed, picking up, here and there some of the cone-shaped cockleshells. Though reassuring to spot one from time to time, nevertheless it was quite frightening to realize, when we arrived at the top of the causeway, that I had probably lost over half of them, that they had been sucked down into the black morass below the sandy cover.

For once, Dickens had slowed so, despite my short legs, I walked ahead of my friend. He was looking from side to side, immersed in the strange, wild beauty of the landscape, whereas I was stepping out as quickly as I could, looking forward to reclaiming my little Carrie and keeping a tight hold of her until I returned her to the care of her mother.

When I reached the sands at the end of the causeway, I did not wait for him, but trudged as fast as I could up to dry land and to the place where the neat cottage stood, high above the reach of the sea. As I lifted the door knocker, I had a smile on my face. Carrie, I guessed, would not be pleased at my long absence and I rapidly prepared a story about being stolen by the fairies. She was a child of great imagination and I planned that I would buy her some of Hans Christian Anderson's fables. I imagined myself reading the *Tale of the Little Mermaid*. But first today I planned to take her in my arms and show her the sea and mist and the shimmering water-covered sands and tell her about those magical beings, those mermaids from the sea.

Mrs Taylor answered my knock with a panic-stricken look upon her face. In her hand, she held Carrie's scarlet cape and the furry hat. 'Oh, sir,' she said, her expression and voice full of anxiety and fear, 'she just went off. I turned my back for a moment, went into my bedroom to get a shawl as the fog was coming in and the damp with it, and when I came back into the kitchen and called her to help me cut the cake, she had gone. Disappeared. And without her cape or hat . . . Oh my goodness, she must be cold . . .'

She stopped abruptly, looking up into my face. I felt bewildered as the situation began to dawn on me.

'What do you mean, Mrs Taylor? Where is Carrie? Where did she go?' For a moment I wondered whether the woman was slightly forgetful, or even senile, but a glance at her sensible face told me that was not the reason.

'I was in the kitchen, attending to the cake and she was playing with the doll's house. Very taken with it, she was, rearranging all the furniture, closing and opening the little curtains that she had helped me to make. I'd been in and out to see her. And then I went to the door, just to look out and see how the mist was getting on. My man, you see, was out fishing for cockles. I couldn't hear the foghorn, but I left the door open so that if it sounded I would hear it and would be expecting the men to come home early. Then I went to get my shawl, like I told you, and went back into the kitchen. I was just sticking a knife into the cake to test it when I heard a noise at the door. I called out to her and went to look and that's when I noticed she was no longer there playing with the doll's house but had run off, out of the house.'

She stopped there and looked at me and I looked back, bewildered. 'But why would she leave, Mrs Taylor? Are you sure she's not in your house somewhere?'

She was stubborn. Like a lot of these women, she could not believe that she had got anything wrong. 'Beg your pardon, sir, but I saw her, flying down the path, she was. I couldn't follow her, not with my broken hip, sir. I just hoped you might have seen her out there on the sands.'

I didn't argue anymore as the reality of the situation hit me, but left her abruptly as fear and panic took over. Mrs Taylor was shrieking after me, calling me to return, but now there was a different tone to her voice. It chilled me. She had accepted the child was lost. Nevertheless, though the voice had been shaking with fear, now it was resolute and determined. She sounded as though she had a ray of hope to offer me, and I returned to her.

'Climb on that chair, sir,' she said with a note of authority. 'Get that horn down from the shelf. We keep it there. Every house in the place has one. If the boats are out at sea and the mist comes down over the sinking sands, or if any poor soul is lost, we call the men home with those horns.'

I was on the chair before she had finished speaking and had grabbed the enormous horn and was flying out of the house and down towards the sands where a crowd of engineers were probing with metal spikes and putting samples of mud into tin boxes. There was a depressed look upon the faces of Napier and Hope, but I had no time for their troubles now.

'Carrie is missing,' I gasped as Dickens came up the path to meet me. I sucked in a breath and raised the horn to my lips.

'Carrie! Carrie! Where are you?' I shouted, realizing with relief that it was a horn loudspeaker.

My voice wailed across the sands. Some distance out to sea a white mist hovered ominously and seemed to be drifting in our direction.

'Carrie! Carrie! Where are you?' I screamed again. There were, I knew, better voices than mine there. Dickens had a wonderfully clear and carrying voice, almost that of a trained actor. And Sir Benjamin had a voice that sounded like his namesake, Big Ben, from Westminster clock tower. But Carrie was a child who had been badly frightened and my voice would be the only one that she would heed. 'Carrie!' I screamed again. 'Shout my name.'

I took the horn from my mouth and held up a hand for silence from the rest of the crowd. All were standing very stiffly, very alert, not moving, their eyes upon the sea that was now flooding the sands, coming in at an almost unbelievable rate, conquering and covering the sands. And the mist, like a ghostly companion, hovered above it. In the distance I thought I could see the dark shape of a fishing boat. It would be, I thought, of no assistance. If a small, frail, five-year-old child were out there in that sea, she would be lost until her body was washed up upon the sands. I took in a deep breath and yelled into the horn.

'Carrie! Wave something. Wave your petticoat. Or wave your jacket. Wave it, Carrie.' In utter despair I was screaming, and my own ears cracked with the shout from the enormous horn. My eyes scanned the mist-filled monochrome of the landscape. I took off my glasses, wiped them and tried to see as they clouded up again.

But it was Sir Benjamin who saw the little signal. He was an immensely tall man. And a man of sharp observation and confident nature.

'She's there, Wilkie!' he shouted. 'Out there!'

I couldn't see what he was pointing at, but I immediately lifted the horn to my lips again. 'We see you, Carrie, we see you. Keep waving! Keep waving, Carrie! Good girl, Carrie!'

And then I saw it, the frail signal. If only she had taken her scarlet cloak, but now I could see something which was not sea, not waves, not strands of mist, but something waving, not from the land, but from where the shallow sea had swallowed up the land.

Sir Benjamin was beside me now. Provident man, he had equipped himself with a pair of binoculars which he held to his eyes.

'By Jove, Collins,' he yelled as I took the horn from my lips and gasped for breath. 'The child is on a shipwreck. Some old boat abandoned on the sand. Give me that horn, Collins.'

He had a chest depth to equal his height and breadth. He filled his lungs with air as he took the horn from me and then he directed it towards the boat coming slowly and cautiously in from the sea and heading towards land. When the words came, they almost split my eardrum.

'Ahoy, the boat!' He repeated these words three times, left a moment while he scanned the ocean and then put the horn to his lips again. When the words came, they were clear as crystal. 'Child on old shipwreck; west, north-west, from the shore. Five hundred yards, east, north-east of lighthouse.'

There was no reply from the boat, but they altered their course almost immediately and something like a fisherman's jersey waved an acknowledgement. It was a rowing boat, and every single man of its crew would now be occupied. Sir Benjamin still held onto the horn and I was glad to surrender it to him. I felt my lips tremble and there was a lump in my throat which would have made it impossible for me to shout. I hoped that brave little Carrie would be able to see that help was coming towards her from that terrifying expanse of sea. I would not distract her by calling from the land. Let her keep her eyes on the fishermen and I prayed that they would bring her comfort and the strength to hold on to the frail mast of the sunken boat.

There was not a sound from the crowd on the beach. All, like me, must be watching and praying.

Quickly I dashed tears away from my cheeks and strained my eyes to peer into the mist. The boat had a dun-coloured canvas sail, and it was only its steady movement and the splashing of the oars that made it stand out from the mist-filled sea. It was making progress, though, and from time to time a rough shout came faintly towards my ears. Whether it was encouragement to Carrie, or instructions to the oarsmen, I did not know, but whatever it was, it would signal to the child that help was coming. Let her remain quite still and focused on the fishermen. I had only known the child for a short number of days, but that had been enough time to inform me that she was fearless and resolute.

'Here, Wilkie!' Dickens was at my side and he thrust into my hands something round and hard. 'Hold on tight,' he said, and he kept his fingers closed upon mine until I tightened my grip. 'That's Henry Austin's telescope and he'll have my head if anything happens to it.'

The scene was still clouded with the heavy mist but wonderfully enlarged by the telescope, and after a minute I could see the small figure of the little girl. Yes, it was an old mast that she clung to. The rest of the wreck was not visible, however. Even in those last few minutes, the sea had made deadly progress. We had noticed, earlier, I and Dickens, that there was a deep groove around the acres of sandy beach and he had surmised that when the tide came in, that it would come in pincer-style, encircling the beach and spreading with huge rapidity over the flat sands. I could see how the little girl must have run gaily across the beach, looking for me, perhaps cross that I had taken so long to come back to her. And then, providentially, seeing the wreck, had climbed it for safety against the incoming tide. The telescope misted over, and I had to wipe it dry with the tail of my shirt. I handed it back to Dickens and he took it eagerly, frustrated, no doubt, by my silence.

'Well done! Brave fellows!' Now he was sharing his information with Sir Benjamin who had lowered the horn and held it dangling by his side. I did not ask for it back. Nothing should distract the attention of brave Carrie or of the fearless

fishermen who were going to rescue her. Could they get near,
though? How big was, or had been, that drowned wreck of a
boat whose mast Carrie had climbed to escape the incoming
tide? I prayed that those fishermen knew the answer to that
question, and I prayed that, as they crossed the water with
long sweeping strokes of the oars, they would have worked
out what they were going to do. I looked back, my eye caught
by some movement, and saw that the dunes above the beach
were filled with people, mainly women, apart from our little
expedition, but there was also a group of elderly men, retired
fishermen, standing somewhat apart and staring silently out at
the sea.

And then, over my shoulder, I heard a splash and saw the
old men turn heads to each other and appear to break into
animated conversation. I wished heartily that I were with them
and that they could tell me what was going on, but Dickens,
telescope in hand, immediately knew what was happening.

'One of them has dived into the water. Brave fellow!' he
said to Sir Benjamin, and then, to me, with rough kindness,
he said, 'Don't worry, Wilkie. These fellows know the sea.
They'll have her out in two shakes of a lamb's tail.'

They conferred together, Sir Benjamin and Dickens, in low
tones, but I did not join in the conversation. For the first time
since I was a young boy, I prayed. Prayed with all the fervour
that I could command. It was a treacherous place and I never
wanted to see it again. I should never have brought a young
child here. Dickens was right. He was a man who knew the
dangers of children and water and I could feel his tension. He
was standing very still, holding the telescope to his eye but
he made no sound, until after that long silence, he said, 'He's
out of the water, the fisherman. He's climbing onto the
shipwreck.'

And then, in the strange and almost eerie silence, when
even those who stood watching from the dunes made no sound,
there was a sudden splash.

'He's swimming with her. He's got her, Wilkie. I can see
the little jersey, still in her hand, brave child, trying to wave
it. Don't worry. He has a rope around his waist. They'll pull
him in if they need to.'

Silence. A dead silence. I dared not say a word. Just stood there with my nails biting into the palm of my hand. I strained my ears. Almost fancied that I could hear the splashing strokes of the fisherman.

'Brave fellow,' said Dickens in a low voice. 'I swear I'll give him a sovereign for this day's work.'

I said nothing. It almost seemed to be tempting fate to say anything.

And then a cheer from the boat. It came across the water, muffled in the mist, but it was picked up and amplified by those elderly fishermen on the beach who could read the signs better than we and then it was taken up and amplified by the magnificent voice of Sir Benjamin, the horn held at a slight distance from his mouth, but amplifying it and making the words clear to all as he sang, 'Brave Hearts of England'.

NINE

I would have liked, if little Carrie were older, to have entered into a conspiracy with her to keep the day's events secret from her mother. If she had been about ten years old she might have been quite happy to enter in a conspiracy of 'saving Mama from worrying', and then I could have carried it off very easily, but, unfortunately, at her age it was impossible. In fact, as soon as we came through the front door, she blurted out, 'Mama, I've been lost! A bad man pretended to be Mr Wilkie. He sounded just like Mr Wilkie, Mama! But he wasn't. He was just like the bad man with the poker! He made me run and run and I nearly drowned.' She threw herself, sobbing, into her mother's arms.

This was the story she had told me as her reason for running off from Mrs Taylor's house. Some evil man, pretending to be me, enticing her away from the house and then disappearing in the mist. The story came flooding out of her, embellished by an extra few inventions! It sounded horrendous. Out there in the hall, with me standing there, feeling like a criminal, unable to reassure her mother. There had been terrible danger and I could not deny that. Beneath her warm cape, the child was dressed in the clothes provided by the kind Mrs Taylor as her own clothes, sopping wet, were carried by me in a canvas bag. For even the most casual of mothers it would have been a frightening moment. For Caroline, still trembling with nerves at every raised voice from the street and at every knock upon my door, it was as if her most terrible fears had come to life again. It seemed as though her tormentor, the man who mesmerized her, had tried to kill her beloved little daughter.

Caroline did not ask any questions, but I knew that they were in her mind and I knew also that she had connected this mysterious voice with the man who had mesmerized her, and with the voice that little Carrie had heard at my dinner table. Her eyes were wide with fear and with suspicion. She shrank

away from me. If the night had not fallen and if the streets
had not worn their ghostly, lamp-lit aspect, she would, I think,
have snatched the child and run out through the front door.
As it was, she just lifted her little daughter in her arms and
took her, without a word to me, right into the room that I had
given to her. After the door had closed, I heard the key turn,
locked securely with a loud click, and then the rattle of the
bolt.

That night, Caroline did not come to my bed and I did not
blame her. She and the child were tucked in together, sleeping
peacefully, no doubt. I rose a few times in the night and listened
at the door, my ear to the keyhole, and there was no sound
from either.

But the next day, also, she was silent and apprehensive. I
remembered, uneasily, that I had left some money in the drawer
of the kitchen table, telling her that it was there in case she
needed anything when I was out. I feared that she and little
Carrie would disappear from my life if I left them alone, would
take a cab and go off to some other part of London where
they could hire a night's lodgings. So I hung around the kitchen
asking needless questions about supplies and equipment and
getting absent-minded answers. She wore the look, I had to
admit, of a deeply frightened woman. She even refused
permission to her daughter to go out with me for a walk in
the park. And shuddered at the very idea that she, also, might
accompany me.

'That child needs fresh air and exercise, and she needs other
children to play with,' Dickens had said to me. And as he was
a father of ten children, I felt uneasily that he must know what
he was talking about. But now, today, was not the time for
me to try to convince Caroline that her little daughter should
come for a walk with me. As for other children, that was a
difficult point. I had friends with children, but would they be
happy to send them to play with the housekeeper's daughter?

'You won't ask these men to this house again, will you?'
It was the first sentence that she had addressed to me and, of
course, I had to hasten to reassure her. At the moment, I would
say anything – anything to tide us over the next few days. I
felt as though I could not possibly plan further ahead than

that. It would, though, be awkward if I could never ask visitors to the house again, just in case one of them might be the man whom she dreaded, the man who had power over her. I said all that I could think to say to reassure her. I exaggerated my connections with the police. Took Dickens' friend, Inspector Field, as a close friend of my own. Told her that this wicked man would not dare to come near me or my household.

And then, when that did not seem to be making an effect upon her, I changed my tone and I told her it would be a good idea if she could see them, all of whom had been on Maplin Sands that day, and then she would be able to reassure her daughter that none of them was the terrible, poker-wielding villain who had mesmerized her and kept herself and her child locked up in his house. I promised her that we would invite everyone here one day next week. I even promised that I would put a screen in front of the door so that she could hide there and listen to the voices, but she began to shudder so violently that I abandoned my efforts and concentrated on soothing her and making promises that I would not force her to do anything that she disliked the idea of. 'Cross my heart and hope to die!' I said dramatically, copying a phrase that I had seen in a cartoon in an American newspaper.

It did not make her laugh, however, and I abandoned my efforts in despair. It was not something that I could put up with for ever, though. I could not change my whole way of living. I liked people, had lots of friends, could not cut myself off from them. Caroline would have to be reassured, would have to be brought to see that her fears were groundless. I even, though I rather disliked the man, contemplated asking Inspector Field to one of my dinners held for those engineers and Sir Benjamin Hall and getting the policeman to cast an eye over the company.

I pondered on the matter for a few hours and then, since it was now half past one and the magic hour of two o'clock in the afternoon was the time when Dickens would have ceased his meticulously observed five-hour session of writing, I took myself off in the direction of Tavistock House and met him at the doorway, stick in hand, all ready for a walk.

'How's my little friend, the butler?' he asked before we had gone through the gate. Typical Dickens! Having bestowed the name of the butler on Carrie, he was probably going to obstinately stick to that for the rest of her life.

'She's getting over it,' I said. 'It's her mother that's the problem. Trying to get me to promise never to allow any of those men, including you, I suppose, into my house again.'

Dickens whistled. He had a wonderful whistle, loud, shrill and very penetrating – so much so that, to my embarrassment, a passing cabbie slowed his horse and looked enquiringly down at us. Dickens beamed up at him and waved him on with a magnificent flourish and the cabbie saluted us with his whip and a smile of recognition and went on, doubtless to tell his wife and his friends about his encounter with the great novelist.

I waited impatiently. When Dickens whistled like that it meant that he was thinking hard. After a few minutes he pronounced judgement.

'I'll tell you what I think, Collins,' he said majestically. 'I think that prince who rescued the long-haired Rapunzel from the tower, the one that let down her hair and allowed the prince to swarm up it, you remember the story, don't you – well, to my mind he landed himself in a load of trouble with a girl like that. And, though I hate to say it, my dear friend, I think that you've done the very same thing. Pay her off, Wilkie, my friend, pay her off. You'll have nothing but trouble from a woman like that. Though I must say that the little girl is a lovely little thing. I wonder, could I adopt her? I've got too many boys and my two girls are grown-up young ladies now.'

'Don't be ridiculous, Dickens,' I said, rather coldly. 'Caroline is an excellent cook and I propose to keep her and to keep her child. I would just like to reassure her. I think that it is all a piece of imagination on the part of little Carrie. She was afraid she would get into trouble for wandering off to look for me and she made up that story.'

'Maybe,' said Dickens. He sounded thoughtful and I could see that he was thinking hard. He strode ahead so quickly that I knew his mind was working fast. I did my best to keep up but felt myself puffing like a steam engine. After a minute or two, though, he stopped dead and faced me. 'I've an idea, Wilkie,' he said, and he sounded so excited that I began to feel hopeful.

'What do you say to me mesmerizing her – mesmerizing your Caroline? If she has once been mesmerized by a man showing her his ring – if you believe that part of the story, and I can see that you do – well, if she has been successfully mesmerized, then that means that it would be easy to mesmerize her myself. And I, my dear friend, let me tell you, am exceptionally gifted in mesmerizing women. I'll get everything out of her – even things that were in the back of her mind without her knowing about them. Don't worry, my friend. I know what I am doing when it comes to mesmerizing,' he finished.

'Yes, I know,' I said, and allowed a note of hesitation to come into my voice. Dickens, I knew, had, according to himself, successfully mesmerized his wife and his sister-in-law, and, also, a woman friend out in Genoa who had been suffering from nerves. Perhaps it would work. Perhaps Caroline would be stimulated to produce a coherent description of this man who had taken her and imprisoned her and kept her as his slave.

'How did you do it?' I asked. 'Not Catherine or your sister-in-law, but what about that woman out in Genoa. How did you mesmerize her?'

'It wasn't difficult.' Dickens had picked up a shade of doubt in my voice and was now inclined to deny me the satisfaction of hearing the details.

'Not for you,' I said swiftly. 'But for anyone else, I'm sure it would be impossible.'

I said no more, just pretended to mull over the phenomenon which was Charles Dickens, a man gifted with so many talents and abilities. It worked, of course. He forgot about Caroline.

'Poor woman,' he said in a contemplative fashion. 'I suppose she had been suffering for years when I met her. Her poor husband, also. She may well have been a comely woman when he met her first, but by the time that I met her, her face was a caricature, convulsed every few minutes with the most terrible spasms.'

'A tic, is that what you would call it?' I asked. He had

stopped, with one of those meditative expressions on his face and I hastened to recall him before he went off on a tangent.

'Only the ignorant call it that,' he said with a crushing verdict upon my knowledge of the world. But then, to my relief, he went on. 'That poor woman, Collins, was a victim of the most terrible anxiety. Trembled with fear at the slightest noise, but that was nothing compared to the inner demons which attacked her continuously. Well,' continued Dickens, 'as soon as I saw her and realized how much she was suffering, I had to have a word with her husband, told him that I felt that I could cure his wife. And, of course, he immediately entrusted her to me. I placed her upon a hillside – in her mind, of course – and then between us, we peopled the hillside, all with people that she knew and trusted and those people walked to and fro, some singing softly, others talking in low voices, saying cheerful encouraging things, admiring the sky, the sun, the song of birds and the scent from the flowers that grew from the grass beneath their fields. And gradually,' said Dickens with a sharp eye upon me, 'she improved. She slept after our walk upon that imaginary hillside. And then she began to sleep at night. Something that her extreme anxiety had previously prevented. I must have treated her many, many times, and did good to the poor woman, until, unfortunately, my dear, loyal wife decided to become jealous, and I had eventually, for the sake of peace in my home, to give up this practice which was so beneficial to that poor woman.'

His face had clouded over with a dark expression of anger and resentment and I hastened to distract him.

'And how would you rouse a woman from a trance that you put her into, Dickens?' I asked and at the note of genuine interest in my voice, he regained his self-possession.

'Not difficult,' he said with a lofty expression. 'I just sit quite near to her, exactly in front of her, and I reach out and stroke her eyebrows, quite gently, using my forefinger only, just gentle strokes until comprehension dawns.'

No wonder poor old Catherine, possessive and unsure of her brilliant husband, felt jealous, I thought, but I said nothing, just bowed my head in silent admiration.

I allowed a few moments of that silence to elapse and

thought about it. This Madame de la Rue, by all accounts that I had heard from mutual friends, had probably been deeply in love with Dickens and so the mesmerizing had worked very well for her. A strong will had prevailed over a weak and neurotic woman. Somehow, I didn't think that it would work with the reserved and self-contained Caroline. Certainly not at this moment when she did not know the man. Perhaps later if it appeared that a good relationship had sprung up between them.

But what would it reveal? I wasn't sure that I wanted to know. As long as mother and child grew in trust of me, became happy and relaxed in my company and that this lovely Caroline cheered my life with her beauty, her companionship and, eventually, her love, well, I really didn't want to know about the past.

For the present I would have to make sure that without alarming her in any way I found out who was the man who had done this to her. People like David Napier were not friends – they were barely acquaintances – and it would cost me nothing to give up their company. I would, however, be relieved to know a name, to fit a face and a voice to this nightmare situation in which the woman and her child had been lodged.

At that stage I didn't think about the police, or about retribution. I just wanted my relationship with both to sail into untroubled waters and for no nightmare past to intrude itself into the pleasant life which I was planning. In the meantime, Dickens had to be placated and to be kept on my side.

'I think that might work, Dick,' I said, 'if you could spare the time, but it might be best to wait a few days or perhaps a week, wait until she settles in with me.'

'You are probably right.' To my relief, he sounded almost glad of the prospect of an indeterminate delay. He was, I knew, extremely busy, totally involved in his latest novel, while producing a magazine, caring for his ten children and running a hostel, Urania Cottage, for destitute girls, and it had been good of him to offer. I turned over other notions in my mind, but wisely held my peace. He would, I know, come up with other solutions. Bringing a problem to Charles Dickens was like putting a pot of small crab apples to boil. Quite soon everything was bubbling, and new ideas kept rising to the surface.

And then we met Joe Bazalgette and the problem with Caroline faded to the back of my mind. He had been walking along Farringdon but was happy to turn back and accompany us. He looked, I thought, like a man with some vision upon his mind. He listened with only half an ear to Dickens' very decided opinions about the folly of digging into the Thames to build channels to house pipes. Incredibly expensive; future generations would curse us if we left them with an everlasting necessity of doing it all over again whenever the pipes needed repairing. 'Whatever the drawbacks of the present system,' pronounced Dickens, 'at least work, if it needs to be done, can be carried out on dry land.'

And then he stopped. He had to. Bazalgette had come to a full stop in the middle of the pavement. We stood looking at him and passers-by, seeing the famous face of the best-known writer in the land, threaded their way around us without a word of protest.

'Let's have a drink,' I said. I could see that Bazalgette was bursting to unfold his ideas, but the place, the middle of a busy street, was not ideal. He needed time, space, quietness, and a solid surface, if, like most technical people, he was forced to pencil and paper to explain his ideas to those who knew nothing of engineering. Beside us was the Jerusalem Tavern, one of Clerkenwell's ancient hostelries. I led the way and they followed.

It was early in the afternoon and so we had the place to ourselves. It had originally been a property of the Templar Knights, right back in the time of King Richard I and the enormous chimney, with its smouldering logs, looked as though it might have dated from that time. The barman knew me, led us to a table, near enough to the window to keep us away from the occasional puffs of smoke, but not too far from the heat of the fire. I gave the order for three glasses of gin punch – a great favourite with Dickens and if Bazalgette didn't like it when it arrived, I had no objection to drinking two of them and getting him something else.

As I had guessed, however, he sipped it absent-mindedly, finished it up and then pushed the glass aside.

'What is the worst feature of the present system?' he said abruptly. He addressed Dickens and I didn't mind about that. If this young man was going to progress, then it was important that he sorted out the important people from the non-important like myself.

'The terrible pollution of our beautiful Thames,' said Dickens, without a moment of hesitation.

'Good,' said Bazalgette, sounding almost like an encouraging schoolmaster. 'Now, why are people thinking of piping the sewage across the Thames and into Essex? Why cross the Thames? Why not use the existing piping, replaced with concrete, of course – that metal piping is forever rusting – and using the existing routes, but don't allow them to empty into the Thames at Charing Cross, but continue the pipes downstream? Why not pipe it down to the Thames Estuary, to where the Thames meets the sea? Get rid of it into the sea itself, let it be carried off into the sea and swept on into the Atlantic Ocean. It won't pollute London from the ocean itself.'

'Yes, but have some sense, man! How can you do that? How can you put in miles of extra piping without digging up the streets in the busiest part of London: Fleet Street, the Strand, Whitehall – man alive, can't you see the problems?'

'No, I wasn't thinking of that,' said Bazalgette slowly. He took a folded notebook from his pocket, straightened it, tore a sheet from it, produced a pencil, and then sketched, rather beautifully, what was obviously a flowing river. 'Let's start with the sewers that empty into the Thames by the Strand. Here they are – most of them were little rivers originally. They flow down, bringing all the filth of the City and the West End, and from further afield, all emptying into the Thames. One of them goes under Buckingham Palace, you know – I think the queen has quite a problem with rats! Now what if we build a giant sewer here to intercept all these sewage pipes – an interceptor sewer.'

'What?' exclaimed Dickens. 'Dig up the Strand, dig up Fleet Street and don't forget to dig up Somerset House, oh and, of course, the Temple Inns – the lawyers won't mind,

will they, Wilkie? Our friend, Collins, spent years pretending
to study for the law at Temple Inn and hates the place. That's
right, Wilkie, isn't it? So, you plan to dig up a substantial area
of London, my young friend, is that it?'

Bazalgette ignored the sarcasm. 'No,' he said slowly. 'I'm
planning to dig, but not there. Not any roads, not any buildings, famous or otherwise. I've got a much better idea. Now,
just look here at this river. You've often looked at it, I'm
sure, and you've seen women and children, even quite small
children, paddling in it, so what does that tell you?'

He shot the question at me and I answered. 'It's very
shallow.'

I was beginning, I thought, to catch a drift of his idea.

'That's right. Now how about if we dredge about two
hundred feet or so down in the centre of the water? Make it
as deep as we can, emptying all the soil and sand onto the
side near to the Strand. We'll be running a giant interceptor
sewer down by the side, and as long as we leave an entrance
and a maintenance path, then we can cover it over with the
river soil. After a while, we will build up that side, build up
a flat bank between the river and the Strand. Make a new road,
well in from the river, of course, just leave a space between
that and the interceptor sewer and that space will be covered
with some sort of bank.'

'You could make it a children's playground,' I suggested. I
thought that it was a clever idea, but Dickens pooh-poohed it.

'Easily known that you don't know much about children,
Collins,' he said. 'Every one of them will start digging to get
to the sewers and will drop stones into ventilation holes and
every other piece of mischief that they can think of. I know
what I'm talking about, Bazalgette. Now, you make some
gardens there, call them "The Embankment Gardens". Plant
lots of red geraniums, my favourite flower. And benches for
old ladies and gentlemen to sit down, rest their legs and admire
the clear, limpid waters of dear old Father Thames.'

'And watch the fish jumping in the clean water,' I said,
pleased to see the flush of excitement upon Bazalgette's face.
'The Embankment Gardens', I had to admit, was a splendid
idea.

Dickens squared his shoulders in a businesslike way. 'Now, how are you going to explain this to Sir Benjamin? What have you planned?'

'Well.' Bazalgette looked down at the sheet he had torn from his notebook. 'Like this, I suppose,' he said. And then he looked from Dickens' doubtful face to mine. I said nothing, however, just left it to Dickens.

'Let me think about it.' As usual Dickens took matters into his own hands. 'In the meantime, you fix up an evening at your warehouse and . . . and, well, if I were you, I would be generous. Invite your colleagues, the other engineers along. After all, this is something that all of London should be getting their brains together over. What is it that splendid poet, John Donne, says: "No man is an island . . ."? Every man in London should want to assist in solving this terrible problem. Even the queen, God bless her, wants to be of assistance.'

And then, having reminded Bazalgette of what was at stake, and of the reward promised by Her Majesty, he downed the rest of his gin and rose to his feet. 'Well, I must be off. Have to see a man about a son.' And with that unusual expression, he was off.

I looked at Bazalgette. He wore a puzzled expression on his face, and I felt fairly sure that, though he might be a brilliant engineer, he found it hard to dream up an effective presentation. Someone would have to assist him. Dickens, perhaps, but Dickens had now started upon a new book and every ounce of creativity would be invested into this. I, Wilkie Collins, would have to dream up something which would win the support of Sir Benjamin for this splendidly exciting plan of Bazalgette's. There was certainly a touch of genius in his idea of reclaiming soil from the polluted river and using it to construct a new road as well as an effective and ornamental disguise for the ugly sewage pipes.

TEN

Carrie was rather quiet and somewhat clingy to her mother for the whole day following her adventure on Maplin Sands, but on the next day she was back to her old self and declaring, quite loudly, that she was bored and that she had nothing to do, and she was tired of playing with Noah's Ark.

'All these animals need a bit of peace and quiet. They want to have a little sleep,' she declared, and I couldn't help a smile.

'Wish I had a doll's house,' she said, encouraged by my amusement.

'Harriet!' exclaimed her mother. 'I think you are turning into a very spoiled little girl. You have plenty of toys.'

'Two isn't plenty,' said her daughter. 'Plenty has to be something like, like one hundred and two,' she added, and I beamed. She was, I thought, a clever child. Could even be good at mathematics, something that I had always hated when I was in school. I would have to find a good school for little girls. I remembered hearing a conversation at a recent dinner party about a certain Dorothea Beale. Miss Beale had taken over a school, named the Cheltenham Ladies' College, and had turned it from a place where young ladies learned to dance, sing, play the piano and curtsey gracefully, into something quite different. Apparently, this Miss Beale believed in teaching mathematics and Latin to girl pupils. And, although she had to accept that universities did not yet accept girls, she was determined that every girl in her school, who had the ability, was coached up to the standard of the newly devised entrance examinations for Oxford and Cambridge. There had been much talk between my married lady friends about how, a year or so ago, I thought, Oxford and Cambridge had started local examinations for boys' schools to make sure that all entrants to their universities were up to a certain standard and that Miss Beale, according to the ladies' conversation at the dinner table, had resolved that her girls would be coached up to that standard as well. By the time my little Carrie was eighteen years old she would be, I was sure, top of her class and ready for any examination which Oxford and Cambridge could throw at her. I smiled at the thought of her in gown and mortar board.

Turning to more practical matters, I said, 'Come for a walk, but I'll only take you with me if you promise to hold my hand all the time.' I added that to reassure the child's mother, but in any case, I planned to get a cab and take her to a toy shop. Why shouldn't she have a doll's house? I had hazy ideas about children and their requirements, but my little godson seemed, already, to have a nursery full of toys, long before he could play with any of them.

Carrie brightened up immensely when I hailed a cab and gave the name and address of the toy shop. To my surprise, once there, she rejected the doll's house. It was, of course, quite a small doll's house, nothing like that wonderfully large home-made one with which she had played when I left her in the care of Mrs Taylor. She explained carefully to the shop assistant that she would come back another day when they had lots of doll's houses in the shop for her to choose from and mentioned, in a reassuring manner, that Mr Wilkie had pots of money, something which amused the shop assistant so much that she called the manager across to listen to this very demanding little customer. He rushed around and then produced from a back room a delightful little village which took her fancy immediately.

'Very educational, sir; so good for the imagination,' he said to me as I watched with pleasure how Carrie was rearranging all the stock figures, giving the fireman a turn of duty in the post office while the post office lady was transferred to stand beside the red fire engine. 'Clever little girl,' he said loudly to the assembled assistants and all murmured exclamations of admiration.

She would, I guessed, as I watched her deliberately amuse them by saying quaint things, soon be in danger of getting quite spoiled. School would do her good, but perhaps before she went to school I should endeavour to get a governess for her. This Miss Beale with the emphasis on Latin and mathematics for her girl pupils sounded a formidable lady and she might well expect that her new pupils could, at least, be able to read and write and add up. After all, a regime of the classics and mathematics would only be successful in the case of intelligent children. For all that I knew, Carrie was already behind. I was sure that my mother had taught me to read at an earlier age than five. I seemed to remember some story about writing a letter to my father when I was four years old. Yet, I thought, a governess might not be the right person for Carrie. Carrie might run rings around a governess and the governess might retaliate by declaring that the child was backward and unteachable.

I would, I resolved, try to teach her to read and write myself. I liked the idea of that and so I left her to entertain the toy shop staff and wandered off to a corner where there were some little sand trays. My mother had taught both myself and my brother, Charley, how to write our names and to practise all the letters of the alphabet and the numerals from one to nine with these trays. I thought that I could still feel the damp grit of the sand underneath my fingernails as I traced a beautifully large letter 'W' again and again.

'I'll have one of these little sand trays,' I said, interrupting the recital of the names of the animals in Noah's Ark with which Carrie was favouring the shop assistant. 'And a large bag of sand – two bags of sand. And this one as well,' I added, spying another enormous and quite deep tray which triggered an idea in my mind.

'That tray is really for a Kindergarten, for a number of small children,' said the girl doubtfully. 'It's a bit big for an ordinary living room or bedroom, though perhaps . . .' She faltered, seeing the manager's eyes on her. Due to Carrie's artless revelations, I was now marked down as a most valuable customer, a man who had lots of money to spend and had no hesitation about spending it on toys for a demanding little girl.

'I want it for the garden. There is a wooden table there where I can put it. You'll be able to make sandcastles,' I said to Carrie, though I could see from her puzzled looks that she didn't know what I was talking about. Poor little neglected thing. The chances were that she had never been to the seaside. Now that I remembered, she had made no effort to dig in the sand by the river but had just raced up and down. By the time I was her age, I had been to the seaside hundreds of times. While my industrious father painted those seascapes, which made him a fortune, my little brother and I ran races on Camber Sands and built immense fortifications to stop the tide coming in. I would, I thought, take Carrie to that clean, sea-swept beach one day quite soon, and her mother Caroline, if possible. We would, all three, go in the train to Rye and get a cab from there to those magnificent sands.

In the meantime, however, I had another use for that enormous sand tray. 'Great George Street,' I said to the cabbie once the toy village, the two sand trays and the two bags of sand had been loaded into the cab.

'Great George Street, it is!' he said in such a flamboyant style that little Carrie mimicked it in an undertone for most of the way through the crowded streets of London. She was, I thought, a little monkey. Once again, I reminded myself that she was in danger of being quite spoilt, but I was fond of her and determined that no harm should come to her, and so I took her by the hand and held her firmly by my side while I hammered on the door of the warehouse.

To my relief the door was opened almost immediately by Bazalgette himself.

'Collins!' he exclaimed and then looked down in a worried fashion at Carrie.

'Don't worry. She has promised to hold my hand,' I said, and Carrie smiled up at him with the charm that she could turn on so easily.

'You're looking nice and dry,' he said to her, while I beckoned to the cabbie to carry in the large metal sand tray and one of the bags of sand. 'You looked like a drowned rat the last time that I saw you.'

She scowled, but then remembered her promises. 'We've got a present for you,' she said quickly.

'What on earth is that?' he asked, but I ignored him, directing
the cabbie to place the sand tray onto a large and fortuitously
empty table.

'Got such a thing as half a pipe, like a trough, I suppose,
as near to the length of the tray as possible?' I asked, thinking
that I should have tried to purchase such an object before
arriving at a busy man's door. 'Carrie and I have brought you
a present for your demonstration,' I called after him as he
went in search of a pipe. He had given a swift glance at the
tray, and when he came back he had a cylindrical piece of
wood in his hand. He measured it against the tray, nodded
with satisfaction as he saw that he had estimated the length
very exactly, and then inserted it into a machine.

'Keep the child away when I turn on the lathe,' he said.
And then to Carrie he said in expressive tones, 'I've seen a
man killed by one of these machines, so you keep well away.
It could chop a little girl in half.'

She shrank in close to me and squeezed my hand hard. I
wondered about picking her up into my arms but did not want
to distract the man in charge of such a dangerous machine and
so made sure that I had a firm grip of the little hand. Within
a few minutes, he had hollowed out the small pole, and then
he inserted it into another of his machines and the machine
neatly sliced it in half all the way down the centre so that he
was left with two long sections, rather like the trough from
which horses drink their water. One of them would, I reckoned,
stretch from one side of the metal tray to the other. This would
be my River Thames.

'Excellent,' I said. 'Now, if you turn off all those dangerous
machines, Carrie can help us. Put the trough in the centre
of the sand tray and we'll fill it and the metal tray with our
sand. But only just about halfway up the trough, this hollow,
Carrie. We're going to pretend that is the river – the River
Thames, so we need room for water on top of the sand,' I
added, and saw how Bazalgette's face lit up with a grin of
comprehension.

By the time we had patted down the sand, the edges of
the trough, which was to hold the River Thames, were
above the rest of the sand and I looked at my demonstration

model with satisfaction. There was a tap with a hose at the side of an enormous sink. I picked out a young boy and beckoned him over. 'Fill up that trough in the centre of the tray, sonny,' I said, 'and keep filling, let it flood over into the sand. Don't worry, the tray is made from metal. It will hold the water.'

I kept the boy at it until the water overflowed its trough and began to soak into the sand, kept him still at it until a film of water covered the waterlogged sand, and the whole tray shimmered like a wide river. To my satisfaction the sand still remained in the lower half of the trough. The smile on Bazalgette's face grew broader and broader. I took from my pocket one of my visiting cards. On one side, it said *Wilkie Collins*. I turned it over, and on the other side, with my pencil, I wrote in capital letters THE RIVER THAMES. I needed a banner but could see nothing suitable and so left it on the table for the moment. By now a little crowd of workers had gathered around my demonstration. I walked over to the sink. There were a couple of cracked mugs there and I returned with them to the table and handed one to Carrie and the other to the boy. And then I held up the card with THE RIVER THAMES printed upon it.

'Now, you two young engineers must scoop out the sand from the River Thames. Let's make it nice and deep,' I said. 'Just take out the sand, not the water. Fill up your cups and dump the sand anywhere on the metal tray.'

The boy did it meticulously, piling the humps near to the metal edge and smoothing them out as he went, but Carrie, becoming excited and competitive, spilled her loads higgledy-piggledy and quite soon the water in the trough grew clearer and clearer and the water in the rest of the tray began to be absorbed by the sand that was being shovelled into it, until by the time the two helpers had scraped 'the river' to be crystal clear, its 'bank' was now looking quite solid.

There was a moment's silence and then a roar of laughter from the audience. Carrie looked a little insulted, but then began to laugh herself and Bazalgette slapped me on the back. 'Wilkie, my dear chap, you are a genius.'

'My dear Joe,' I returned, 'the genius is yours. I'm just

the son of an artist with an eye for an artistic effect. And I have the best little helper in the world.'

I scooped up my little helper, gave the other helper a shining sixpenny coin and went back to the cab and returned her to her mother with her new toys to display. During all the excitement and the bustle, I slipped into Caroline's room and placed a parcel on her bed. A helpful assistant had picked out a dress, a lovely blue dress, which she told me should suit a lady with blue eyes and, since it was meant to be loose and floating, just girdled with a sash, it didn't really matter that the lady hadn't tried it on. In any case, she assured me that the dress could be returned and exchanged for another model if the lady didn't like it.

She would like it, though, I thought as I slipped it out from its package and spread it over the bed. It was a lovely shade of blue and the flounces would float along when she walked. I would say nothing, I decided. Just be quite surprised if she said anything. Pretend that I knew nothing about it. Make up a story for mother and daughter about how the fairies must have flown in with a gift.

Carrie was immensely pleased with her toy. She loved the post office with the little old lady at the door, the red-and-yellow fire station with its fireman, the vegetable shop with its owner, the butcher shop with the butcher, wearing a nice, clean, white apron. And Caroline laughed at the story of the fairies and their gift, so we all had a happy day together.

It was about a week later when Carrie summoned me into the kitchen because she had a job for me to do. She wanted me to number all her little buildings, but when it came to the church, the largest building in the village, I told her that a church never had a number upon it. She picked it up and looked at it doubtfully.

'Who lives here?' she asked.

'God,' said her mother, as she left the kitchen with some wine glasses in her hand.

Little Carrie looked at me dubiously. 'Who is God?' she asked of me.

'A big old man with a long white beard,' I said frivolously. My father had been an ultra-religious man. I had had religion stuffed down my throat from the earliest days of my childhood, had been bored by church services at an age when I could not possibly understand what was going on. I was determined that was not going to happen to any child for whom I had responsibility. 'He's not important,' I said firmly. She was, I thought, getting tired of the village, having played with it non-stop during the last week and it was time for me to institute my latest idea. I would take Carrie for a daily walk. It would do both of us good. The air in London wasn't too wonderful, but on a spring morning with the sun out and a breeze blowing it must be fairly healthy. I had mentioned my plan to Caroline earlier on and she had instantly agreed. By now, I thought, she trusted me with her little girl.

'Walk time!' I said firmly. 'Go and fetch your new cape and your furry hat,' I added when I saw that she was about to object. She did like that scarlet cape and everyone in the shop, where I had spent such a lot of money, had admired it immensely.

By the time that I came back with my own coat, hat and walking stick, she was already buttoned into her coat by Caroline, and off we went.

'Where are we going?' she asked. It was a good question, and I was stuck for an answer. I had thought of walking around the streets for about a quarter of an hour and then turning to go back home again. But that, I thought, might not suit a child. The idea of exercise was probably alien to her. I pretended to think hard, dramatically stopping in the middle of the pavement and closing my eyes while prodding my forehead with my forefinger.

She giggled. She was an enchanting child, I thought. So easy to amuse.

'I know where we'll go,' she announced. 'I knowd it all the time, but I kept it a secret. Let's go and visit Mr Bazalgette again and then he can see that I am still nice and dry and warm.'

I thought about that for a second or two. Bazalgette was a busy man and would probably not welcome morning visitors. On the other hand, Great George Street was just about fifteen minutes away and, I told myself, we need not stay long. Just

a minute or two and then we could go back again. It would
be an excellent start to my resolution to take more fresh air
and exercise for myself as well as for her.

Of course, she had an ulterior motive. Carrie, even at the
age of five, always had a clear mind and very definite ideas
about what she wanted. As soon as we had been admitted to
the warehouse and while I was explaining the situation apologetically to Bazalgette, she whipped out the miniature church
from her pocket.

'That can go on your riverbank,' she told him, placing the
little building on top of the sand. 'It's a church and God lives
there, and I don't want him in our house,' she added carelessly and was delighted when the cluster of workers started
to laugh.

'It looks just perfect there,' said Bazalgette.

Carrie looked demurely up at him. 'I like you and I like
Mr Wilkie, but I don't like God.' And then she beamed at
Bazalgette's assistant, Andy Wainwright, who was admiring
the little church, picking it up in his hand and feeling its
weight, and she informed him that she liked him, also, much,
much more than God, who was a horrible old man with a long
white beard and a poker to beat people.

'We'd better go,' I said hastily. The little church, I thought,
did look rather good on the riverbank and I whispered to
Bazalgette to keep it for the moment. I would remove it after
the exhibition next Friday. Children being children, by next
Friday she would probably want her church back to provide
the finishing touch to her village.

'See you Friday,' I said aloud. 'I'll be along just after my
dinner. Don't worry. You'll wipe the floor with them all.' I
crossed my fingers for luck as I said that. It would be a
wonderful thing for Joe Bazalgette to win the award and
a knighthood. His scheme, I thought, was by far the best.
This business of tunnelling under the Thames was too difficult and London city and its outskirts could not stand any
more digging up of its streets to lay new pipes. The metal
pipes and small rivers, at the moment, all carried sewage
into the Thames and the Thames had to be preserved from
such pollution. Bazalgette's scheme to dig out the river and

built a new system on the bank, then cover it with sand and gardens, would solve most of London's problem. The demonstration next Friday evening would, I hoped, be successful.

ELEVEN

Dickens invited himself to dinner with me on that auspicious Friday evening. We would, he said carelessly in a note to me, be good company for each other afterwards on the walk to Great George Street. For a moment I was slightly annoyed, but then I began to be sorry for him. Despite the shortness of the letter, there was a slightly lonely note, a plea for company.

Poor Dickens! There was, I couldn't help knowing, serious trouble between himself and his wife, Catherine. He was the most obstinate man in the world, having got it into his head that his wife, who had borne him ten children, had insulted the actress Ellen Ternan and her mother, and had refused to believe a husband who had done so much for her during more than twenty years of marriage. Everything had piled up and he had resolved to separate himself from her, telling all and sundry that it was the last straw, sharing rather stupidly his matrimonial troubles with the world. His pride and his determination to protect the reputation of Mrs Ternan prevented him from telling the whole truth. In fact, I think that I was the only one of his friends who knew the true story about Ellen Ternan.

Of course, being Dickens, he did not just move quietly out of the family home but demanded that Catherine, having so deeply and terribly misjudged her husband after twenty years of marriage, should be the one to move out, should live in an apartment that he bought for her and should have the company of their eldest son, while Catherine's sister, Georgina, remained to look after the rest of the large family of her nieces and nephews. He had, I knew, made a very generous settlement upon Catherine, but the feeling of most of those who knew the couple was of deep sympathy for the woman. Catherine was a good-natured, kind woman. She had never been right for Dickens, not after the first few years, but that, I felt, was no excuse for Dickens' behaviour and I determined to stay friends with both husband and wife.

In the meantime, though, Dickens shunned his own house and spent long hours at the office. He even rigged up the top storey as a 'bachelor's quarters' where he could occasionally spend the night.

And he dined out as often as possible. I was delighted to have him.

Caroline, I hoped, would be less shy, less retiring with just one guest and Dickens made such a pet of her daughter, encouraging her to give her opinions about everything and playfully addressing her as the butler, that I thought Caroline's motherly feelings would get the better of her diffidence with strangers. I lingered with him in the hall, inviting Carrie to show him her new bedroom and the shelves where the toys were very neatly arranged now, I noticed, and guessed that her mother had been in to make order amongst the chaos. The Noah's Ark was now on a tray, and the toy village upon another. Dickens and I agreed that we were both tempted to play with one of those enticing displays and Dickens teased Carrie about a plan to steal a plaything when she was asleep. She sedately told him that he might be allowed to borrow if he asked politely and made sure to look after it carefully and not lose anything.

Then we went into the dining room and drank some of the wine which I had carefully decanted. Carrie came too and brought some of her Noah's Ark creatures to make the table look nice. Dickens entertained her by singing the old nursery rhyme song 'Who Built the Ark' and she happily joined in with the chorus of 'Noah, Noah.' It was a very homely scene, and it would have been easy for Caroline to have joined us.

She didn't, though. She served up a delicious dinner, but I carried it in and carried out the plates when we had finished, lingering for a while, telling her how much Dickens enjoyed her cooking and how he said that he would have liked to thank her in person, but she looked at the door in such a terrified fashion that I had to hasten to tell her that he wouldn't come in, unless she was happy for him to do so.

She shook her head, told me that she had left the cheese

and a cold dessert on the sideboard and then whispered to me that she wasn't well and that she and the child would go to bed early and that she would do the dishes later.

I suggested that I should send a messenger to fetch the parlour maid who came a couple of times a week, but she refused absolutely, got almost hysterical at the idea.

So, I left Dickens with a carafe of wine, scooped up his little 'butler' and deposited her in her mother's arms. Caroline was pale and heavy-eyed, with dark shadows under her eyes and obviously in need of a good night's sleep, so I took her into my room, gave her some of my own supply of laudanum and told her that it would help her to sleep. I mixed the dose myself, carefully putting in less than half of what I would take myself. She would drink it down, she said. She would sleep for a couple of hours, would be better by then and would be able to do the dishes. She was so agitated that I gave up arguing and allowed her to do as she wished.

Little Carrie was sleeping well these days. We took a daily walk to different parts of London and the pallor had begun to fade from the child's face. She was an entertaining companion, immensely enjoying a visit to the real River Thames, looking with great interest at the enormous buildings of King's College, Somerset House and of the Savoy, and seeming to understand how the sand could be scooped out of the river and piled up to make a foundation for the new road, named the Embankment, and how the piles of sand would be covered with grass and plants which would hide all the ugly pipes, but could easily be dug up if the pipes needed to be repaired. On that very day, I had taken her for an even longer walk and showed her a real church, St Mary Le Strand Church, and we had finished our walk at Great George Street and even peeped in from the door as I told her how all these men were going to come and sit on the chairs that one of the apprentices was setting out and watch Mr Bazalgette explain the idea of digging out the big River Thames and making it deep and narrow, and how everyone would see her church on the riverside. It would be, I told her, a model for the real church, St Mary Le Strand, and would help to make everyone understand Mr Bazalgette's plans. She had nodded gravely with an air of understanding

all, though she turned a deaf ear to my suggestion of lending
some more little buildings.

We took a cab home but, even so, it had been a long walk
for five-year-old legs and as soon as she had her supper she
had gone off to bed without any protest. When I looked in on
her before Dickens and I went off to walk to the warehouse,
she was now curled up, fast asleep, Teddy in her arms, the
two of them forming a satisfactory hump under the bedclothes.

'You go to bed, too. Leave the dishes until the morning.
Leave them for a week. Who cares?' I said to Caroline and was
glad to see a ghost of a smile come over her face. She was
genuinely ill, though. I could see the pallor of her face and the
heaviness of her eyes. It would do her good to have a few hours'
sleep. The laudanum which she had taken was already beginning to work. I could see that. She was, I guessed, anxious to
have the house to herself and her sleeping child, so Dickens
and I set off a little earlier than I had planned. He was pleased
to do that, checking his watch and telling me that we could
make a quick visit to his office in Wellington Street as he
wished to have a word with his manager about some details
concerning the weekly magazine *All the Year Around*.

The visit to Wellington Street took longer than I had
expected. Dickens was meticulous about the stories that he
published. Any contributing author had to get used to having
his work scrutinized and alterations made, again and again,
until Dickens was satisfied with the result and was able to
assure the original writer of the work that the story was now
far, far better.

So, we were one of the last to arrive at the warehouse in
Great George Street. Everyone was milling around, inspecting
the works. All his fellow engineers, or competitors, were there,
as was Bob Smith, his landlord, all dressed up for the occasion
in a very stylish suit with a diamond tiepin stabbed through
his necktie. Sir Benjamin Hall was there and so, to my annoyance, was Disraeli. He soon wandered up to the seats in the
gallery where I lost sight of him. I had wondered whether Joe
Bazalgette would corral his guests in the safety of the gallery
upstairs and send the others up to join Disraeli, but he didn't.
Wanted them nearer to him, wanted it to be less of a lecture

and more of an experimental enterprise, I supposed. Not too
many people, of course. There were some chairs at a safe
distance from the machines, and a few more up in the gallery,
but most were left unoccupied for the moment while the guests
clustered around Bazalgette, examined the wonderfully complicated machines and nodded wisely at the names of Peaucellier's
Parallel Motion, Bucket chains, Archimedes' screws, the
Centrifugal Governor, and my personal favourite, the Boomer
Double Screw Toggle Press. It was a warm night with no wind,
and once the Boomer had been set going, the warehouse began
to smell of smoke and to become rather airless, even though
the top windows of the warehouse had been opened.

Bazalgette had prepared some refreshments at the bottom
end of the warehouse, some rather inferior wine and a plateful
of cakes, but the engineers ate and drank heartily and so did
I, though I noticed Dickens sauntering over to the sink and I
guessed that he disposed of his wine while pretending to
admire the little model, which now had a splendid noticeboard
propped up on a stand with THE RIVER THAMES written
in enormous black letters across it. Carrie's little church stood
on the bank quite near to the enormously wide expanse of the
river and now, to my astonishment, I saw the little fire station
as well. Had Dickens surreptitiously removed it before we
departed? I wondered.

Once all had their fill of cakes and wine, Bazalgette ushered
us all to the top of the warehouse and opened the evening by
demonstrating his brick tunnel coated with Portland cement
which had been placed in an empty bath, balanced on a couple
of bricks, and was to be tested as a reliable drainpipe. Two of
the boys were armed with buckets to empty the bath when it
began to fill up, and then the demonstration began. One of the
apprentices hosed the surface of the Portland cement, moving
the hose up and down and even increasing the velocity of the
water by placing his thumb over the nozzle of the hose and
enjoying himself immensely by directing a powerful jet of
water at the white surface of the drainpipe and surreptitiously
spraying his companions from time to time. When enough
water had sprayed upon the drainpipe, the bath was completely
emptied and volunteers were invited to test the pipe surface

with their fingers and see how resistant the Portland cement
was to water.

After this excitement, Bazalgette gave a long explanation of
his idea of an interceptor sewer, during which I scanned the
warehouse and saw with pleasure that by now more people
had arrived through the open door and that there were quite a
number in the audience up in the gallery including some women
– wives of engineers, no doubt.

Next came, from my point of view, the most interesting
part of the evening. First, Bazalgette gave a talk about the
problems of maintenance of pipes – quite a good talk, I
thought. Not too many technical details, but a lot about the
inconvenience to the public when roads had to be dug up to
repair the pipes that ran beneath them. There were quite a few
murmurs of 'Hear! Hear!', a few laughs and exaggerated shud-
ders of horror from the gallery as he detailed the disgusting
work that the mudlarks were forced to do with the present
system and of the terrible danger to health and to drinking
water that system caused. After that short preamble, Bazalgette
began to explain his brilliant idea about dredging out the River
Thames.

Perhaps deprecating the rather childishness of the sand tray
model, he then handed the explanations over to the elder of
his two apprentices and the boy made an excellent hand of it,
speaking in a loud and confident voice, displaying the expanse
of river, where the water filled up the entire sand tray. He was
a very competent boy and far outdid my original explanation
by being able to name the machines that would be used to
dredge out the real River Thames instead of the two metal
scoops which he and his companion were about to use. Some
of the explanations were a little too technical for me and I
lost track from time to time.

Nevertheless, I admired the way that the two boys made an
excellent display of the whole process, energetically excavating
the sand from the trough which represented the river and
winding up with a simulation of a narrow and deep River
Thames and a wide expanse of sand. They had improved upon
my model by laying a long strip of canvas, painted with hardened cement, to simulate, they announced, a new road to be

called 'The Embankment' which would run on top of the
embankment, between the river and the road named 'The
Strand'. The model of the church had been slightly raised by
being placed on a small mound of sand, and the fire station
was placed a good foot away and on top of another little
mound. I was still puzzling over where the fire station had
come from. Perhaps one of the apprentices had that model
village in an old toy box at home and had decided to add it
to Carrie's church on the Strand. I imagined I could see a
number on it – the number I had written on it for Carrie, I
told myself – but my eyesight was poor, so I could not be
sure.

Bazalgette's evening was proving to be a great success, I
thought, looking around at the faces of the audience as people
clapped and laughed. Even Disraeli had deigned to come down
and examine the model at close quarters. Cautiously, and
without making any disturbance, step by step I moved nearer,
but could not get close enough to see whether there was a
number on the little building. But, yes, it did look like Carrie's
fire station. Worriedly I scanned the crowd, but there was no
sign of a little girl, though there were several little boys. I put
the matter from my mind. That shop may have sold hundreds
of those toy villages, I reasoned. One of the apprentices might
have a little brother or sister and had borrowed one of the
little buildings to enhance the embankment. Forget it, I told
myself and, as always, those words worked as well with me
as a dose of laudanum. Another bad habit of mine, but removing
worries from my mind allowed me to present a calm and
relaxed face to the world around me.

The model of the proposed river and embankment was
going down extremely well, and I congratulated myself on
my idea. Once the murmur of excitement had died down at
the sight of a new road on top of that surplus sand, the
apprentices then built up the gardens by heaping the sand into
little piles and solemnly sticking a few clumps of grass and
some daisies and buttercups into them, and again the audience
showed its appreciation by clapping and laughing.

'Ladies and gentlemen,' said one of the boys, 'behold
London's latest road, The Embankment, and behold The

Embankment Gardens which disguise the pipes and the
Interceptor Sewer from the public.'

There was a cheer from the audience at this and then the
two boys, shepherded by the assistant Andy Wainwright,
bowed to the audience and retreated to a place at the back of
the crowd. Now came the more serious part of the evening as
Bazalgette stepped forward and began to explain the machines
that he would use to dredge the real River Thames and turn
it from a meandering estuary into a much narrower and
deeper river, less than half its present width, only about a
quarter of a mile wide instead of almost a mile, according to
Bazalgette.

By now the smell from these combustion engines had heated
up the warehouse, and the air was much warmer and stuffier
than when we had arrived on this unusually mild spring
evening. I'm not sure who had opened the doors to the road.
It was a relief, though, as the doors were about fifteen feet
high and quite wide enough for the largest loads to be pushed
into the warehouse. It made the place much brighter, also, as
the lamps in the warehouse were mainly clustered around the
machines and now that night was falling little light fell on
the rest of the warehouse.

And, of course, human nature being what it is – naturally
curious – the open doors brought a new and expanded audience. The crowd clustered around the doors had initially been
the usual small boys, but now quite a crowd of men and a few
women had joined them. There were also some small children,
not many, but lots of babies in arms. A few of these new
spectators ventured over the threshold, mainly the better
dressed and more self-assured. Some stayed near to the doors,
but others climbed the steps to the gallery. Only the street
urchins, who had, so often, been warned off, stayed obediently
outside, and the efficient Andy Wainwright and one of the
apprentices came and tied a rope across the open entrance. As
far as I noticed, none of these shabbily dressed little boys
ducked under or stepped over the rope and they were doing
no harm, seeming to watch with interest. I saw Bazalgette
glance at them a few times, but he was a fanatic, hugely
interested in his subject, determined to communicate to all

minds the engineering problems of solving 'the Great Stink of London', and so he ignored their presence.

Andy Wainwright, however, had a better idea. He summoned the apprentices and organized the moving of the heavy table with the model of the new embankment road and its gardens and placed in front of the crowd of eager small boys at the open door. It made an additional barrier, but even more importantly it kept people's interest focussed at a safe distance from the machine. I smiled to myself as I saw some of the audience sidle over to be near to the model, including a lady with a small boy, wearing a cap and well wrapped up in a warm coat.

Bazalgette, though, was in his element. Many of these machines had been invented by him, with the dredger being the most important part of his plan. He explained how the dredging of the River Thames would work efficiently and effectively by using a machine which didn't just scoop out the sandy, polluted mud, but could fling it at a distance – a sufficient distance so that the water could not reclaim it again. This was, I gathered, the kernel of his plan. I was amused to see, though, when looking away, that my sand tray and the model of the embankment still had quite a crowd around it – in fact, the audience was almost divided into two sections. And all the time, more people were walking along the street, stopping to peer in through the door. In fact, there was huge interest from the crowd outside. I was glad that my sand tray and Carrie's little model of a church were close to the crowd and I heard a few gasps and murmurs as the two apprentices, at Andy Wainwright's instruction, whispered explanations about the whole process to the crowd, and even the small boys at the door were silent and attentive and did not attempt to encroach upon the workshop within.

It was, I noticed, with a quick glance at my watch, now about eight o'clock in the evening and the lights of Great George Street were being lit by a lamplighter carrying his ladder from one streetlight to another. It made, I thought, an interesting scene, something that only a great painter could have done justice to. The crowd of urchins and working men outside, and inside the cluster of men in evening dress, top hats, overcoats, white shirtfronts, and intent faces – all staring at the strange machines which spluttered and whirred with an occasional harsh grinding sound.

'Stand well back, everyone,' said Bazalgette. 'Now, this is the dredging machine. Of great importance to all of us, gentlemen. No matter whose scheme is adopted, dredging will be needed. Let me introduce the Robinet, gentlemen!' he said with a flourish. 'This works by using low fall and large quantity – as you can understand, I'm sure, the effect is gained by low pressure acting on a double-acting piston. The valve, of course, is reversed by the motion of the engine. Keep well clear, gentlemen. This is highly dangerous, and no one wants a weight like that iron bucket on the top of their head.'

At this everyone on the ground floor stood back hastily, while those in the gallery got to their feet and craned their heads over the balcony railings.

Sir Benjamin's voice boomed out above the noise of the engine. 'Good way of getting rid of all your enemies, Bazalgette – bang them on the head! That would be the way, wouldn't it?' he said.

Everyone laughed, including those up on the gallery, but there was a slight uneasiness in the company and I, having no false pride, moved myself to the back of the crowd. I couldn't see so well from there, but I didn't worry. These machines with their strange names; their snorting, stinking, deafening performances were beginning to pall as an evening's entertainment, and I wished that I had slipped away after seeing the success of my sand tray and gone over to Covent Garden and watched Macready play his magnificent version of 'King Lear' using Shakespeare's original words and plot.

I lost some of the intervening explanations and only came back to consciousness of my surroundings when Bazalgette told everyone to stand back. There really was a big crowd there, many now up in the gallery, standing behind the rails and looking down. It was a fine evening, very warm for the time of the year and few wore coats or cloaks. I even thought I glimpsed the pale blue flounce of a woman's dress up there behind the bars, and a small boy in a cap beside her.

Bazalgette gave an approving glance up at the gallery and

then a worried glance at those who pressed so closely around him. Once again, he ordered them to stand back, this time with a sharp note of authority in his voice. I wondered why he did not wear some protective headgear himself, perhaps something like an iron mask or a steel helmet, but reckoned that he probably understood his own machines and trusted to his own skill. I obeyed his instruction though and stepped well back, leaving quite a space for those ahead of me to move out of harm's way.

All did so, except Bob Smith, the landlord, who, dressed in his best suit, had stood by his tenant's side throughout the whole evening and seemed to take a proprietorial interest in all these strange machines. Instead of standing back, the man moved a little closer, but slightly out of the sight line between Bazalgette and his audience. By now, I thought, with some amusement, the portly landlord fancied himself as a fully-fledged engineer and what looked like a most expensive suit, silk neck cloth, fancy diamond pin and sparkling ring were all donned to make him worthy of the part.

Knowing that Dickens would doubtless want to talk about it all as we walked home, I tried to listen and understand as Bazalgette embarked upon an explanation of how he would show the difference between an ordinary screw press and a hydraulic press by demonstrating first with a Screw Fly Press and then with my favourite machine, The Boomer, telling everyone to observe very carefully the central isosceles triangle. This here was a tall, thin example of that mathematical expression which I remembered from my unhappy school days, and I started thinking about that appalling maths teacher whom I loathed and rather lost the thread of Bazalgette's explanation of its triangular shape being important in something to do with pressure. Surreptitiously I stuck my fingers in my ears and waited for The Boomer to live up to its name.

The scream that sounded out at that moment could not have been blocked by anything as petty as a finger in the ear. It was a shocking sound. High-pitched and full of agony. I felt my heart thud as I strained to see what had happened. Joe Bazalgette was still there, had leaped aside, but was standing looking down at the floor. And then a man in front of me shifted and I could see the horror; I could suddenly see what was causing the cacophony of screams from the gallery.

On the floor was a body, twisted into an animal-like shape, drenched in blood. As I watched in horror, the fountain of blood which had squirted astonishingly high in the air began to waver, to diminish and then finally stop. It all happened so quickly that nothing could have been done, and even I, with no medical knowledge, no experience of fatal accidents, knew that the victim's heart had stopped and the man on the floor was now dead. It was at this point that I registered the identity of the body on the floor. It was Bob Smith, Bazalgette's amenable, flamboyantly attired landlord. The jovial elderly man who had so kindly provided us with our picnic and had amused us all by his intense interest in his tenant's inventions.

Bazalgette was standing next to the landlord's body, quite upright, quite shocked, and very white-faced, looking down as the blood sluggishly oozed from the man's neck and then ceased to flow. Andy Wainwright was standing beside his master, also looking down at the mangled body. Then Andy turned away, grabbed at one of the apprentices near him and began to shout, his voice shaking, 'Get a doctor, Harry – run outside, ask where the nearest doctor is, though God help him, I think he is past any help from man. And then when the doctor is on the way, go on until you find a policeman. No,' he contradicted himself, 'no, get the policeman first. Tell him that we've had a terrible accident. Go on, scoot! Tom, you go with him. Keep together, the two of you.'

Then, with a quick glance at his master's dazed face, Andy Wainwright began to organize the crowd, ordering, appealing, escorting them, and soon he had everyone moved back from the gory scene and as many as possible sitting upon the chairs that had been lined up in a row for the visitors. Others went back up the stairs towards the gallery, meeting those coming down and stopping to talk with that instinct to gather around the scene of a disaster that seems to be in all Londoners.

I evaded Andy and took a few tentative steps forward towards Joe Bazalgette. The man's face was a deadly shade of white and he looked as though he were about to faint. I resolved to

take his arm and bring him to a seat, but he waved me away
with bad-tempered impatience.

'Get that door shut, for God's sake. Keep those children
out of here.' It was a sensible thing to do. I should have thought
of it myself. I went towards the door, followed by Dickens,
and then Andy and one of the apprentices followed, and
between us all we managed to get the crowd to stand back as
we rolled the doors forward in their groves and gradually shut
the crowd outside the door. Andy went back inside, but I stayed
with some vague idea of manning the door and keeping the
crowd under control, and I slipped out into the street, keeping
my back to where the two doors met. No one, I resolved in a
fuzzy fashion, would get past me, though I soon found the
task beyond me and gave up the struggle. The crowd was quite
dense by the time that the first policeman arrived, and he was
soon followed by a cab-load from Scotland Yard, led by
Dickens' friend, Inspector Field. I thankfully handed over my
task as doorman to the police force and went back inside to
look for Dickens.

The inspector was an efficient operator here on his patch
in London. I had to admit that. He spent a while examining
the dead man, making notes and occasionally bending over
him, examining his clothes and accessories, even his ring,
before turning to a new page and making another detailed
note. Eventually, though, after another few long and appraising
looks, he nodded at his assistants. The body was lifted onto
a wheeled stretcher and taken away upon a horse-drawn ambu-
lance. A couple of policemen were then given the task of
keeping the crowd under control while positioned by the
doors, which were left open a few feet in order to admit more
light and air; another couple of policemen were busy taking
names and addresses from all present before dismissing them.
I was guiltily aware that I should inform the inspector that
many had already left the building before he had arrived and
that I had done nothing to stop them as I considered that the
place was overcrowded already, but I decided that I wouldn't
involve myself. Dickens and I were nodded at by Inspector
Field and we both got the impression that he wished us to
stay in the background while he interviewed Bazalgette, who

looked shaken and ill. I was glad to see that Andy stayed valiantly with his master, bringing him a chair to sit upon and helping to explain the demonstration in layman terms to the inspector who tended to get irritated with people who uttered words which he did not understand.

Gradually the policemen were going through the crowd in a most efficient way and the big, echoing space of the warehouse was getting emptier by the minute. I wandered around, looking sadly at the big tray of sand and the little church sitting upon the bank.

TWELVE

t did not take long for the police to switch the enquiry to
a different track. While the second-in-command policeman
noted down the names and addresses of Sir Benjamin Hall,
Disraeli and the engineers present, Dickens had a brief conversation with Bazalgette and then went across to the inspector.
Now he and Inspector Field had their heads close together
and the inspector seemed to be listening to Dickens and
nodding wisely as he spoke to him in a rapid undertone. I
was intrigued by the meaning for this intense tête-à-tête and
so I strolled as close as I could towards them, pretending to
examine an intricate engineering drawing made with charcoal
on the whitewashed wall, and listened for a few minutes. I
even caught the words: 'You could be right, Mr Dickens,'
followed by another emphatic nod. Wasn't this just a straightforward accident? Or was there some doubt about it?

From time to time, with quick, furtive glances at the pair,
I observed that Inspector Field looked across at Sir Benjamin
and then back at Dickens, acknowledging, doubtless, the background which Dickens, in his usual authoritative way, was
filling in for him. Then there was some more conversation.
The queen was mentioned, I guessed, as I saw that both men
bowed their heads in reverence. So, Inspector Field was being
told about the prospect of a knighthood, and a prize and the
part which Sir Benjamin had played in setting up this huge
incentive for the engineers of London to find a solution to
London's sewage. Both men were now looking at Bazalgette,
Dickens talking rapidly and the inspector nodding wisely.
There was no doubt now, in my mind, that Dickens must be
telling Inspector Field that the death of Bob Smith, the landlord, was suspicious and not at all an unfortunate accident.
Although the murderer was unknown, perhaps the focus on
the victim had been shifted in the inspector's mind. I saw him
give a final nod to Dickens, look once more in the direction

of Sir Benjamin and then he went across to the famous man;
would have known him well at Westminster, I guessed, as the
two shook hands. And then the inspector proceeded to have a
confidential, whispered conversation with Sir Benjamin,
nodding his head very wisely at the baronet's words, from
time to time making a note in the small book that he took
from his pocket.

I, more lowly than Sir Benjamin or Disraeli, had to wait
my turn. Eventually I was accosted, and I gave my name and
address to one of the Scotland Yard policemen but had little
to say when my turn came to be interviewed. I had, I told the
policeman, rather lost interest after the practical demonstration
as I had neither knowledge nor interest in machines and how
they worked. I emphasized that I would not have the slightest
interest in dredging machines and if anyone had wanted me
to do something as practical as engineering, then I would
probably have run away to sea as I loathed hard work of all
kinds.

To my slight alarm, this seemed to act as a challenge to the
policeman and he began to question me very closely on all
aspects of my misspent youth, seized on my confession that
I had not liked the law and had given up my studies. He wanted
to know whether I'd had any training for work in engineering,
even if I had given it up, and seemed to regard something like
writing books, which he, personally, had never read, and of which
he had never heard any report, as an unsatisfactory way of
explaining my wasted years. I suspected that he was filling in
time and endeavouring to discover something interesting from
his examination of me, but eventually he finished, leaving me
rather shaken and wondering whether I had protested too much
about my lack of knowledge of engineering matters and had
aroused his suspicions by those protests. Perhaps he took
that as a sign of guilt – he who protests too much. Still, I told
myself, as an author I was unlikely to want to murder the
landlord, who had been unknown to me until just a few weeks
ago. I tried to put the matter from my mind and endeavoured
to listen to what was going on amongst the small group of
engineers corralled in a space behind the deadly machines
with their heads together and eyes on the broken dredger.

And then the inspector came forward and addressed the whole group. 'Can anyone explain to me exactly what happened?' he asked, his eyes going from one to the other but ending up looking very directly at Joe Bazalgette while Field's assistant, probably by a prior arrangement, scanned the faces of the rest of the engineers.

'Someone fired a piece of metal right into the works of this machine that we call The Boomer.' Joe Bazalgette was calm, perilously calm. White-faced. A man who had been within inches of a person who had been killed, who had himself barely escaped death. I realized, looking around, that others thought the same as Bazalgette stated, 'I have no idea who did it, Inspector. Or why.'

'Could it have been an accident?' The inspector's voice was quite neutral but his glance was keen as his eyes travelled from one man to the next, sweeping across the whole group who were now standing in a semi-circle, still facing that murderous machine.

There was a silence after his question. I longed to cry out, 'Yes! Yes, of course it was an accident!' but all the engineers present just looked at one another and said nothing. The inspector waited. There was something deeply ominous in the way he stood there and moved his eyes from one person to the next. Henry Austin, Dickens' brother-in-law, was the first to crack.

'Perhaps a piece came off the machine, perhaps something broke off, got entangled in the works, got . . .? What does anyone else think?' He finished in a tone of desperation, looking at each man and then flushing slightly as his eyes rested upon Joe Bazalgette's rather scornful face. I and everyone else, I should have imagined, had watched Joe check the machine meticulously after the accident. All waited now for Joe to speak, and eventually the inspector's eyes rested on him.

'What do you think, Mr Bazalgette?'

'I can demonstrate, if you can procure me another similar machine, Inspector, but perhaps for the moment you can take my word for it that the machine was functioning perfectly until someone maliciously fired a metal object into its works. That was what killed the man. The machine itself did not misfunction. But you have a roomful of engineers here, Inspector. Perhaps someone else would like to disagree with me.'

The inspector went back to his notes after a keen look at the man who had been operating the machine at the exact moment when the fatal accident occurred. Did Bazalgette think himself under suspicion? I wondered. Was that the reason for the irritated note in his voice? Could there have been any reason why Bazalgette might have wanted to murder his landlord? After all, the simplest assumption would be that the man who was operating the machine could have dropped some piece of metal into its works. And of all present, Bazalgette was the one who knew the machine best, who would be confident of how it would react. He could also have privately asked the landlord to step forward at some stage of the proceedings; he could have given some pre-arranged signal that would not be noticed by anyone else. It was, I thought, a fascinating theory. The only problem was in finding out why a successful and talented engineer, who might soon be knighted by the queen and might be the saviour of the health and happiness of the inhabitants of London, why a man like that should murder a fat, old landlord. The rent, surely, could not have been a problem. Apart from any question of Bazalgette's successful career and probably large income, he was on the crux of receiving a huge commission to manage the drainage of all London. He might well end up as a millionaire. No landlord in the world would have pressurized a tenant like that for some paltry sum of rent. And no one in Bazalgette's position would need to owe rent. We had also been witness to Bob Smith's generous offer to forfeit any rent at all from this genius of an engineer on the cusp of finding a successful solution to London's horrendous problem.

I could not wait to discuss the whole matter with Dickens who always seemed to have an encyclopaedic knowledge of even casual acquaintances.

There was a silence for a moment. No one took up the challenge, no one ventured upon disagreeing with the man who had owned and operated the deadly machine. Joe

Bazalgette, was, I reckoned, as well as being the owner of the machine, estimated to be the best engineer in London at this time. I had noticed how respectfully everyone listened to him when he was demonstrating the machine. But now things were different. A man had been killed by that machine which had spewed out a piece of metal. Now, it occurred to me, there was something strange in the way with which he was being regarded by all who stood around.

'You saw the piece of metal in the man's neck. Now, do you, Mr Bazalgette, or anyone else – after all, you all saw the metal in his neck – do any of you know where that metal came from?' The inspector's eyes went to the damaged machine and then back to Bazalgette.

'No, I don't,' said Bazalgette, sounding most irritated. 'And I didn't know in the first place! How could I recognize it! All I saw was a terrible wound with a piece of metal sticking out from it. But I didn't examine the metal. The man was dead. I did try to find the pulse at his wrist, but I had known beforehand that he was dead. No one could have survived with his head half blown off and blood pumping from him. I didn't examine him, if that's what you mean.' He stopped for a minute and then resumed in a more animated manner. 'But I did examine the machine, Inspector. Nothing appears to be damaged; nothing broken,' he said. 'I inspected everything. It's a model of a dredger. I made it myself, made it for testing, but it is made of the correct strength, grey-cast steel, Inspector.'

I had no idea of what 'grey-cast steel' meant and I was quite sure, by his expression, that the inspector was no wiser than I on that subject, but he bowed his head and said, 'Thank you, sir.' He cast a swift glance around, scanning the faces of the other engineers, but none showed any disagreement or even hesitation. And so, the inspector nodded at his assistant and the assistant continued writing the words into a notebook and all waited respectfully until he had finished and then the inspector resumed.

'So, as far as you can see, nothing had been damaged on your model of a dredging machine,' he said, speaking rather slowly and in a meditative manner. And then with a sudden change of expression and pace of speech, he said rapidly, 'So what's your explanation, Mr Bazalgette, as owner of the machine? What do you think happened?'

Bazalgette was ready for this one. 'Someone flung a piece of metal into the machine when it was working. Anyone who knew anything about machines would have known that would result in a terrible accident, that the piece of metal would be spun around and fired out with accelerated velocity. It's something that I always warn any apprentice of mine about. Anyone caught throwing objects while machines are working is immediately sent home, thrown out. I never could tolerate that sort of behaviour in the workshop. It could kill a man, I tell every one of them on their first day of work and again from time to time. And so, it did kill. Severed the artery in the man's neck. He bled to death in front of our eyes. Surely you can see that.' The words came out abruptly and were spoken in an irritated manner. I grimaced slightly. It was a mistake, I thought, to antagonize the police. They had their job to do.

The inspector looked around the room. 'All here are engineers except Sir Benjamin and Mr Disraeli, who are Members of Parliament and, of course, Mr Dickens and Mr Collins, who are writers. Is that correct?'

'I *am* an engineer, a civil engineer, Inspector.' Sir Benjamin was irritated, though I thought that the inspector could not have known that unless he had been told. Sir Benjamin and Disraeli were here to represent the government and to report back to the queen. The inspector probably regarded a Member of Parliament, with clean hands, as being immensely superior to an engineer who grubbed around in mud and metal. I was slightly amused at that thought but kept a very solemn face as I stood there and waited to be released.

'I stand corrected,' said the inspector, unperturbed by the irritated note in Sir Benjamin's voice. 'But, perhaps, I might put the question to all the engineers present: has any one of you anything to add to Mr Bazalgette's explanation?'

No one spoke for a moment. And then Sir Benjamin said in rather icy tones, 'Inspector, Mr Bazalgette is not only the owner of the machine, not only the one who made the machine, who has worked with the machine, but in his field of civil

engineering, he is at the top of his profession. I, for one, would
readily accept his explanation.'

There was a murmur of agreement, though I noted that
Dickens' brother-in-law, Henry Austin, grimaced slightly in
the direction of David Napier. There would inevitably be, I
reflected, a feeling of professional jealousy amongst engineers,
all of whom were striving to provide a solution to one of the
worst problems of this generation. And, of course, the offer
of a knighthood and a substantial prize from the queen would
only add to the jealousy and the sense of competition between
these engineers. At this moment, after that most successful
demonstration of an efficient and imaginative suggestion for
getting rid of the terrible pollution of the river which should
be the crowning beauty of our capital city, well, even the
dullest mind could guess that young Joe Bazalgette was at
the front of the queue when it came to knighthoods and prizes.
I looked thoughtfully at the young man and then something
occurred to me. I turned to look at Dickens with widened eyes
and saw his lips tighten over an amused smile. So, he was
ahead of me! The thought that had just occurred to me had
been in his mind. I looked at the inspector, wondering whether
the same idea was in his mind, but I could read little from
that deadpan face.

'The man was a landlord, an owner of property, warehouses
and such-like, Officer. I know little else of him,' said Joe
Bazalgette, and he looked around at the rest of us as if for
help. 'I paid him rent on the first of every month; he came
around for it. And I paid it into his hand. I don't even know
where exactly he lived, though I suppose he did tell me at one
stage. But if he did, I have forgotten it, or thrown away the
piece of paper on which it was written. So, I know nothing
about him, not even whether he had any near relatives. I
suppose you could advertise. Put . . . put out a . . . a verbal
description . . .' His voice faltered at that last word and he
looked around helplessly.

It was, I thought, in everyone's mind that the landlord was
now and would always be quite unrecognizable. His head had
been almost blown off and no feature could be identified. I
shuddered a little as I thought of the image of the dead man.

I had always hated the sight of blood and now blood was everywhere. The piece of metal had been lodged in the neck and he had bled so copiously that even the surrounding machines had been splattered and stained a dark red with his blood.

'And an owner of houses, also, I think,' said Andy Wainwright. 'We know nothing of him, really, Inspector. Certainly we know of no reason why anyone should have killed him. He may have had a hundred enemies for all that we know. And, since the night was warm and the engines were burning, we had those big doors open. I put a rope across to keep the boys out but, of course, I'm sure that none of us could swear that someone could not have slipped into the warehouse without our knowledge. I kept a sharp eye to make sure that no one came too close to the engines, but I don't think that any of us could swear that no stranger came in and stayed at the back of the warehouse, or even went up the staircase to the gallery. I don't think that I would have cared, really, so long as they kept well out of the way once the engines began to work. The first part of the evening was just a bit of play-acting. The apprentices put on a little demonstration of Mr Bazalgette's ideas. It was only when it came to using the machines that I put up the rope and then kept a sharp eye out to make sure that no one came near to them. We are always most careful about safety in this workshop. It's the first thing that Mr Bazalgette teaches the apprentices and it's the first thing that he thinks of if ever we have a visitor to the warehouse.'

He spoke for the firm and it was, I thought, kind of him to lend his support to his employer. There was almost a hint of a sigh of relief from the other engineers and the two Members of Parliament. Feet were shuffled. Everyone was anxious to get out of this terrible place and go home to their own firesides, away from the memory of the horror and from the pungent smell of blood which still filled the area where we all stood.

The body had been removed but the concrete floor was still stained with that large, ugly, dark-red blotch. One of the apprentices had come forward with a bucket and mop but was waved away by the policeman. I wondered whether the stain

could ever be removed or whether that patch of the floor would
have to be covered with a new layer of concrete. The place
seemed to smell of blood and I wished that the inspector would
finish up and allow us all to go home. I was sick with anxiety
and couldn't wait to leave. After another five minutes or so,
I planned, I would get Dickens to intervene on my behalf. Tell
him that I had a terrible headache and needed to take some
of my medicine. After all, I was not an engineer and had
nothing to do with this experiment. Most of the crowd that
had been at the door had either melted away before the arrival
of the police or had, like good citizens, given their names and
addresses and been dismissed. The two politicians had left
after shaking hands with Bazalgette. Those who remained were
the police, the engineers and, of course, myself and Dickens.
Our presence was certainly not necessary. I sidled up to my
friend and whispered in his ear.

Dickens, however, unfortunately for me, was deeply interested and watched the little crowd, his keen eyes going from
one engineer to another. 'Won't be long now,' he whispered
back and then left me and went to have a word with Sir
Benjamin before he went through the door. I watched them
impatiently as they stood nodding to each other and then the
inspector, with a sidelong glance at the two most distinguished
men present, stepped forward and whispered something into
Joe Bazalgette's ear.

It came as a shock to the man. There was no doubt about
that. He turned very pale and then shook his head vigorously.
'No, certainly not. No, I can't think that you are right,
Inspector.'

And then, probably to the inspector's deep annoyance, Joe
Bazalgette addressed the engineers, friends, colleagues, fellow
workers, men whom he had probably known for years, men
with whom he shared a sense of purpose and who were
members of the same profession, all of them qualified civil
engineers.

'This is totally absurd,' he said vigorously. 'The inspector
here thinks that the victim was supposed to be me, not that
poor fellow, my landlord. What do you think of that, my
friends? How absurd it is, isn't it? You must understand the

absurdity, Inspector. These men here are friends, co-workers. We all want to solve this problem. That's what we were trained for. Who cares about a silly knighthood?' he went on, looking, perhaps accidently, at Sir Benjamin. 'Who cares? What use is a knighthood to any of us? We want clean air for the citizens of London. No, Inspector, I'm absolutely certain that no one here tonight tried to kill me, and you will never persuade me otherwise. You keep your enquiries to finding out about the man who was killed. None of us know anything about him except that he was a landlord, but landlords can arouse anger and fury, can throw people out of their houses. Who knows what his history is? I don't, but I'd advise you to start digging into it and to cease to endeavour to stir up bad feeling between myself and my colleagues. We have work to do, and that work will only be achieved with all of our efforts and with a professional sharing of expertise and ideas. Now I'd like to go home, if that is all right by you, Inspector. And I think that my highly valued, highly esteemed colleagues would like to do so also. May I bid you and your men a good night, Inspector. Andy, you have the keys, haven't you?'

And with that brave and impressive speech, Joe Bazalgette wound up the evening. The inspector could say nothing. He and his men had interviewed all present. All had given their names, their addresses and details of their professional qualifications and expertise. There was nothing for Inspector Field to do but to wish everyone a good night and to remind them that he would be in touch with further questions if necessary and then he went, escorted to the door by Andy Wainwright and followed by myself and Dickens who, with a rare show of restraint, said nothing beyond wishing everyone as good and peaceful a night as possible.

Now came my opportunity. And in the bustle of engineers moving in one direction, police in the other, all with an eye on Andy Wainwright who was now flourishing an impressively large key, I managed to slip unobtrusively through the crowd and come up to the table which held the model of the River Thames inside my enormous sand tray.

It was undisturbed: the trough, symbolizing the River Thames, where the clear river water glinted beneath the gas lamp; the new road, the strip of cotton sprinkled by the apprentices with cement on top of the sand in order to make it look realistic, christened 'The Embankment' road; and beyond the road the newly piled-up bank of sand which would hide the still-to-be-built interceptor sewer and the sewage pipes and would be named Embankment Gardens, beautified with plants and shrubs.

Somerset House, the Savoy, King's College, St Mary le Strand and the other buildings that skirted the riverside of the Strand would, of course, still be on the far side of the embankment gardens. For the moment, their positions were signified only by one model. The little church belonging to Carrie's toy village was still there, still mimicking St Mary le Strand. I stood and looked at it. It was alone. No other toy building beside it. The fire station had vanished. It occurred to me, with a sickening feeling of apprehension, that a little cast iron model, thrown from a distance, but with deadly accuracy, right into the heart of its works might have been used to foul the workings of the dredger machine. I wrestled with my feelings. I was imagining things. No doubt, I told myself, whoever had supplied the fire station, identical to Carrie's, had retrieved it.

It would have been such a terrible thing if a child's toy had been used to kill a harmless old man. I felt sick at the thought and resolved to try to banish the whole scene from my mind until I reached home and could take a calming dose of laudanum from the box in my cupboard.

THIRTEEN

However, despite my wish to banish the scene from my mind, I knew that Dickens was made of sterner stuff and that his initial silence was purely out of concern for me. And so, I weakened, gave into him and we had no sooner traversed Great George Street and were making our way across St James's Park when we began to talk about the matter, and it was I who broke the silence.

'Do you really think that it was a murder?' I asked.

'I believe Bazalgette,' said Dickens shortly. 'He's a competent man, a man who knows what his machine is capable of, and I take his word for it that the machine did not malfunction and someone maliciously threw a piece of metal into the works. Well, that, to my mind, was attempted murder.'

I bowed my head. It did seem to make sense. 'And do you believe that the murderer, whoever he was, intended to kill Bazalgette, not the old man, the landlord?' I asked. I wished that we could talk of something else, but even I felt quite unable to avoid the subject. My mind was full of it – that terrible image of the man with the gaping wound in his neck would not leave that inner eye of mine, and so I hoped that Dickens' matter-of-fact manner might calm me. He didn't seem in the least worried. Just walked along the pavement, whistling softly to himself, his face bright and alert.

'Of course I do,' he said in an off-hand manner. 'Goodness gracious, Collins, why on earth should anyone want to murder an elderly landlord? What on earth would be the motive?'

I gave up. I should have known better. I was never a match for Dickens during an argument. 'Why do you think that the victim was more likely to be Bazalgette then?' I asked weakly.

'You just think about Bazalgette, Wilkie, and you will admit that he was destined to be the queen's knight and the saviour of London. And a man to make a fortune for himself and all of his children. But let me tell you about the man.

I've been finding out some details about him and have noted them down here.' Dickens sounded as vigorous as if it were eight o'clock in the morning and he had just emerged from one of those icy showers from the machine he had installed in his house.

He stopped under a gas lamp and began to read from a notebook. I could see that there were pages filled up, and not for the first time I was most impressed by the man's energy and huge industry once a subject interested him. He had taken so much trouble to find out about Bazalgette. Hardly glanced at his notes as he walked rapidly along, enunciating facts and figures. The man was apparently born in Hill Lodge, Clay Hill, Enfield, London, the son of a Joseph William Bazalgette who died in 1848, a retired Royal Navy captain and the grandson of a French Protestant immigrant to London who had become extremely wealthy. He had spent his early career articled to the noted engineer Sir John MacNeill working on railway projects and amassed sufficient experience (partly in China and Ireland) in land drainage and reclamation to enable him to set up his own London consulting practice in 1842. In 1845 he married Maria Kough, from County Kilkenny in Ireland, the daughter of a justice of the peace and an heiress to a fortune.

'Some men,' he said rather bitterly with a note of envy in his voice, 'have wives and relatives that bring them wealth, while other poor, hardworking souls spend their energies supporting wives and relatives, not to mention large families.'

I said nothing. As I was quite convinced that I would never marry, that would ensure that I had neither wives nor many relatives on whom to spend money. I turned an attentive face towards Dickens who was beginning to wind up his peroration.

'Now, what do you think, Collins? Isn't it likely that this man, a man who may be about to receive the high honour of a knighthood from the queen as well as a substantial money prize, might be the envy of his fellow engineers?'

I thought about that statement but could find no reason to disagree with it. 'You think it's possible that someone meant to kill Bazalgette, perhaps because it looks as though he is the one who is going to be the successful engineer who receives a knighthood and a prize and will get the job of freeing London from that dreadful miasma which is killing so many of his citizens? Is that what you are thinking, Dick?'

'Yes,' he said, and watched me meditatively without adding anything else. And so, knowing my role as a sounding board, I went over in my mind the gathering of engineers around my table that night and remembered the conversation, the genuine exchanging of ideas and the interest shown in results observed by a fellow professional. Pleasant fellows, all of them, I thought. I had envied their camaraderie. And then I remembered the one slightly unpleasant note.

'Disraeli,' I said aloud. 'I wonder, was it he?'

'Disraeli,' said Dickens. He sounded genuinely startled. 'Why on earth should a politician like Disraeli kill Bazalgette? My dear Collins, Disraeli is the man who put forward the bill which might save us all from a summer like last year. He's the man who forced the House to sit in that terrible heat and stink of summer until they voted through a sum of three million pounds for works to solve the problem of London sewage and cleanse the Thames, to be paid by the taxpayer, of course. Three pence from every pound.' Dickens winced a little at that, but then nodded his head. 'An excellent decision,' he said firmly, 'and Disraeli's name is so attached to the bill that it will be important that a competent engineer is put in charge in order to accomplish the transformation of our city and the Thames. No, my friend, Disraeli regards Bazalgette as his saviour, as the man who will help an ambitious politician to the top of the tree. Mark my words, some day we will see Disraeli as prime minister and if we do, it will be Bazalgette who will have been largely instrumental in placing him in that position.'

I thought about that. It made sense. But I brushed it aside. I had great faith in my intuition and little Carrie, I told myself again, had shrunk from him.

'But he didn't kill Bazalgette, did he?' I felt rather pleased with myself. It wasn't often that I managed to startle Dickens. 'He killed the landlord, and none of us, not even you, Dickens, knows anything about the landlord.'

'Seemed a nice, genial sort of fellow,' said Dickens decisively.

'How do you know – "There is no art to find the mind's construction in the face"?'

'Go on,' said Dickens. 'Let's hear your reasons.' Shakespeare had gone down well with him. He saw every Shakespearean play on the London stage at least once – three or four times if he liked the production.

'Politicians are always at risk if they have a guilty secret and Disraeli is ambitious. He wants to be prime minister, you said that yourself. Queen Victoria won't permit that if there is any scandal attached to him. He might have a secret mistress,' I finished triumphantly.

Dickens winced perceptibly and I was sorry.

'Or, more likely, he has embezzled some money,' I said hastily. 'All I know is that he has the sort of face that a murderer would have.' I didn't like to say that my little Carrie didn't like him, but I thought that a child's instinctive judgement was as good as that of any old man in a long wig sitting enthroned in a dusty courthouse.

'Nonsense,' said Dickens decisively.

I gave in, as I always did when Dickens took that curt tone of voice, but his face was relaxed. He glanced sideways at the window of a bookshop. Most of the display was taken up with multiple editions of his latest success, *A Tale of Two Cities*. He gave a nod, flourished his stick in the air and turned an animated face towards me.

'Now, let's consider which one of those engineers present might have wanted to get rid of Bazalgette and put forward his own ideas. After all, I suppose there wasn't a man there whose heart did not sink as he listened to what Bazalgette had to say.'

'Enough to fill the others with jealousy and make them feel, perhaps, envious of him,' I said. 'But then I suppose that people always accept that there is someone in their profession better than they. For instance, you sell a lot more books than I do, but I wouldn't kill you to get your market.'

Dickens gave a short laugh at the ridiculousness of that very idea, but then went back to the engineers. 'Someone is going to have to endeavour to solve the terrible problem of London being flooded by overflowing cesspits, leaking pipes and poisoned rivers. The money for the works is there. It has been voted in by Parliament – all three million pounds of it. If Bazalgette were to die, why then, another engineer would have to take up the cause and struggle for a solution. And, of course, since Bazalgette has been very generously sharing his ideas with his fellow engineers, then even if he were to be killed his ideas would still live. Someone could employ the efficient Andy Wainwright and probably have access to Bazalgette's hard work.'

I turned that over in my mind, tried to find a weakness, but had to acknowledge its truth. 'It wouldn't be very fair,' I said, but knew it was a weak argument.

'Life's not fair. It's not fair on me that American pirates can copy and print my books and sell them without giving me a penny from their profits,' said Dickens bitterly. 'This would be less unfair, as any engineer taking over Bazalgette's ideas would still have all the hard work and all the designing to do. And remember what I said, "Life's not fair". After all, Bazalgette may have started with advantages that other engineers could only dream of, and who knows, he has perhaps picked up ideas from others. I didn't like to mention it, but I think that dear old Christopher Wren, who did so much for London, also had the idea of dredging the River Thames and making the river narrow and fast-flowing.'

I knew little or nothing about Christopher Wren, other than a vague idea that he had something to do with the Great Fire of London, and so did not argue with him about that. However, my mother, always a fund of information, had known Bazalgette's father who was, she thought, in the Navy and certainly not well-off, though the grandfather had money, she had remembered as an afterthought, so I delivered that piece of information to add to Dickens' already considerable wealth of knowledge on the subject and then added, 'Perhaps he was industrious and intelligent. Others may not have had that luck, even if they had access to his working notes, so the idea of someone killing him for the sake of some notes, and access to his assistant, seems a bit ridiculous to me.'

Dickens pursed his lips and shook his head doubtfully,

signalling disagreement. Dickens always claimed to know
human nature so much better than I, and so I said no more as
he held forth.

'My own feeling,' he said in his positive manner, 'is that
Bazalgette is far advanced in his plans. He gave us an outline,
but he is not the sort of man who would do that unless he had
put in all the hard work, all the testing beforehand. He's not
one of these people who get an idea and hope that it will all
work out. That might do for novelists like ourselves, my dear
Wilkie, but an engineer needs to test and to retest, and of
course be sure that he has the finances behind him that will
allow him to take his time and do all the work that is needed
before informing the public or selling his services and his
ideas to those who can afford to pay for them. A man like
Bazalgette is at the stage when his client will be governments
and people in high places. They will pay the bill when the
work is done and is deemed satisfactory. I'd say that if you
went through that desk of his you would find that everything
is in order, that every piece of machinery needed has been
acquired and tested, or at least a model of it. And I'll also lay
you a bet that the instructions for its use have been written
out so carefully that he can make no mistakes due to a lapse
in memory and, of course, as no man can do all of the work
himself, he will have to train up his assistants. I'd lay you a
sum of money as a bet that the sober-faced Andy Wainwright
could deputize for his master on most occasions.' Dickens
stopped for a minute, his face thoughtful and then, quite unex-
pectedly, he said, 'I admire that man Bazalgette immensely
and, do you know, Collins, I envy him. He gets a machine,
studies it, notes its peculiarities, remedies its faults, keeps it
well-oiled and whatever else you do to machines and then,
you know, he can rely on it. Now take us, my dear friend. We
rely on the book-reading public, not a predictable machine in
any way. Impossible to rely upon. Moves this way and that;
likes this one year, and that the next. And take money. Well,
if Bazalgette is offered a job, he goes and checks on his
machines, knows he can rely upon them, so he sits down with
pen and paper, works it all out, how many hours, days and
months it will take his machines, factors in the wages for the

men who will be working those machines and then he gives a price – and if he's sensible he builds in something for delay due to weather. Otherwise, he knows he can rely on these dumb and obedient machines and he tenders his estimate and makes sure that he gets half of it in advance and there he is – he has the money in the bank to maintain his household and he can devote all his resources to doing a good job, knowing that he has already received a substantial payment and that his machines won't let him down. And, above all, that his contract is with one firm, or, better still with one government. Now, you contrast that with you and me, Collins!'

Dickens stopped dead in the centre of the pavement and wagged an admonitory finger in my face. Despite the interested glances from passers-by, he began to enumerate the contrasts on his fingers. 'We get a paltry advance, not enough to feed my raven for a year, then we have to slog away, day after day, never knowing whether that fickle customer, the "general public", will like our offering or not. We cannot say, if the book is a flop, well, I have fulfilled my contract, I have built you a road, or laid down one hundred pipes. No, my friend, we must swallow the fact that that paltry advance is all that we are going to get, and we just have to take our unsold books and stack them in an attic, just as I had to do with *Barnaby Rudge*. No, if any of my sons have the brains for it, I would like to see them become engineers rather than hanging on the tails of their father, who, goodness knows, already has enough relatives looking to him for money.'

I wondered whether he was thinking about his brother-in-law, Henry Austin, who always seemed to be getting into money trouble, but then he surprised me by changing the subject to something quite different.

'You compare Bazalgette's background with someone like poor Phillips who went to work when he was five or six years old and who has never been inside a school in his life,' he said, looking at me keenly. 'Don't tell me that Phillips doesn't resent Bazalgette and his ideas and that he doesn't think that if he were twenty years younger and had the resources to furnish a warehouse with all of those fancy models of machines that he too might have a chance of being knighted by the queen and given a substantial money prize.'

I thought about that. There had been, I noticed, a slight stiffness between Phillips and Bazalgette. It must be difficult for one not to be envious of the other. I thought about my own upbringing and how my father had never even hinted that I should abandon my studies and go out into the world and how he patiently went on paying my law school fees well after it was apparent that I had no interest in becoming a barrister. There were times when I thought that Dickens, rich and famous though he was now, rather resented how easy life had been for me and how little incentive I had to work as hard as he did, and Dickens was the most generous of men. If that were the case, perhaps some of these engineers might have resented Bazalgette to the degree that they felt the world would be an easier and more pleasant place for them if this ambitious, young, gifted and monied engineer were to be nudged out of it.

'You see, Collins, old friend,' said Dickens, tapping his notebook, 'this is a very impressive man, this Joseph Bazalgette. I've written quite a few details about him here in this notebook of mine. He's got it all – qualifications, plenty of experience, a rich grandfather who left him a fortune that has helped him in gaining qualifications and in setting up that extremely impressive workshop of his. And, of course, he has been working for years for the Metropolitan Board of Works and rose to be their chief engineer. Became convinced, like most people, that this dreadful miasma, or stink as you and I would call it, is responsible not just for the discomfort of our esteemed Members of Parliament, and, of course, the rest of London, but for also destroying the beauty of our river, our Father Thames, and for spreading cholera all over the city.

'Now, all these engineers have schemes, most of them hugely expensive and not, in my judgement, terribly practical. I'm fairly convinced that running pipes under the sprawling mass of the Thames is not going to work. The installation would be almost impossible, and even if it did succeed, the maintenance would be hugely expensive and would leave a burden on the people of London for generations to come. But these ideas of Bazalgette's: the replacement of broken old pipes with these well-built brick pipeways, lined with this waterproof Portland cement of his; the building of an interceptor sewer; and, above all, to my mind, that brilliant idea of creating a narrow, fast-flowing Thames and using the spoil from the river to build an embankment and to create not just a new road to relieve our terrible traffic problems on the Strand, but to build those lovely, imaginative, decorative gardens to hide the pipes while still leaving them accessible for maintenance and repairs . . . No, my friend,' finished Dickens, in his most impressive fashion, 'there is absolutely no doubt whatsoever in my mind that Bazalgette's scheme would have been chosen above the ideas of all those engineers and that he would have been the man to win the prize and to be knighted by the queen – but not, of course, if the man were dead.'

Dickens then stopped and relieved his feelings by simulating a shot at a flying duck, aiming the point of his stick at the bird and uttering a very realistic 'ptt' noise.

'I agree,' I said, and he beamed approval at me.

'And so, being an intelligent man, you would also agree with me that a harmless, overweight and quite elderly man like that landlord would be unlikely to be assassinated by any of those engineers present.'

'I agree,' I said absent-mindedly.

'Especially,' continued Dickens, 'as the unfortunate man had only, a minute or two earlier, stepped close enough to that dredger machine to put himself into danger. So, it wasn't – could not have been – a premeditated murder. Anyone who had wanted to murder him would have had to have done it purely on the spur of the moment, and it might well have failed if the man had moved back to his original place. It could not have been planned! Whereas Bazalgette had been standing there for the whole time of his talk – talking, mind you, not moving, standing in the same place for all the time that he was speaking. He stood there, explaining it all so clearly, and there may have been one man who felt that his own hopes were being washed away and who decided to get rid of the man who had formulated such splendid ideas.'

'I agree that an engineer would be the one who would realize what would happen if a piece of metal were thrown against the works of the machine,' I said. And I did agree, and I did admire his explanation. I always marvelled at the way that Dickens could sift ideas and present them in such clear form.

'But,' I continued, 'which one of those respectable, hard-working engineers do you think would be so burning with ambition that he would murder a colleague just to win a money prize and become a knight of realm?' I bet he won't mention his brother-in-law, I said to myself while I turned an innocently blank face toward him. 'Speaking in complete confidence, of course,' I added.

He hesitated for a few seconds and then said, with a sidelong glance at me, 'Any one of them, I suppose. Any man who needs money. Especially married men, of course. London is an expensive place for a man with a family.'

So, he does half-suspect his brother-in-law, I thought. Henry Austin was not a successful engineer. But he was the husband of Dickens' younger sister. Dickens had had to draw on funds to rescue him from bankruptcy on one occasion, and in general played a generous part in his brother-in-law's finances. He had hoped, I guessed, that Henry Austin would have come up with some good scheme that would have ensured that he and his family would have been self-sufficient from then on, but Henry, as even I could see, did not have as many brains in his whole head as Bazalgette had in his little finger.

'It will be a valuable money prize, then,' I ventured, speaking cautiously, and making sure not to look at him as I said the words.

'The knighthood, man, the knighthood,' he said impatiently. 'That would have been the golden key to wealth. For every single one of these men a knighthood would have guaranteed success,' he added. 'Orders would have come piling in from all over the world.'

'I agree.' I said the words very quickly and then added to them. 'And I should imagine that Inspector Field will agree with you if you put the matter to him.'

Dickens swung his stick in a nonchalant way. 'Well, of course, if he were to ask me . . .'

'You know that he will,' I said. 'But which of the engineers do you think might have had the burning ambition and, of course, the ruthlessness, to murder a man in that dreadful way? You make your choice and I'll make mine and then we'll argue.'

'John Phillips,' said Dickens, never a man to hesitate. 'And I've explained all of my reasons. He has the toughness not to hesitate and the burning desire to succeed. His past history shows that he is a man who can overcome obstacles. No, I think that if he decided to get rid of Bazalgette, he would not allow himself to falter.'

'And yet it wasn't Bazalgette who was murdered, but the landlord,' I reminded him.

'Chance in a million,' said Dickens. 'And Inspector Field shouldn't waste his time investigating the background of the landlord. It was obvious that was an accident. It was the first time that the man had moved forward. Before that he was standing behind that big desk and could hardly be seen. No one could have planned a murder which relied on him standing in front of the one working machine, the machine that spat out the piece of metal – The Boomer, wasn't it? And, according to what Bazalgette said to Inspector Field, the metal had to hit the shaft, not any other part of the machine, for it to be spun out and turned into a deadly killing weapon. So, unless the whole thing was a terrible accident, then it had to be aimed by a man who understood the consequences – in other words, one of the engineers.'

'I agree with you one hundred per cent,' I said, nodding my head emphatically. 'As for my choice among the engineers, I'm a bit stuck. I like them all. It seems a terrible thing to murder a man just to succeed in business, but I suppose that if I have to choose one, it will have to be David Napier. There's something a bit odd about him, and he is obviously not a good engineer if he blows up two ships when repairing their boilers. Perhaps he needs to steal other engineers' ideas just to get commissions. And there was that odd story of him keeping his mistress hidden. But I don't know, really,' I finished in my usual indecisive fashion and was not surprised when he laughed.

'We're back to Rapunzel and the tower again,' he said

mockingly. 'Now, I turn off here and you had better go back to your Rapunzel and my charming little butler, of course. Goodnight, my dear fellow!' And Dickens, flourishing his stick, made his way down the street and I turned to go back to my home.

FOURTEEN

My key turned easily in the lock when I arrived at my house. There was a satisfying click and then, with a gentle push, the door slid back and showed a hall with a candle and a box of matches standing ready on the hall table. I lit it before I closed the door upon the light from the street gas lamps and looked all around me. It was nice to be home, I thought. There was a tidiness about the place, a cared-for look, even a smell of polish. Somehow these lodgings of mine seemed different, seemed more like a home. The soft blue-grey shawl that I had bought for Caroline hung upon the coat stand and Carrie's little cape dangled beneath it. The air was scented with the aroma of smouldering logs and there was a lovely perfume of baked cake coming from the half-opened kitchen door.

And then I heard something, and I smiled. A homely noise. The sound of someone snoring coming from Caroline's room. It was so loud that I knew she was there and was sleeping peacefully, and so I didn't disturb her. I peeped into Carrie's room, though. She was there, by herself, sleeping happily, a small lump of child and teddy bear wrapped in each other and half-covered by the bedclothes. Gently and quietly, I straightened the blankets and the pink eiderdown over the two of them. Caroline was still snoring loudly, but the child was undisturbed and seemed to be sleeping peacefully, so when I tiptoed from the room, I decided to leave the door open a little in case she cried out in the night. Caroline was sleeping so heavily that she might not hear the child. I would, I decided, leave my own door slightly ajar too.

Those snores from her mother were very loud and I had not heard them before. After another moment of listening, I went into my own room and opened the door of the small cupboard by my bed. My faithful companion, my box of laudanum, the soother of headaches and the killer of the sharp pain of gout, was there on the top shelf, but when I opened the lid of the box I could see that a few extra spoonfuls were missing, and possibly some from the cough syrup also. I smiled to myself. So, she had helped herself, had found the stuff useful. Well, I didn't begrudge her, though I would have been pleased to have found her warmth in my bed. I took a small dose of laudanum myself to blot out that terrible, bloody sight and then filled a stone hot water bottle from the kettle of warm water left upon the hob and got into bed, resolutely determining that all thoughts of the evening's bloody horror would be banned from my mind.

Nevertheless, it was a long time before I ceased to toss and turn, before the faces of all those who had stood facing that line of strange machines began to fade from my mind's eye. Eventually, and as it always does, the laudanum began to do its work and a pleasant feeling of warmth and relaxation came over me as I fell asleep.

When I woke up, the sun, getting stronger each day as spring progressed, was filling my room with warmth and a bright light. I stirred and yawned loudly and then, just as though she had waited for that signal, there was a knock on the door and Caroline's voice calling out, 'Good morning' and telling me that my breakfast and shaving water were ready. She had been in sometime earlier, silent as always, and the stove in my room burned with that dark red mixture of coal and embers that showed it had been alight for at least an hour. I smiled a little at the pleasant sight and then put on my dressing gown, went to the door to take in my breakfast tray and to place the shaving water on the top of the stove.

I didn't close the door, though, and I stood there for a moment, listening intently. The child was quite happy, singing a nursery rhyme about Humpty Dumpty and her mother joined in from time to time and seemed to be energetically bustling around the kitchen, stacking pots and closing cupboard doors.

So, Caroline had suffered no harm from her dose of laudanum. She must have been up long before I was and so had little Carrie. I guessed that both had breakfasted before I heard them singing nursery songs in the kitchen and the sound was a very pleasant one.

I closed the door as quietly as I could and did my best to avert my mind from the horror of that terrible evening in the warehouse as I swallowed down my breakfast and then washed and shaved.

By the time I came out, they were both sitting at the kitchen table and Carrie's little finger was tracing over the imprint of her name, HARRIET. And then, being a little show-off, she rubbed the word out and displayed her ability to write it without any help.

'So now you know six letters of the alphabet: A E H I R and T,' I said, sitting down beside her. 'Only another twenty letters to go. There's a song, isn't there?' I said, looking up at Caroline and she sang it very sweetly, bending over the child and giving her a kiss after she had sung the last words: '"Now I know my ABC. Next time won't you sing with me?"'

They sang it together three times and then Caroline shooed us out to go for a walk as she wanted to clean the kitchen, but at that little Carrie looked mutinous. 'I don't *zactly* feel like a walk today. I'm tired of walks.'

'Well, let's go into the sitting room and play,' I said, and I watched her carefully. There was something slightly different about Carrie this morning, after all. Now that she was not so animated, I could see that her colour was not as good as usual and that her eyes had shadows under them, almost as though she had not slept well. I wondered whether she had, in truth, been asleep when I had peeped into her room last night. I hoped that Caroline's large dose of laudanum, a dose that might well have knocked her out almost immediately, had not frightened her little daughter. If so, we might never know. Another child would announce all her worries, but Carrie, I knew from experience, tended to bury anxieties under a show of carefree chatter. There was an odd mixture of small child and worried adult in Carrie. Most of the children, my godchildren, and others that I knew belonging to friends of mine, always blurted everything out instantly, but Carrie had a side to her that seemed to hold hidden secrets. She went with me, now, slightly reluctantly, and I saw how she paused in the hallway and looked up at her cape and cap as though about to change her mind about the walk. I went on to the sitting room, though.

'I'm tired,' she said, dramatically throwing herself upon the couch. 'I'm too tired to play. I need a bit of peace and rest.'

I bit back a smile. All little girls copied their mothers, I supposed, but Carrie did it very well.

'Well, I'll just play by myself, then,' I said and pretended to think, placing my forefinger theatrically in the centre of my forehead. 'Now what will I play with?' I said. That, I guessed, would fetch her out of her lethargy. Carrie liked to be the one who was in charge of all games. However, there was a different reaction on this occasion.

'No!' She was on her feet instantly. 'Let's not play. *Childrens* get bored with playing. I've changed my mind. Let's go for a walk. Let's go to Regent's Park. I like that place. I like it much better than the river and the Strand and all those places.'

'Very well,' I said, and tried to inject a reluctant note into my voice, though I was pleased at the suggestion as I thought she was looking rather pale. 'You win. You go and ask your mother to brush your hair and wash your face and then we'll go to Regent's Park.'

'And bring bread for the ducks, will we?' Now the colour had come back to her face. She did love to determine what we were going to do, and I loved to indulge her in that. However, something else was on my mind.

'Ask your mother,' I said. I needed to have her out of my way for a few moments. I needed to make sure. After all, I tried to tell myself, half the children in London may well have that toy in their possession.

I walked into the hallway and waited there until I heard the tap running. Caroline was washing her daughter's face and singing the ABC song again. The sound of the tap and her voice would drown any sounds that I might make. I went into the little room and opened the linen cupboard. Not much linen there, but the shelving had proved ideal for holding Carrie's toys in tidy rows and Caroline kept it looking very neat. Noah's Ark was on its tray and beside it was the tray holding the toy village. Everything was there, at first glance. No noticeable gaps. The post office with its little old lady, the greengrocer, the butcher, the baker – no church, of course. But, also, no fire station. I could no longer deceive myself.

How had she done it? How was it that I did not see her? Even with my bad eyesight, surely, I would have seen a little girl. But the answer was there, in front of my eyes on the shelves. When I had bought some decent clothing for Francis to wear every day, I had also bought another set to please Carrie, who had demanded that he should have good clothes for Sundays and for going to parties. I remembered how she had directed her mother to put the clothes on the top shelf.

Yes, they were there. The shirt, trousers and waistcoat were neatly folded, just in the way that Caroline, who was neat about everything, had placed them on that day.

But the coat and the cap – were they rather out of place, rather untidily thrown up, rather than placed and folded? I wasn't sure, but I thought so. And I remembered seeing a boy wearing a coat and a cap who had climbed the steps up to the gallery on that terrible night. Was it a boy? Or was it a girl wearing boy's clothing? Was it Carrie?

There was, I feared, one answer. When Caroline had taken that big dose of laudanum and had fallen into that heavy sleep, her small daughter, now repenting that she had denied her toy to Dickens who made such a favourite of her, self-willed and determined as Carrie always was, had slid out of bed, dressed herself, slipped out of the basement door, probably, and had made her way, very easily, as we had walked those streets so often, to Great George Street and had brought her toy, as the final touch, to be added to the model of the future embankment.

But what, I asked myself, had happened next?

I sat on a hall chair and went over everything in my mind. I had, I told myself, two alternatives. One was my usual way of dealing with difficult matters – do nothing. The other was to interrogate the child, get the truth out of her, even at the risk of upsetting her, and then, of course, she would probably run weeping to her mother. There would be recriminations and investigations. And what if the child, in all innocence, spoke of it to others such as Dickens, for instance, who never came to the house without having 'conversations' with his 'butler'.

If the five-year-old were upset by my questioning, she might well pour out her story of what happened that night into his sympathetic ears.

And then . . .?

I knew the answer to that instantly. I did not want any investigation. I did not want Caroline and Carrie to be involved in this murder investigation. If I was being honest with myself, when I said nothing after the murder about my suspicions of that fire station model which had been added to the embankment scene, I had known the answer already.

I knew nothing about this woman and her child, nothing but a fantastical story which was now never mentioned, not even by the five-year-old.

Dickens had pooh-poohed it. Had put the whole rigmarole down to a woman who wanted to escape from a jealous lover, or even a pimp who wished to exploit her. Perhaps he was right, but now I thought that perhaps he was wrong. I thought about Carrie's story of the voice that had tempted her out onto Maplin Sands and how perhaps she hadn't made that story up after all. I thought about the ring on the dead body. A man who owned houses.

And Carrie? Reluctantly my mind went back to her.

Perhaps the child as well as her mother had been frightened out of their wits. She had come to the sanctuary of my house, had been happy in my care, but then, quite shortly after her arrival, she had stolen into the dining room – a piece of childish mischief – and hidden under the table. She had heard a voice that was familiar, the bogeyman of her dreams, the man who might beat her with a poker if she were not hidden in the attic before he arrived. It had never occurred to me that it might have been Bazalgette's landlord. But now that I had seen the distinctive ring on his finger, I wondered about the dead man, wondered whether he had recognized the child, his attention drawn by her dread of him, perhaps. And so, fearing that if he were recognized by the child and knowing that recognition would mean the end to his lucrative business and imprisonment, he had decided to get rid of her.

And that terrible place, Maplin Sands, which had swallowed so many human lives was, of course, the ideal place to lose a child and have no questions asked. And so, he had mimicked my voice, tricked her into leaving her safe place with Mrs Taylor, had tried to drown her on Maplin Sands on that dreadful day. I wondered whether Carrie, in her clever, secretive way, had known who it was that had been calling her and had decided to cause his death when she saw him that night standing down there beside that spluttering, thudding engine?

I shuddered slightly at the thought. No, I reasoned, no five-year-old could think like that. What was much more likely was that the child, wanting to reclaim her property after the apprentices' demonstration, had slipped it into her pocket and was about to go home when she noticed the landlord, heard his voice, perhaps, and then, in a fit of childish petulance, had thrown that piece of metal, the toy fire station, at the man whom she had known was her mother's tormentor. It could have been an innocent childish act, no more than throwing a stone. It missed the man but hit the shaft of the machine. At five years old, it was impossible that she could have known of the deadly consequence of her act.

Nevertheless, she and her mother were now under my protection and I could not betray their trust. I would get rid of that toy village. It was, after all, lacking two of its charms as a village. I never wanted to see the little church again – Bazalgette was welcome to retain it. And as for the fire station, the less said the better. I would deny all knowledge of it. There had been plenty of witnesses to my dramatic setting up of the sand bank and the church. Nothing else would be connected to me. And then my mind went again to that terrible day on Maplin Sands and I hardened my heart. If the landlord, from that company of men on Maplin Sands, was the devil who had tricked the child into going out onto that dangerous quagmire where so many had lost their lives, then I was glad that he was dead and would do nothing whatsoever to help identify whoever caused his death.

'Hurry up, slow coach,' I shouted, and Carrie was out in a few seconds, face shiningly clean, hair brushed, swathed in her scarlet cape and her fur cap placed neatly on top of her head.

'Have you got the bread?' she demanded.

She loved to find fault with me, so I dramatically clapped my hand to my forehead and admitted that I had forgotten all about the bread. I was so old that I forgot things easily, I told her. She informed me that I had to keep on 'minding myself' and I promised that I would do that and never again forget anything important like bread for the ducks.

And Caroline, smiling at her daughter's scolding of me, went back into the kitchen and reappeared with a paper bag filled with crusts of bread. And so, we set off.

It was, I reckoned, about a mile's walk between my lodgings and Regent's Park. She was a sturdy little girl but a mile was about as far as she could walk without having a rest. We would sit on a bench for a while before undertaking the return journey. That, I decided, was the time for careful questioning – if she had forgotten all, had not realized that her action had caused the machine to have that deadly effect, well, I was not going to remind her. Children, I knew from my own past, do not always make connections between occurrences. The man was killed by the machine blowing up. That, in Carrie's mind, if she had been the one to throw the fire station, would have had no connection with her action.

The ducks proved to appreciate the stale bread very much and Carrie forgot her tiredness as she raced around, tossing bread into the lake and trying to induce a favourite duck to come a little nearer. And then a mother duck appeared from the island followed by an enchanting line of little ducklings and Carrie was brimming over with excitement and pleasure. We named the twelve ducklings after the first twelve letters of the alphabet, watched them swim around, sang to them and then when they obediently followed their mother back to their hidden home on the island, we sat together on the bench to have a rest before going home.

She was quite tired, I realized as she snuggled into me. I took her upon my knee and sat very quietly, and soon she dropped off to sleep while I stayed there, staring absent-mindedly at the island, wondering why the child had fallen asleep so quickly at this early hour of the day.

There was one answer. She had been late to bed.

These words came to my mind and stayed there. Something

had happened last night, and I had to know the truth about this complicated situation into which I had been plunged when I took into my household not just a strange woman, but a child. When she woke and stretched sleepily, I put the question to her instantly before her defences were built up again. There may have been something worrying both mother and daughter, something that they had decided not to reveal to me.

'That bad man with the poker, Carrie, was he the one that pretended to be me when you got so wet on Maplin Sands?'

She looked up at me with one of those sharp looks of hers. She was, I thought, not for the first time, a highly intelligent child, and I diverted myself for a few moments by planning to seek out an excellent school for her and swearing that I would spare no expense on educating her. But all the time I kept my eyes steadily on that little face.

Eventually she spoke. 'I don't want to talk about him,' she said.

'No, I don't either. Don't worry, you will never see him again,' I said and almost held my breath waiting for her response.

She didn't respond in the way that I had half-dreaded she would. She didn't say anything about the man being dead or that she had seen him die. She just nodded her little head firmly and said, 'The bolts and locks will keep him out. I'm not worrying!'

And then, suddenly regaining her energy in the way that children can do, she jumped to her feet and pulled me by the hand. 'Come on, lazy bones,' she said. 'Time to go home. You'll be late for lunch and Mama will be cross.'

As I got to my feet, she looked up and shook her finger at me. 'You're a very naughty man,' she said. 'You took my fire station. It's not on the tray. I noticed that this morning. You took it for your friend, now don't tell me a fib! I know that it was you. Don't forget to go and get it back.'

I laughed, greatly relieved. No child of five could have told a lie with such conviction. Her scolding voice and her faith in locks and bolts quite convinced me. The fire station . . . could it be that Dickens had taken it? That would account for its presence on the model that terrible evening. She was very sharp, and he had spent some time exercising his charm upon her. She probably knew by now that I would admit to it if I had taken it.

'I'm afraid I've lost it,' I said in as contrite a way as I could. 'But I'll buy you a new one.'

She turned that over in her mind and then pursed her lips. 'You have to buy a box,' she said firmly. 'The shop only sells boxes. They *doesn't* divide them up, you know. That wouldn't be fair.'

A huge wave of relief swept over me. Again, I thought, no five-year-old could lie as convincingly as that.

'I'll do that,' I said. 'And then you'll have two villages, won't you?'

'And they can share the fire station and the church,' she said after a moment's thought when she stopped walking and stood quite still. 'I know what they'll do. They can do without the church. We don't bother about churches, do we? But they need the fire station so if they have a fire, then they'll tell the post office lady to send the postman with a message to the other village. That will be fun, won't it?'

'That will be great fun,' I said with huge relief.

'Let's go,' she said, and I allowed her to lead me through the park, swinging hands in the way that she liked.

After all, I decided, the police were surely right. Joseph Bazalgette was almost certainly the designated victim of whoever threw a piece of metal at that machine. And in a warehouse that was an engineering workshop, pieces of metal must have been readily available to a man who wished to clear the way to laying claim to a substantial money prize and a knighthood.

I would buy her that new toy village and, I planned, a beautiful doll with sets of clothes for every occasion. I would ask my dear friend Nina to help in the choosing of a doll and present it as a great surprise.

In the meantime, I would follow the lead of the police and ponder upon who might have wanted the death of Joseph Bazalgette. It was of the utmost importance for the sake of a man that I liked very much, but also for the sake of the welfare of the people of London who were being choked to death by the terrible miasma which rose out of the River Thames. If Bazalgette's scheme could work, then every right-minded citizen should put their mind into finding the person who had tried to kill the man who might save them and their children from the deadly cholera.

FIFTEEN

Dickens and I went for a long walk that night. I could tell that he was full of ideas as he met me at his front door, racing down his staircase as fast as a boy. He donned his coat and his scarf, then picked up his stick with tremendous alacrity. His eyes were gleaming with excitement.

'I've got an idea,' he said as we went through the gates to Tavistock Place. I waited while he tipped the custodian, who had instantly left his fire and come confidently out to open the gate for us and to enquire about the hour when we would return. Dickens was in a good humour, I noticed. He joked with the man, telling him that he planned to walk all the way to Gad's Hill in Kent and back again, but once we were pounding on the pavement I saw how his face grew dark and determined and he swung his stick with the air of one who is thinking hard.

Nevertheless, when he spoke, it was just to throw a question at me.

'Well, Collins, my friend, what's your instinct about this? I presume that we both now agree that the victim was intended to be our talented friend, Joe Bazalgette, not an obscure and amiable old gentleman like that landlord, poor man, may God have mercy on his soul,' ended Dickens piously, but he eyed me sharply and with that veneer of impatience which was always barely beneath the surface with him.

'Yes, I agree,' I said in as definite a manner as I could produce to satisfy his eager nature. There was, I suppose, a note of strong agreement in my voice and for once he seemed satisfied with the warmth of my response.

'I've been thinking about Phillips and his ideas,' he said without preamble. 'Good ideas but, you know, I could see by the thoughtful expression on his face after that experimenting in the Thames, and seeing the difficulties about laying pipes beneath it, that he was willing to move onto a different track. Now it's an interesting thing about people, Wilkie, my friend, that they are moulded by the experiences of their youth. Time and years can apply a veneer over that initial shaping, but believe you me, the initial contours remain there for an entire life and they mould all that is essential to a man.'

I bowed my head. He was about to subject me to a lecture, and he wanted nothing from me other than careful attention and, of course, complete acquiescence once he had delivered his thesis.

'So, you see, my friend, as we know, John Phillips didn't have a youth as you did with attentive parents, years of schooling. No, as he told us, he had no schooling whatsoever. He went to work as a bricklayer when he was eight years old, and before that, during what he called his "childhood" – up to the age of eight, mark you, my dear Wilkie, I suppose from about four years old to eight years old – he ran, to and fro, with buckets of clay, carrying them to the brickmakers and carrying trays of shaped clay to the furnaces – you can see how bowed his shoulders are and that terrible scar on his arm. He told me that he got that from a furnace when he was six years old and that he saved his own life by plunging into a bath of water where mud was soaking before being formed into bricks.

'Not many people would realize how hard a man like that would have had to work to get to where he has,' said Dickens in that voice which presupposed that he, Charles Dickens, was exempt from the masses who showed such a lack of understanding. 'Just think of it, Wilkie. Carrying mud for the brickmakers, becoming a brickmaker, perhaps, and a brick-layer, but then moving from that to be a housebuilder, from that to be a designer of houses, and from a designer of houses on to be an engineer, to be a professional man, graduating in engineering – think what an effort that must have been to a man with his lack of education, Wilkie, and remember he was not a young man at the time, but graduate he did, and then rose to be chief surveyor to the Westminster commissioners. So, somewhere along the line, there he was, managing to become literate as well as numerate; literate to the degree, apparently, that he bombards the commissioners with proposals and solutions to our terrible problem with our polluted city and poisoned river. And,' said Dickens in his most impressive manner, 'this, my dear fellow, is not a man who gets an idea and sticks to it, come what may. No, this is a man who picks up an idea, puts it forward and then if rejected, or if he himself rejects it, why he drops it and tries again. His whole past life fits him for this flexibility.'

I listened with interest. 'What you are saying is that after the testing of the difficulty of laying pipes beneath the Thames, then Phillips might have relinquished his idea and thought that Bazalgette had a better solution. But wouldn't he perhaps have offered to go into partnership with Bazalgette?'

Dickens laughed gently and patted my arm. 'My friend, it's easily seen that you, brought up as you were in comfortable circumstances and never having felt the sharp tooth of destitution, could not understand a man like Phillips. He would want it all, would want to be the man who got the solution, the man who was given the prize, the man praised by all, the man who would be knighted by the Queen. In any case, why would Bazalgette take on a man as an assistant who is so much older than himself, especially as he already possesses such an able assistant as young Andy Wainwright?'

He was probably right. I was probably incapable of understanding someone like Phillips. I did have an easy boyhood with plenty of stimulation – I even remembered my dear mother teaching me some Latin when I was a small child and then boasting about my cleverness to all and sundry. In fact, almost too much interest was paid by my parents to my progress, but, above all, I wasn't the driven type. I wanted to do well but I could never have studied late into the night to teach myself to read and write and, even worse, to learn the complicated mathematics that engineers had to master.

'He's such a nice man,' I said feebly. And then, more decisively, I said, 'I just could not imagine him hurting a fly.'

Dickens looked at me with scorn. 'Permit me, as so much an older man than yourself, Wilkie, to advise that you, as an aspiring novelist, should rid yourself of the habit of assessing people by their outward appearance. Dig deep, my friend –

learn what lies behind the cheerful exterior, the friendly smile. Watch the eyes, my friend, watch the eyes. Watch and see what is burning in the soul of a man.'

I was, I thought resentfully, a mere ten years younger than himself, and as for being an aspiring novelist, well, no one who had received the praise that I had garnered after the publication of *The Woman in White* could still be called 'aspiring'.

Still, I never argued with Dickens, so I nodded my head and accepted his words obediently. I was, I had to admit, rather intrigued at the possibility of Phillips deciding to get rid of Bazalgette and then taking over his ideas so swiftly that after a while no one would realize that they had not been his in the first place. Bazalgette, I thought, had been trusting of his fellow engineers to explain his ideas so fully. There had been an atmosphere of cooperation between them which had appealed to me very much and I had envied them their spirit of camaraderie. Wrongly perhaps! Perhaps an attempt at murder had resulted from that generosity of his.

'But still . . .' I said aloud and then stopped. However, when Dickens looked down at me with one of those sharp glances of his, I was forced to explain myself. 'I know that it was terrible that the man, the landlord, was killed, but let's face it, Dick, wouldn't it have been so much more of a tragedy if Bazalgette were to have been killed? It was lucky that the man stepped forward at that moment and he was the one whom the metal struck. And no one could accuse Phillips of having a motive for killing that landlord.'

And then I stopped talking and walked on in silence, thinking hard. I did not want Phillips to be accused of murder. That story he had told, about working so hard at the age of four – one year younger than my little Carrie – had gone to my heart and I wanted nothing to do with convicting a man like that. Still, I liked and admired all those engineers so there was always going to be the possibility that someone I liked may have had something to do with that fatal event. I resolved to muddy the waters to a degree where the terrible murder of that night could remain as one of those great unsolved mysteries.

Dickens was still talking, taking little notice of my silence as he was immersed in one of his favourite subjects – the worth of certain individuals to mankind – but my mind was on a different subject. If the missile had been fired at the landlord, well, it had not hit its target. It had gone into the machine. If it had been fired at Bazalgette, well, it had not hit its target either. In any case, as far as I could remember from one horrified glance, it had not looked to be a large piece of metal. I remembered with a shudder how the lump had protruded from the man's neck, bathed in blood. I was certain that it would not be enough to kill a man if it just struck him, though it might have caused him to fall. But aimed at a machine – well, that was a different matter as it turned out.

But I wouldn't have thought of that as a way of killing a man. Nor would any of my friends, I decided. It was only an engineer and one who understood the workings of that machine thoroughly who could have calculated that the missile fired at that moment and to a pre-decided spot within the machine could kill a man standing nearby – purely because the workings of the machine would turn it into a deadly weapon. Yes, I said to myself, Inspector Field must be convinced of the theory that an engineer, and only an engineer, could have caused that death.

And Phillips was an engineer.

The whole of his background would have made him ruthless. Even as a child he had to be quick-thinking and agile. Imagine a small child, in terrible pain from burning flesh, having the quickness of reaction and the courage to dive immediately into a bath of muddy water. Yes, I thought that Dickens had made a very reasonable case for Phillips to be the murderer.

And I? Who could I put forward? He had rejected my idea about Disraeli.

As I mentioned to Dickens before, I had another idea in my head. I wished that I had thought it through a little longer before I subjected it to Dickens' criticism, but he was waiting expectantly and so I had to come out with it.

'I wonder whether it wasn't David Napier,' I said a little reluctantly.

Dickens gave me a sharp look. 'And his partner, William Hope.'

I shook my head. 'No, they may have been partners in this enterprise but there is little other link between them, I'd say. I noticed that when we were down on the shores of the Thames and everyone was teasing David Napier about blowing up two ships, one after the other, that William Hope kept away from the group, isolated himself, didn't come to his partner's rescue. At the time I didn't take much notice of it, thought it was good-natured banter, but no, William Hope may not be too fond of his partner, may not trust him too much. And then there was the strange business about the man's mistress . . .'

'Yes, him and his Rapunzel mistress,' said Dickens. 'I knew it would catch your attention. A strange coincidence was it not? One of them said something about Napier leaving the bits of ships lying around and going home to his mysterious mistress who was kept locked up, didn't he? It was John Grant, wasn't it?'

I nodded. I remembered the words and I quoted them. 'Yes, it was John Grant and this, I think, is what he said: "And when he saw pieces of metal fly up into the sky, he just shrugged his shoulders and went off home to his secret mistress. He keeps her locked up in a tower." That's what he said, wasn't it?'

'It has certainly stayed in your memory, but you know, if you detach the interesting story that your Caroline told to you, there is nothing very strange about John Grant's observation. Many men, including, perhaps, yourself, my friend, keep a mistress whom none of his friends have seen and who could, therefore, be deemed to be locked up, or locked away from society. Especially if the man has a wife, and since David Napier is a good twenty years older than me, and quite a bit more than thirty years older than you, the chances are very strong that he has a wife and probably a long line of children, some grown up but still living on their father, all of them ready to be appalled by the thought that their father might have a love interest,' said Dickens.

'Yes, I suppose so,' I said, slightly embarrassed by the note of bitterness in my friend's voice. Certainly, Dickens' eldest son, and many of his other sons perhaps, also, had been angry when their father separated from their mother.

'In fact, my friend, if it were not for your Caroline and her Rapunzel fairy tale of being shut up at the top of a tower, there would really be nothing to cast suspicion upon Napier. It's a partnership between himself and William Hope, and I reckon that Hope is the man with the money and the brains, though the other man might have had longer experience. No, I'd put them both out of your mind for the moment, but what about John Grant? Now that we are quoting him, what do we make of him?'

'I can't remember anything very much, apart from the time when he was teasing David Napier.' I thought about John Grant for a while and then shook my head. 'I can't remember much that he said about engineering matters. He didn't seem all that interested, did he? No particular ideas or points of view to put forward. A colourless sort of person would have been my impression of him.'

'Ah well, my friend, that's because you don't know the family. John Grant doesn't need to have ideas, or drive, or even money. His wife has all three. And of course, ever since that wretched Married Women's Property Act came in over there in Ireland, she is probably eagerly anticipating it being made law here in London, and when that happens she will have complete control of her money. In the meantime, she turns up at every job that he undertakes, bosses the men around, wears a man's watch looped onto her girdle and pulls it out from time to time so that she can time how long they are taking to complete a job of work. I heard a story in the coffee house last week, that when they were doing a job on the railway and had to send a man up to the nearest station from time to time to report their progress, she wouldn't allow any of them to leave their work but trotted to and fro on her little pony, just as though she was one of the team. Yes, she'll want her husband to get his chance at that business of the Great Stink – at least have him involved with it and if energy and bossiness can work, she'll achieve her purpose. The last time I saw her she was cross-questioning me about Mr Bazalgette and who worked for him and what sort of a man he was.'

'You seem to know a lot about her,' I said. 'Take care that you don't make her husband jealous.'

I meant it as a joke, but he looked horrified. Living on his nerves ever since the adoption of pretty little Nelly Ternan and the trouble with his wife. Poor old Dickens. Never a man to take gossip lightly or to brush aside criticism. He always had to be in the right.

'Don't be ridiculous,' he said, sounding most irritated. 'The woman is a sister of one of my employees. That's how I know all about her. Comes into the office occasionally with news about their daft old mother. Bosses her brother around as well, tells him what to do. I feel sorry for poor John Grant. I hate to see a fellow man downtrodden like that. But mark my words, Collins, by hook or by crook that woman will get him working with Bazalgette. To give the woman her due, she has a fair number of brains herself and by now she probably knows that her husband is nothing but a plodder.'

I digested that. It looked as though Dickens was ruling out John Grant as a suspect. After all, why should the man kill Bazalgette if he hoped to work for him? He didn't have the capital or the experience, or possibly not the brains, to set up on his own. His best bet would be to be named as one of the engineers working on a successful scheme.

'An indecisive sort of fellow, too,' I said. 'Yes, I would rule him out. Can't see him deciding to kill someone on the spur of the moment.'

'That's right, my friend, you are quite correct. But you may be interested to know that, as I am not an engineer and was getting a little bored by listening to all those technical terms, I allowed my eyes to wander around the balcony and who do you think I saw up there in the front row?'

I looked at him apprehensively. 'Who?' I asked.

'Mary Grant,' he said. 'There she was, up in the front row, wearing a blue dress and leaning over the balcony, listening to every word like the intelligent little woman that she is.'

'Well, she's not going to kill Bazalgette if she wants her husband to work for him,' I pointed out, conscious of a feeling of relief.

'Ah, but, my friend, what about if, being clever, she decides that she and her husband could hire Andy Wainwright? He's a man that knows all these engineering secrets. Buy Bazalgette's business and continue with his ideas.'

'But would he have the money to buy up Bazalgette's business? It sounds as though he is not too well off if his wife has to act as a messenger boy for him?' I didn't care much either way, but Dickens demanded an active response from his walking partner and that was about as good as I could come up with.

'My dear Collins, a pretty woman like that can always lay her hands on some money, especially if it is money that will keep the woman's husband happy and engaged to the degree that he has no time to spend investigating what his wife is getting up to while he is busy building pipes and dredging rivers,' said Dickens at his most cynical.

I raised an eyebrow at him but did not argue. I had not seen any very ravishingly beautiful women up there on the balcony and so I didn't know whether his surmise could be correct about how John Grant's wife could get her hands upon enough money to buy up a flourishing engineering business. Dickens, of course, was probably more in touch with what went on in high society than I was. Nevertheless, I was sceptical about John Grant and his wife.

However, it was always easier to agree with Dickens and so I expanded his theory.

'Of course, Bazalgette explained his idea, didn't he?' I said. 'And there are probably detailed drawings in among his papers,' I went on, remembering the splendid desk which had taken my fancy. This was a meticulous and most careful man. He would certainly have made extensive notes. 'No use to anyone if Bazalgette were still alive,' I went on. 'However, if the man were killed it might be possible for another man to buy his way into the practice with the use of his or his wife's money, or even a loan from a member of his family. Especially if he moved fast while the family were still mourning. He has young children, Bazalgette, doesn't he? If anything happened to him, his wife would be in a terrible state.'

Dickens nodded and so I went on with his own idea. The

more I thought of it the more it seemed to be a well-thought-out one.

'Bazalgette's splendid idea could easily be taken on by his successor and, you know, Dick,' I said, 'there is no doubt in my mind that Bazalgette was the sort of man who would have meticulously documented his ideas and his experiments. A less talented man, taking over his practice, and his assistant, and having access to these notes, could make a fortune, don't you think?'

He looked at me in a slightly strange manner. It was almost as though he were scanning my mind, wondering what lay behind the words. He was, I guessed, thinking once again about his brother-in-law, Henry Austin, one of his many responsibilities, and I hastened to expand the field.

'This could have applied to any one of them: Phillips, Grant, Hope and Napier – especially Napier – and, of course, even to your brother-in-law, Henry Austin. Not one of them is as talented as Bazalgette.'

I finished there and allowed him to think about the matter. He didn't like it; I could see that.

'Has your Caroline ever come out with anything more about this mysterious man who mesmerized her and kept her locked up?' he asked, changing the subject with a sharp glance at me.

'No,' I said. 'And I'm not going to ask her anything, either.' I added this in as firm and resolute a manner as I could achieve, and for a moment I thought that I had won, although Dickens and I did not have that sort of relationship. We were friends, yes, but it was an uneven friendship. He was the benevolent one and I was the grateful one. It was for him to ask the questions and for me to answer them. Still, I told myself, relationships change as years go by. And so, I decided to add nothing but walked as briskly as I could.

Of course, that didn't work.

'What about the child?' he asked. 'Bright little girl. Plenty to say. Full of courage, too. I like my little friend the butler. I would not like to think of her worrying about something in the privacy of her room. It would give a child nightmares, a vision like that of a mysterious man, never seen but wielding a poker. Had she ever heard his voice?'

'Yes, that was how she knew, that was why she told her mother . . .' I stopped and regretted my words. Now you've done it! I said to myself. Now Dickens would get the whole story out of me.

And so, weak character that I was, I gave in and told him all that his little 'butler' had said on that night after she hid beside his knees under the dinner table.

'Hm!' The story fascinated him. I could see him glance at me from time to time as we walked along in silence, but when he spoke, to my relief he returned to the question of David Napier.

'Do you think that he could have been the man who locked up your Caroline? Mesmerized her, of course, and kept her as his secret mistress?'

I said nothing. The whole subject was distasteful to me. I didn't care for the look of David Napier with his unruly frizz of white beard and his tight, downturned mouth. It was the mouth, I thought, of a man who could be cruel.

I walked on as fast as I could, but, of course, Dickens kept pace with me. 'I think, my dear fellow, that you will have to try to find out the truth from the lady; remember that one death has already occurred. We can't allow another,' he said with the rough kindness which so often surfaced in his dealings with me.

Again, I said nothing. The thought of that fire station model was in my mind. How had that appeared upon the sand tray in Bazalgette's warehouse? And where did it disappear to? Was it possible that the little model, only the size of a fist, but made from solid cast iron, could have killed a man? Reluctantly I had to admit that it was not only possible but highly likely. Bazalgette had a very tidy workshop. That desk which I had admired so much was an example of his way of working. 'A place for everything; and everything in its place.' Benjamin Franklin's famous quote certainly applied to him. The chances of odd pieces of metal left lying around in that meticulously tidy workshop were exceedingly small. But the two models, the church and the fire station, had been there ready for any murderous person to help themselves. Dickens was my friend and I trusted him, but I would say nothing about that second model. After all, the first model, the little church, had been there for days and all were used to its presence.

'What about young William Hope?' I said abruptly. 'We haven't discussed him. Don't tell me that you don't have all the details about him off pat,' I added and saw him smile at the implied compliment.

'Did a lot of work in Spain and in Majorca,' he said. 'He was telling me about the place. Told me that he reclaimed some huge number of acres and set up irrigation schemes when he was working there. Had quite a talk with him after dinner at your place. He was telling me a lot about the Spanish women, the senoritas and thought I should write a novel about one. He had a description off pat and was willing to help me with it. You'll find this, Collins, when you are famous. Three-quarters of everyone that you meet for the first time have an idea for a novel at the back of their mind. The sensible ones keep it there. The hopeful ones try writing a book and then give up when they discover what hard work it is and the generous ones make me a present of a plot. As far as I could judge this book was going to be about a good-looking young engineer from England who met a beautiful Spanish girl who led him to fame, fortune and blissful happiness.'

'Sounds an ideal plot,' I said.

'Well, you're welcome to it,' he said in that careless way that he had when talking about my future books, though, to give him his due, he never failed to praise books that I had already written and so I did not take offence but went back to the subject of William Hope.

'Did you say he was rich?' I asked.

'He's rich,' said Dickens, with that undertone of envy, which he, though the most generous of men, felt for those who inherited riches and did not have to badger his brains every morning without fail in order to sustain his lifestyle and large family. 'He's the son of the Lord Chief Justice in Scotland, a university man – Cambridge I think – but no milksop. Has had quite a career, though he is a young fellow, about ten years younger than yourself. I think that he was only about twenty-one years old, just a lieutenant, during the Crimean

War, and he left the trenches to go to the aid of a soldier
who was injured. After trying to pick him up and realizing
the man was too badly injured, he went back again, back to
the safety of the trenches, got a stretcher and, so I've heard,
under very heavy fire, went back with a trio of foot soldiers
and managed to bring him to safety. Clever fellow, too –
invented some sort of shrapnel shell for rifled guns. And when
he left the army, he went into business. Had great success in
reclaiming land in Spain and Majorca, so perhaps he might
make a success of this Maplin Sands idea. That's if they can
get the funding. Too complicated, to my mind, but there you
are – he's a young man who would let nothing stand in his
way. Those dare-devil army types are all like that. Life is
cheap to them so they will take any risks, venture all.'

I brooded over that. *Life is cheap*. A strange phrase. I knew
that Dickens meant it to be complimentary, but a man who
was willing to sacrifice his life for a fellow officer, that was
William Hope. But did being willing to sacrifice your own
life bring with it the implication that all life is cheap and that
fortune is to the brave? This was a man who had been used
to success, who had the golden touch, who could go to and
fro, not once, but twice, under heavy shelling and yet escape
unscathed. A man who left one successful career in the army,
embarked upon something totally different, invested money in
draining and reclaiming land out in Spain and in Majorca and
made a huge success of that, also. It would, I thought, be
another feather in his cap to solve the terrible problem of
London's sewage. All London, his entire country, would be
grateful to him. And still not thirty years old. This was, indeed,
a man who was favoured by the gods, the sort of man of whom
people say, 'He can fail at nothing'. But what if it became so
important not to fail that life itself became cheap?

'Oh, come on, Collins, put a spring to your step!' said
Dickens impatiently. While I had been musing, he had got
well ahead of me and was now standing looking back impatiently. 'You take too much of that laudanum,' he said in his
schoolmasterly tone as I came breathlessly up to where he
stood. 'Look at you, out of breath, on a pleasant stroll. I'm a
good ten years older than you, a man burdened down with

cares, but look at the two of us. I'm as fresh as a breeze, raring to go, and there you are wheezing like an old man. How much of that laudanum do you take?'

'Not much,' I said defensively. 'I have to have it for my aches and pains.' I didn't like to tell him that laudanum was not the only drug in my cupboard. I had an array of them. They got me through episodes of poor health, and I had to admit that some of them were very pleasant to take.

'What else do you take?' As usual he read my mind and was interrogating me with one of his most piercing looks.

I passed a few names on the bottles and packages in my medicine cabinet through my mind and fastened upon the most innocuous-sounding of them all. 'Oh, just a few things – Ayer's Cherry Pectoral when I have a cough. My mother used to give me that when I was a child; it used to help me go to sleep,' I said defensively, and remembered the pleasant picture of three sweet-looking children on the bottle.

Dickens frowned at me. 'What an extraordinary thing for your mother to give a child. Do you know what's in that stuff? Opium and strong alcohol. I wouldn't have it in my house for anyone, and certainly not for children. No wonder you used to sleep after it. I hope you don't still take it. You would be poisoning your system. Make sure that child doesn't get hold of these things. Have you a lock to that medicine cabinet of yours?'

'Yes, of course,' I said, and justified the lie with the resolve that I would have a word with the obliging man, my landlord.

SIXTEEN

It must have been about three days later when Dickens and I once more walked through the streets of London. I had got a note from him earlier in the day, one of these numerous notes which Dickens penned with such rapidity and which our efficient post office service delivered to me within an hour of the ink drying upon the flourish of his signature.

> My dear Wilkie,
> Something most interesting, something quite amazing has turned up and I told Inspector Field that you, as a novelist, would be intrigued to be allowed to have a look at what he has uncovered. Meet me at the office at about eight o'clock this evening.
> My regards to you, your household and, above all, to my little friend, the butler.

And then below it was his signature, written, I could guess, at top speed, and with a certain amount of excitement.

That evening Caroline, Carrie and I had our supper early, at six o'clock, in the kitchen, sitting at the well-scrubbed table in front of the glowing stove. It was very homely and very enjoyable. Another one of her deliciously cooked goulashes and some potatoes mashed with butter. She even relaxed enough to taste a new bottle of wine which I uncorked and asked her opinion of, and I had a feeling that she enjoyed it very much. Carrie kept us amused. I had read Dickens' letter to her which she listened to very gravely and said to tell him that she would visit him soon and help him to look after his boys. And after that we talked about her going to school and she decided immediately that she wanted to go to a school for training butlers. I had to give a detailed demonstration of what butlers do and managed my best with a napkin over my arm, though I was forced by incessant questioning from her to confess that I had never actually had a butler in my household and had only occasionally met one at a public dinner.

'I'll ask Mr Dickens about the school for butlers. Tell him to come to see me,' commanded my little lady, and I bowed my head obediently and promised to tell him.

It was such a pleasant supper that I was sorry to leave. I didn't care all that much for Inspector Field and one of his discoveries might not prove to be of any interest. If my dawning suspicions of the dead man were correct, then I did not care who had murdered him. Nevertheless, now, of all times, I could not let Dickens, in his lonely state, down, and so, under Carrie's supervision, I washed my face and hands and then brushed my hair.

By the time that I arrived at Dickens' office, only three minutes late, both he and the inspector were standing at the door with a subordinate policeman beside them. As soon as he glimpsed me, Dickens closed his front door with an efficient slam, locked it and then tested the efficiency of his lock, just as though all the thieves of London would be waiting around the corner to steal manuscripts in his absence.

'Let's go,' he said and off we went, walking at Dickens' usual hectic pace with the inspector keeping in step, and me, with my short legs, panting behind, shepherded by the policeman, who initially kept a decorous few steps behind me, but then was forced by my slow pace to draw level with me. He was a nuisance as he did not allow me a few minutes to catch my breath, but when we got into a crowded spot even Dickens had to slow to normal speed and my new friend the policeman became confidential.

'Dreadful business, this, Mr Collins,' he said.

'Dreadful!' I echoed, thinking that he was talking about the murder.

'When the night-watch brought the news in this morning, it gave me such a shock. Couldn't believe my ears!'

This morning – it couldn't be the murder then. I still had to pretend to know all about it, though, as otherwise he would clam up. I shook my head gravely.

'Things like that give you a shock, don't they?' he said.

'They do, indeed,' I said.

'Lovely young lady, so they say. Pretty as a picture. Blonde hair, big blue eyes, so I'm told. Brought her back to the police station, he did. Couldn't do nothing else, could he? The sergeant-in-charge was giving her a cup of tea when I left, and he had sent a message for his wife to come and sit with her.'

'Best thing to do.' My response was mechanical, but I scanned my mind for enlightenment. A young lady! Were there any young ladies at that gathering of engineers? A few wives well wrapped up, but they were all I had met. And then I remembered the blue flounce of dress. But surely the man wasn't talking about a murderess. The police wouldn't be giving a murderess a cup of tea and the sergeant-in-charge, no matter how kindly, wouldn't be sending for his wife to care for a woman who had committed murder.

And then I remembered Dickens' words about John Grant and his efficient wife, pretty enough to take the attention of a rich man who might finance her husband's engineering business to keep his attention off what she was getting up to with her lover. It had seemed a fantasy from Dickens, a man whose imagination was always working overtime, but now a beautiful woman was at the police station, being fed tea and succoured by the sergeant's wife. Perhaps John Grant had been arrested and his wife had come along. And yes, from Dickens' description, Mrs Grant was pretty, pretty enough, according to my cynical friend, to attract a rich man who would finance the husband while seducing the wife. Not our big, fat landlord of Bazalgette's, though. Surely no pretty and monied young woman would take a man like the landlord as a lover.

'Where are we going, Sergeant? I asked breathlessly. The crowd had thinned out and we had turned into an empty side street. Dickens and the inspector were storming ahead, and the sergeant had quickened his pace considerably, forcing me to keep in step with him.

'To the house, sir, the house where she was found. And I'll tell you a strange story, Mr Collins, about that place. You, being an author, will like this story.' To my relief he slowed down enough to give due emphasis to his story. A romantic story, it was, too, about a lamplighter who fell in love with a beautiful girl peering out of the window. 'Came along and told us the story this morning,' said the sergeant. 'Thought it was his duty when he heard about our men finding another girl in a house nearby. He saw her, this girl that he fell in love with, night after night, you know, sir, every single evening, when he was lighting the lamp. Peering out of the window. All nailed up, the window was. So the lamplighter told us. But he could see her when he shone his lantern on the glass. Beautiful, she was, Mr Collins, that's what he said. Long black hair, silky-like – them were the words that the lamplighter used. Beautiful big brown eyes, he told us. Most beautiful girl he had ever seen! So he said. Night after night, she came to the window and peered out at him, and she seemed to be trying to say something. Beautiful mouth, opening and closing. And after a while he made out what she was saying. "Help me! Help me!" That's what she *were* saying.'

'And did he? Did he help her? Go to the police?' I found myself getting most interested in the story. I had a certain amount of fellow feeling for the lamplighter.

'Nah, of course he didn't. Stupid, that fellow. Came along on a very dark night, no moon, no stars, nothing. Puts his ladder up against the window and there she was, right inside, and her lips, *them* beautiful red lips according to him, were saying the words, "Help me! Help me!" And so he cut the glass, took out the pane as neat as anything – the inspector had a few questions to ask about that, but he pretended his old grandfather had been a window maker and had left him his tools – say anything, some of these fellas – well, he opens the window, helps her to climb out, lets her go down before him while he stands on the windowsill, holding the ladder for her, and then he puts back the windowpane into the frame with some caulking. And guess what? After all his trouble, she no sooner put foot to ground than she was off, running as fast as she could. By the time he got down there was no sign of her – searched everywhere and he a married man with ten children, if you please. Couldn't stop talking about her, though. Most beautiful girl he had ever seen. Like something in a picture with her lovely long black hair and her big black eyes and her red lips.'

'What does the inspector think?' I asked, but it was the wrong question. It made him worried about revealing official business by telling me the story of the romantic lamplighter and the beautiful dark-haired goddess, so he became reticent and said that he didn't know, to be sure.

I subsided. It was hard enough keeping up with him and I had no breath left for detailed questioning. In any case, we had arrived at the house where the latest girl, now safely ensconced in the police station and being comforted by the sergeant's wife, had been found. I resolved, however, to tell Dickens the story of a beautiful girl who sounded like the Roman goddess, Luna, with her lustrous long black hair.

The house was newly built, one of a row of similar houses on the street, and it reminded me of something. It was only when I saw the damaged lock that I remembered. It was in a different part of London but it was almost identical, in size, shape, number of windows, hall door and front garden, to the house from which I had rescued Caroline and her daughter. An idea suddenly came to me and robbed me of my remaining breath. I slowed down and allowed the sergeant to go ahead of me, which he did eagerly.

By the time that I came up to them, the sergeant had joined Inspector Field beside the door at the top of the stairs where he was talking to a constable. Dickens had waited at the bottom of the stairs for me.

'Another Rapunzel,' he said with a quizzical look, and suddenly I understood everything.

'Our departed friend, the benevolent landlord, was not quite as benevolent as we thought,' continued Dickens in my ear. 'A man of many parts. As well as building houses and letting out warehouses, he was in the white slave business. Your Caroline had a lucky escape. I wouldn't tell her, if I were you. Women get upset about things like that.'

I didn't know what a woman would feel, but I felt sickened to the heart. And what would that monster have done with my little Carrie? I knew, of course, what he meant by 'white slave business'. It was a euphemistic term for stealing women, mostly young and pretty, and forcing them into prostitution and selling them abroad to places on the other side of the world. There had been, I remembered, a campaign against white slavery which had culminated in a rally in Hyde Park about a week ago. There were demands that white slavery should be more investigated by the police and some extremely passionate speeches were made, someone had told me. I had been very moved by some of the stories, though oddly had not thought of it in connection with Caroline. But now everything became clear to me.

'Pity he's dead,' I said through gritted teeth. 'I'd have enjoyed killing him myself. Slowly and painfully.'

Dickens quickly put a hand on my arm and squeezed it painfully. 'Not another word, Collins,' he said warningly in a low undertone. He was right, of course. I had been present on that night and I had recently rescued a beautiful girl who had been imprisoned by a dastardly scoundrel. Not just Dickens, but my brother and his friends knew all about it and that probably meant that the whole of London knew about my Caroline and her little daughter. I closed my mouth firmly and tried to contain my anger. I would say no more, I decided, and would not contribute anything to the anecdotes which, no doubt, would be told.

There were heavy footsteps on the stairs and then the inspector was back and full of information for Dickens.

'He had these houses ready to rent out, Mr Dickens. That's how they were listed. We found the addresses in his safe. We had to break it open to see if there were any relations' addresses or anything like that. Fine, healthy bank balance, he had. A very wealthy man. Paid in cash, he was, for those girls. Lots of the pay-ins at the bank were of cash. Big sums of money, not from the sale of houses or anything like that, all of that was listed separately. I've looked through his bank deposit book and there is no clue to where the money came from. Paid into his hand, so as to speak. And, of course, he probably didn't bank all of it. Used it to buy things. I must say that I spotted that valuable ring of his right away. Did you notice it, Mr Dickens? Hallo, I says to myself. If that ain't a diamond, well, I'm a Dutchman. We had a jeweller along to have a look at it. Stunned, he was! Turned white, he did! Take their job seriously these people. Should see some of the sights that we

see, Mr Dickens. I could show him a few things!' And the
inspector laughed heartily. 'Never seen such a magnificent
diamond in his life, so he said. Didn't know anything about
it, of course. No use to us. We'll just have to keep poking
around. They'll have been a gang of them, you can bet your
bottom dollar on that.'

And it was only then that it hit me. I had seen the ring on
the man's finger – had merely thought that it was all of one
piece with the good suit and silk neckcloth and the bejewelled
tiepin. It was, though, now that I remembered it, very much
identical to the ring which Caroline had described to me on
that first night when I had met her. I remembered her words:
'He told me to look at his ring . . . I've never seen a ring more
beautiful, a huge stone, a strange colour. It was blue, but when
he turned it under the gaslight, it flashed like moonlight, like
rays of moonlight. I couldn't stop looking at it. I just stood
there, and the rays seemed to go into my brain.'

Probably he used that ring every time he kidnapped a girl.
The flash of the moonlight-like beams helped him to
mesmerize them.

I wondered, boiling over with fury, how much the man got
for each piece of flesh that he sold, for each girl whom he
had mesmerized and abused, and then I remembered something
else. This man was dead, but he was part of a chain. The
inspector was right. There would have been a gang of them.

'I think I might be able to help you, Inspector, in laying
my hands on another one of the mob,' I said eagerly. 'I was
only half-listening, not really understanding, but on the day
when the engineers were testing the possibility of laying pipes
under the sea, down there beside the Thames, I overheard the
landlord, the man who is now dead, on the beach chatting to
the skipper of a schooner tied up to the bridge. Something
about a trip to Belgium, and wanting a full load, I seemed to
make out. I thought he was talking about goods, but, of course,
now I can see he was talking about human flesh.'

The inspector had his notebook out in a flash. 'That's
extremely helpful, Mr Collins. Where was this?'

'Down by Westminster Bridge, Inspector; the schooner was
tied to the bridge, on the side near to the Strand.'

'And the schooner, what did it look like?'

I had no idea, had hardly looked at it and only vaguely remembered the words 'Belgium' being mentioned and 'full load'. Young Andy Wainwright had been somewhere near, also, I remembered, but he had not been as close as I had been, and his interest would have been focussed on the work of directing the men with the load of wood. So, it was up to me to remember. I shut my eyes in an agony of thought, trying to visualize the prow of the boat, and heard Dickens come to my rescue and occupy the inspector.

'Extraordinary, isn't it, Inspector. Why take girls to Belgium? Don't they have girls of their own in Belgium?'

'Halfway house, Mr Dickens, halfway house, and, of course, if you take some of these girls and lock them up on their own in a strange country, where they don't know the language, well, they're much more manageable than they would be in their own country.'

'Extraordinary,' repeated Dickens, and to my astonishment he took out a notebook and started to scribble.

He's surely not going to pen a book about white slavery, I thought, distracted for the moment from my mind which was frantically trying to visualize that scene on the river shore. The schooner, I remembered, had been tied to the bridge and it had rocked gently as the waves came in and out on the tidal waters of the Thames. Why couldn't I remember the name . . .?

It had been a pleasant name, I thought suddenly. And I remembered thinking that the skipper, if he had selected the name, must have been a pleasant character, a fond, loving husband of a devoted wife and the loving father of an affectionate daughter. Two names. Yes, that was it. That was why I had thought of a wife and a daughter.

And then, suddenly, in the way that these things happen, the name just flashed across my mind.

'The *Frances Mary*, that was the name; I could swear to that,' I said triumphantly. I was sure! Frances would have been the wife and Mary the daughter, I had thought at the time. The memory injected a note of confidence into my voice and the inspector's face lit up like a huntsman who had caught a glimpse of his prey.

'Well done, Collins,' said Dickens, but the inspector had vanished. Gone to despatch some underlings to Westminster Bridge, I guessed. I approved of that. After all, it was more important to save the living girls from such a terrible fate than us all beating our brains out to find the murderer of a scoundrel who was killed quickly with probably no lingering pain, rather than left alive to rot in the clutches of men like himself, a fate which he had planned for Caroline and her little daughter.

'Let's go, Dickens,' I said urgently. I had decided that I wanted nothing whatsoever to do with the matter. I wanted to leave this house, shut away the memory of the blood and the one terrible sound that had been heard just before the man fell dead on the ground. I looked at Dickens. He was reluctant to go. I knew that. He loved to feel part of these investigations but I had made up my mind. I was going to go home, and I was going to tell Caroline about what had happened. I didn't care whether it was police business or not. I was going to tell her and hope that she might find the news of that evil man's death closed a door on a terrible time of her life. She would stay with me. She would be happy and no longer terrified. I would protect her and her little girl and the three of us would live happily together.

So, with a brief nod at my friend and a few words for the constable on duty, I heard myself uttering the lying words about urgent private business, and I was outside the house and striding as rapidly as I could through the streets.

I would finish with the whole business, I decided. I didn't care who killed the landlord. He was better dead.

And then I heard the sound of rapid footsteps behind me, gaining upon me, would soon catch up with me, I knew. So, reluctantly, I slowed down, stopped and looked back. It was, of course, Dickens. I expected reproaches, but he said nothing, just fell into step beside me, walking more slowly than his usual rapid pace and, I realized, keeping in step with my short legs.

'By George, Wilkie, you're a wonderful fellow to have remembered that schooner and to have remembered the name of it, also. You may have saved some unfortunate girls from a fate worse than death,' he said after we had left the noisy traffic of Whitehall and were heading north.

I looked at him. I was suspicious of Dickens when he was in one of those conciliatory moods of his. They usually ended with me being talked into something that I didn't wish to do.

He gave me a nod as though he wished to signal that he had read my thoughts, but then continued calmly. 'I have a problem, my friend, that I would like to consult you about. You see, I have only just realized that I was the one who was responsible for the death of that man. The police surgeon has started upon the autopsy and sent a message to the inspector. He has extracted the piece of metal that killed the villain. And he told me all about it.'

I stopped dead at that and looked at him. He nodded gravely. 'Yes, indeed, I was responsible for that death, not by my hand, exactly, but I provided the means for his murder. Do you remember your discussion with my little friend, the butler? You wanted to take another of her toy buildings and she, like all women, turned stubborn and refused. Well, when her mother called her, I just slipped that fire station into my pocket. I'd have given it to you to replace before she ever noticed that it was missing, of course,' he said calmly, 'but, unfortunately, by the time I went to look for it, it had disappeared. Our murderer had taken it, thrown it at the machine and killed the late, though not lamented, landlord. Or, at least, it looks highly likely. It was a piece of metal that had been painted red and yellow and they even managed to distinguish the word "Fire" engraved into one section – such are the miracles of magnifying glasses in this wonderful new world of ours.'

He was silent for a moment and so was I. It seemed a dreadful thing that a child's toy had caused such a terrible death. I did not bewail the loss of the man. He had captured these girls and intended them to be white slaves. Girls like my beautiful Caroline, like the girl at the police station and like the goddess with the long, flowing, black hair and red lips who was rescued by the romantic lamplighter, good fellow that he was. And there were, I knew, other girls who had been sent across the sea to an indescribable fate. The man who had committed these crimes was a villain and deserved to die, but, somehow, I was sickened at the idea that his death was caused by the child's toy.

Together, we walked in silence. We were approaching his office when he suddenly said, 'I suppose I will have to tell the inspector that I was responsible for putting the object, the fire station, there.'

That roused me instantly. I opened my mouth to protest but then shut it again. Dickens was a man who had a high opinion of his opinions and a low opinion of mine. Tact would be needed if his mind were to be changed.

I thought for a moment. 'You're very brave,' I said admiringly. 'I couldn't do that. I suppose the thing to do is to be like you and never read the newspapers.'

He winced. Visibly. Dickens had suffered a lot with newspapers during the last few months. He declared that he never read them, but I doubted that and had, though I would never tease him about it, proved the assertion to be incorrect on many occasions. Yes, he read them and yes, he suffered acutely when he saw details of his private life in them.

'I suppose I might appear, also. I can't bear the thought. Unfortunately, I am documented as providing the church already so they will assume that it was mine,' I said gloomily. 'You remember that Bazalgette publicly thanked me for providing the sand tray and the toy building on the Strand.'

I didn't look at him as we walked on, but I could sense him turning over matters in his mind. One toy building was like another.

'No point in confusing the police with different toy buildings, I suppose,' he said eventually.

'I'm hoping to keep my name out of the papers,' I said. 'After all, a piece of metal is a piece of metal.'

That rather feeble aphorism seemed to please Dickens and he swung his stick in a determined fashion which seemed to indicate that he was banishing a thought from his mind.

'Come in and have a gum-tickler, my dear Wilkie,' he said as soon as we reached his office, and I took this affability for a tacit agreement that he would not inform the police that the missile which killed a man had belonged to a small child with a strange background. I shuddered at the thought of what the newspapers might have made of that juicy piece of news, particularly if they had got wind of Caroline and her child's history. The words 'white slavery' would have sent journalists howling down the track after any connections between the murder and such an exciting subject. Dickens' name, of course, would have been added to the brew.

And so, cheerfully and gladly, I agreed to have a 'gum-tickler' and went in with him to his office.

SEVENTEEN

When Dickens' key unlocked the door, we found that all was chaos in his office premises. Wills, his faithful assistant, editor, secretary for many a long year, had tumbled down the stairs and was lying awkwardly at the bottom, his face white with agony and his left leg bent at an odd angle.

Dickens took over instantly. A cursory glance, an instruction to one of the sub-editors to fetch a bottle of brandy and a glass and then he was at the desk, scribbling a note with immense rapidity while beckoning to the office junior with his other hand.

'Take this to Dr Frank Beard, Jim. I've written down the address. Take a cab and bring him back in it.' He rummaged in his pocket, took out some silver and handed it to him. 'Be as quick as you can. Tell Dr Beard that it looks like a fracture to me.'

The boy was through the door and out in the hallway almost before he had finished speaking and Dickens turned his attention to poor Wills.

'Courage, my friend,' he said, bending over the half-fainting man as soon as the boy had crashed the front door behind him. 'Help is on the way. Now, try this brandy and I'll guarantee that you will feel better.'

He poured the spirit with a generous hand and stood over Wills until the glass was empty. Then he took out his watch, unhooked the silver chain and held it dangling. 'Your leg, eh, that's the trouble, isn't it?' he said in a low, almost sleepy voice. 'Yes, I can see that you are in pain. What about your eyes? Now keep them both fixed on this watch. Don't close them; watch the watch, Wills, watch the way the watch swings. I want to check your eyes – watch the watch, Wills.' His voice had sunken almost to a whisper and he kept on murmuring the same words: 'Watch the watch, Wills.'

The pain-filled eyes of the injured man were obediently fixed on the revolving watch which now spun in slow circles. I watched too. Almost mesmerized! To my alarm, I found the term 'mesmerized' rising in my mind and realized that Dickens' voice and the revolving watch were having that effect upon me.

'Now close your eyes, my friend,' he said, his voice low and soothing, and for a moment I almost felt my own eyes closing. I rapidly stepped back, behind Dickens and out of sight of that revolving watch. I had no wish to be mesmerized.

The watch had worked with Wills, though. The face of that pain-racked man, with the twisted leg, lying on the floor at the bottom of the stairs, had, by some almost miraculous power, smoothed out and he was now sleeping peacefully. Dickens looked down at him with an air of satisfaction, glanced around in a businesslike manner and began to throw orders about to his subordinates, sending one flying for a rug to put over the sleeping man and others to fetch a large wooden noticeboard which could be used as a stretcher when the doctor arrived. Such was his command over his staff that all was done in silence and with the minimum of bustle and words were whispered rather than spoken aloud. From time to time men and boys looked with awe at the man who only minutes ago was a groaning, agonized figure and who now slept peacefully at the bottom of the stairs, well protected from draughts by the warm rug around him.

Dr Beard, when he arrived, expressed no surprise. Just gave a nod of satisfaction when he looked at the man and then at the watch still swinging from Dickens' hand. 'You'd better come with us and keep him under sedation,' he said to Dickens. 'I've brought plaster of Paris and the bandages, but it would be better and easier if I could do it when he is safely in bed in his own house.' He inspected the board lying beside the patient and nodded approval as, with a pair of scissors, he cut Wills' shirtsleeve and then took a syringe from his medical bag. 'I'll give him a shot of laudanum. I've made it good and strong. It will knock him out and be more effective than those fancy tricks of yours, but all the same, you might as well come

along and be ready with some mumbo jumbo just in case the
pain wakens him. I wouldn't dare give him any more
laudanum than that in case it kills him. Now, lads, gently does
it; easy now; easy; just slide him onto the board. Now with a
one; and a two; and a three! That's it. Well done, lads. Now
carry him out to the cab.' Frank Beard bustled out, calling
instructions to the men carrying the injured Wills and Dickens
turned to me.

'Stay here till I get back, old chap, will you. The men will
be worried if they have no one to refer things to. It's always
been either me or Wills here, until the pages have been checked
and printed. There are usually a couple of last-minute problems. A few words which must be added or cut out to balance
the column. You'll do it perfectly. I have great confidence in
you. I won't be long. I'll be back as soon as I see poor Wills
safe in the hands of his wife, tucked up in bed with his leg
set in plaster of Paris. You'll do that for me, old friend, won't
you?'

I assured him that I would. I was, I had to admit to myself,
quite flattered by the request. I suspected that there would not
be too much to do, but his trust in me was heart-warming and
so, once the cab had gone, I settled myself in Wills' office
and waited with a certain amount of self-importance.

However, either my opinion was not required or not
esteemed. No one came to consult me, so after about twenty
minutes of boredom I decided to occupy myself. Borrowing
a large piece of paper and a well-sharpened quill from Wills'
desk, I set myself to write down my thoughts about the latest
development in the case of the death of the landlord.

The revelation that this landlord was involved in the white
slave trade meant that all my previous ideas had been turned
upside down. I was now quite sure in my own mind that the
right man had been killed. And the latest evidence made it
increasingly likely that the murder of this man had been
intended, not the result of an accident.

Bazalgette's fellow engineers had been unfairly suspected
of his murder by both Dickens and me; and more seriously,
by the inspector from Scotland Yard as well. I thought back
to the spirit of camaraderie and genuine intellectual interest

shown in Bazalgette's theories and knew that I was happy to have come to the decision that we were wrong.

Bazalgette was not the intended victim, I decided. The discovery of the evil crimes committed by the murdered man made everything look different – Bazalgette's landlord was a man who deserved to be murdered.

What about the women whom that evil monster had planned to ruin, women who might have escaped his clutches? I could not rule out either Caroline or even her daughter, or both, if they had been there on that night. I remembered the woman in the blue dress, and I remembered what looked like a boy in a jacket and cap and knew that they could well have been Caroline and her daughter, wearing Francis's Sunday outfit which she had stored so carefully in her little bedroom. But had either of them had gone near the table that held the model of the fire station? If they had, I had not seen it, I told myself. But would they not have avoided my gaze and waited until I was engaged in talking with someone? As far as I could remember only the engineers were near to that table and had the fire station close to hand, but I was never the most obser- vant of men and my eyesight was extremely poor, even with glasses.

But surely only an engineer could have known the effect of throwing a piece of metal into the works of that machine, straight onto that shaft.

This fitted neither Caroline nor the child, though the child, in a fit of petulance, might have thrown the metal toy at the man who had frightened herself and her mother and, in that case, the death might have occurred completely by accident.

When we thought Bazalgette was the intended victim, it seemed quite feasible that an engineer would have been the person to have known the deadly consequences of throwing a piece of metal into the whirring bowels of the machine and somehow, despite the new evidence, it still felt as if that were the most likely solution. But why should an engineer kill the landlord? Even if he had been involved in the white slave trade!

If only there had been a motive.

Was it David Napier with his mistress locked up in a tower?

And then it suddenly came to me. I knew exactly who had murdered the landlord and why. I should have guessed it as soon as I heard the policeman's story of the romantic lamplighter.

'Rapunzel,' I whispered, and wished that Dickens were here to admire my brilliance.

Not Caroline, nor Carrie, not the woman at the police station being comforted by the sergeant's wife, but another one of his victims, locked up in an empty house and awaiting a full load for the schooner, the *Frances Mary*, to take her from London to Belgium; to take her to a life of utter degradation and slavery.

The romantic lamplighter's story!

A beautiful girl. Long, dark hair, black eyes, red lips, dark skin. Not English – not one of the blue-eyed, blonde beauties of London streets. Somebody far more exotic. I had thought of the Roman goddess but now I knew. Another face, dark-skinned, with brown eyes, jumped to my mind. Andy Wainwright.

Quite a Lancashire name, I had thought when we first met, but certainly not a Lancashire face. This Andy Wainwright had jet-black hair, dark brown eyes and, despite the long, wet winter, his skin was deeply tanned. His twin sister, I had guessed, when he told us that she modelled clothes, was probably a beauty. He had been quite reticent about her and I remembered suspecting at the time that she may well have strayed from her occupation as a clothes model in her friend's shop. Strayed. And then, what? Disappeared? It would not have been the first time that such a thing had happened when it came to a beautiful young girl, living alone and unprotected in the vast city of London. Her brother must have made contact when he came back to London, but she, when she strayed, she would have been ashamed to go near him. So, when she fell into the hands of the white slavers' gang, she was friendless and alone.

But when the romantic lamplighter rescued her, her brother Andy would have been the first to whom she would turn. There was no doubt in my mind that he would have heard the story. I sat and thought about it and worked things out.

Andy had, I remembered, been near to me that day when the landlord had his conversation with the captain of the schooner *Frances Mary*, may well have already suspected something about that particular ship, may have gone back and asked his sister details about the man who had mesmerized her and kept her locked up.

Then, when the landlord arrived at his demonstration that night wearing that strange ring, he knew the truth. Or perhaps his sister had been there to see the triumph in which her brother was involved – there, cloaked and veiled, she would not have stood out among the women in the gallery, but at some stage of the evening she may have recognized her tormentor and whispered the truth to her brother.

And he? Resourceful and clever. He had seen what to do. Had sent his sister home and awaited his chance. The landlord, I remembered, had been fidgeting for most of the evening, determined to share the glory, walking forward from time to time and peering at the machine which was being talked about.

And Andy Wainwright? Like a good assistant, he had been standing in the background, behind the row of machines, behind that machine known as 'the Boomer'. It would have been an easy matter to drop the metal fire station into the machine when the landlord was within reach of the deadly missile spewed forth by the revolving triangle.

I sat very still thinking about the whole matter. The busy hum of Dickens' staff passed over my head and when someone looked in through the door, I gazed at him blankly and he instantly disappeared.

It was only when Dickens came back that I was disturbed. I listened with half an ear to his dramatic account of how, eventually, after the leg was set and the patient well dosed up that, at Frank Beard's request, he brought poor Wills out of his trance and left him sleeping a natural sleep with his wife sitting beside him.

'And then,' said Dickens, 'Frank Beard and myself walked home and who do you think we met? Joe Bazalgette.' He had answered his own question very quickly so as to avoid the tedium of listening to me go through his hundreds of London acquaintances who might have been walking the night streets.

'Yes,' he continued. 'He was just coming back from the East India Docks. He had been to say farewell to his assistant. You remember Andy Wainwright? The man with a Lancashire name and an Indian face?'

'I remember,' I said slowly. 'And what about his sister?'

'You have a good memory,' said Dickens with an air of approval. 'You know, I had forgotten that he had mentioned a sister. Worked as a clothes model, wasn't that right? Yes, she went, too. Bazalgette was not too forthcoming about her, said that she had gone straight down to her cabin, he thought. Was more concerned about the fact that Andy Wainwright would be missing for so long. Apparently this holiday had been planned and booked quite some time ago, but, of course, now with all the bright prospects of his scheme being chosen for solving London's sewage problems, it may not be the best of times to have his assistant missing. Still,' said Dickens buoyantly, 'I cheered him up by telling him that it will be a lot of paperwork this spring and the real work probably won't start until the early summer. Andy Wainwright should be back by then.'

Unlikely, I thought, but Dickens had already turned away to check the first printing of *Household Words*. Over his shoulder, he wished me a good night and I went down the stairs meditating. *Planned and booked quite some time ago.* That could well be right. It could have been arranged as soon as his sister had escaped. But now, of course, it was an escape.

I turned the whole matter over in my mind as I walked home. A man had been killed, but he was a man who had caused unspeakable suffering and sorrow to young girls, and perhaps to their families, also. Once again, I thought of little Carrie and shuddered. If that man had been left to carry on, he undoubtedly would have caused more suffering, been guilty of more crimes. The state had been saved the expense of hanging him. I was neither judge nor jury, and no action was required of me. I could keep my thoughts to myself. And I would.

I would also, though, I thought, ask Bazalgette for Andy Wainwright's address in India. After a week or two had elapsed, I would get a good, strong envelope that could be well sealed and in it I would place a card with no name, no address, no signature – a card with just three words printed upon it. DON'T COME BACK.

Dear Reader,

What is true and what is fiction?

Since about three-quarters of the characters in this book are
real people who lived during the reign of Queen Victoria, it
is, for me as author, more difficult than usual to say what is
true and what is invented.

I suppose that it would be fair to say that most details about
these real characters are correct as to their families, their
occupations and in the main, their actions. The dialogue is
mainly invented, of course, although less so in the case of
casual observations by both Dickens and Wilkie Collins since
I have read most biographies written about these two characters. I think, as far as a non-technical person can go, with the
help of my engineer son, William, I have recorded the main
achievements of Joseph Bazalgette, to whose wonderful engineering works the people of London are still indebted almost
two hundred years later.

The story of Wilkie Collins' mistress, Caroline Graves, and
her daughter, Harriet, or Carrie as she was called by Wilkie,
is either a very ordinary and slightly sordid one or else a very
strange one, and I have gone for the strange version. It has
been ridiculed and not taken seriously by any biographer, but
I feel that Dickens' influence was strong in this case. He never
liked Caroline and always hoped that Wilkie would give her
up. Most of their acquaintances in London followed Dickens'
example in this, though, strangely, Dickens was very fond of
Caroline's child, Harriet, and most amused by her. He always
called her 'the butler' and I have ventured to give authenticity
to the nickname. The story of Caroline's daughter is an interesting one as Wilkie Collins was, for all his life, devoted to
Harriet, who was five years old when Collins took the two
under his protection. His bank account at Coutts enumerates
substantial sums for school fees which he paid out, term after
term, until Harriet was grown up. He liked to use her as his
amanuensis and insisted upon paying her for her work. When
she married the solicitor, Henry Bartley, he not only gave a
substantial wedding present but transferred most of his business to her husband. She is also a beneficiary in his will, and
she remained hugely fond of him for all his life. Somehow

this story, I think, paints a most attractive picture of Wilkie Collins.

Cora Harrison